TRICKS

OF THE

TRADE:

MAGICAL GAY EROTICA

Edited by Jerry L. Wheeler for Bold Strokes Books

Riding the Rails: Locomotive Lust and Carnal Cabooses

Dirty Diner: Gay Erotica on the Menu

Tricks of the Trade: Magical Gay Erotica

Visit us at www.boldstrokesbooks.com

TRICKS
OF THE
TRADE:
MAGICAL GAY EROTICA

edited by

Jerry L. Wheeler

A Division of Bold Strokes Books

2013

TRICKS OF THE TRADE: MAGICAL GAY EROTICA
© 2013 By Bold Strokes Books. All Rights Reserved.

ISBN 13: 978-1-60282-781-3

This Trade Paperback Original Is Published By
Bold Strokes Books, Inc.
P.O. Box 249
Valley Falls, NY 12185

First Edition: January 2013

Credits
EDITORS: JERRY L. WHEELER AND STACIA SEAMAN
PRODUCTION DESIGN: STACIA SEAMAN
COVER DESIGN BY SHERI (GRAPHICARTIST2020@HOTMAIL.COM)

CONTENTS

INTRODUCTION:
LON CHANEY, MAME DENNIS, HARRY HOUDINI & ME

When I was a kid, sick days at home from school were the best. The mornings were cereal with reruns of *The Real McCoys*, the old *Dick Van Dyke Show*, and game shows like *Match Game* and *Concentration*, followed by chicken noodle soup and Vernors ginger ale for lunch while watching cooking shows like *The French Chef* and *The Galloping Gourmet*.

Having finished her housework, my mother would wake me up after my lunchtime nap, gather up either her sewing or her ironing, and we'd settle on the sofa for Bill Kennedy's Showtime Movie (broadcast in Detroit on CKLW out of Ontario). Bill Kennedy had been a bit player for Warner Bros. in the forties and fifties and had parlayed that into a retirement career as a movie host, affecting a bored, jaded persona telling tales of old Hollywood between segments of the movie.

Every time I was home sick, he seemed to show one of three movies. The first was *The Man of a Thousand Faces*, the Lon Chaney biopic starring James Cagney. As a young boy who knew he was different from other young boys, masks and artifice appealed to me, plus I knew Lon Chaney's name from my *Famous Filmland Monsters* magazines and the *Phantom of the Opera* plastic model I'd spent hours meticulously gluing together and painting.

Of course, none of the events occurring in that film were remotely true, but I was not to find that out until years later. The scene that I recall most vividly, however, was Cagney's rendition of Chaney's performance in one of his earliest silent films, *The Miracle*

Man, where he plays a crippled, deformed man restored by a faith healer. Watching Cagney unclench, uncurl, and snap his bent and broken frame back to normal posture was a horrifying, yet fascinating experience. Considered a lost film, Chaney's transformation scene is all that remains of the original *The Miracle Man*. You can find it on YouTube.

The second movie was *Auntie Mame*, a film Bill Kennedy himself—who always came across a little fey to me—seemed to genuinely admire. *Auntie Mame* spoke to my gay sensibility before I even realized I had one. Its sophisticated wit was as accessible and charming as its broad slapstick, capturing an urbane world so far from my own it might have been Mars.

Mame Dennis was the rich, madcap aunt I never had but always wanted. And as I watched the look of longing on my mother's face while she sewed and watched Mame's antics along with me, I suspected she wanted to *be* her—living that New York City life on Beekman Place, surrounded by movers and shakers and intellectuals and people who mattered. I know I wanted to be Patrick, and for the record, I thought the kid who played him was a lousy actor. By far the weakest part of the movie. I could have done much, much better.

The third film was, again, a Hollywood biopic more fantasy than fact—Tony Curtis and then-wife Janet Leigh in *Houdini*, about the life and times of Harry Houdini. Though Houdini was more escape artist than magician, he was still a man onstage doing seemingly impossible feats, an image and idea that has stuck with me all these years. He represented skill, showmanship, and sheer audacity, something that appealed to the nascent queer kid inside me. And looking at a shirtless Tony Curtis certainly caused a reaction as well.

For what better way to deal with the bullies and taunts and fear of physical confrontations than to amaze your potential opponents into submission? Make them fear you, admire you. Astonish them and they won't gang up on you after class or laugh when they see you coming. So what if it's all a trick? It's the effect that matters. If you can inspire wonder in them, they won't care how different you are.

And don't you find magicians hot? Mysterious men who can do wondrous feats with style and panache—cool, unflappable, sure of themselves. Who isn't turned on by a handsome, well-dressed man who can perform impossible acts? And we have a lot of handsome men performing impossibilities for you between these pages. Try getting out of the irresistible trap laid by Jeff Mann in "Inescapable" or the bonds holding a magician on vacation in Ralph Seligman's "Magic Takes a Holiday."

Looking for feats of legerdemain in other times? We can pull something out of the hat for you with Jay Neal's tale of hypnosis and Victorian lap dances, "The Mesmerist's Assistant," the vengeful erotica of William Holden's "Magic Lantern," Dale Chase's Old West wizard three-way in "Manly Magic," or Rob Rosen's buckboard fuckfest "In Through the Out Door."

If stylish illusions with a twist are more to your taste, you're sure to be amazed by Lewis DeSimone's eerie "And Now, For My Next Trick," Joseph Baneth Allen's Atlantean efforts in "Old-Fashioned Expectations," 'Nathan Burgoine's cruise ship fantasy "Transposition," or the lyrical "Sons of Orion" by Xavier Axelson. But magic is more than swirling capes, dry ice smoke, and red lacquer coffins, as Todd Gregory proves in the ritualistic "Let's Just Kiss and Say Good-bye," and Mel Bossa reinforces with her tale of prestidigitating street kids, "The Assistant." But even with the professionals, the magic isn't always onstage. Sometimes it's in the job interview, as with Logan Zachary's "The Magician's Assistant."

No matter where it happens or how the illusion manifests itself, you're sure to be entertained by our marvelous masters of magic. So sit back in the most comfortable seat in the house, nibble on your popcorn, and prepare to be amazed. And if you're so inclined after reading a few of these tales, try and pull a rabbit out of your own hat.

Or wherever you have it stuffed…

INESCAPABLE
JEFF MANN

(for JW, in return for a fine premise and a certain phrase)

Spring's come to northern England. Despite today's chilly weather, crocuses are already pushing up in Sackville Gardens, a medley of purple, yellow, and white, and the cherry trees are in full bloom. After winter's long, gray months, I'm delighted to see a little color. Smiling, I run my fingers through the cherry blossoms' wet pink, then move a little faster through the March drizzle.

Here's the Eagle, Manchester's leather bar, my favorite place for an end-of-the-day pint. I should be heading home for a quick dinner and another evening devoted to research materials, but I'm tired after hours at the university library, and besides, as a bear and devoted gourmand, I figure I should take advantage of my new job in England by enjoying the local ales as often as possible. Dropping my backpack on a stool at the bar and peeling off my biker jacket, I greet George, the bartender, and order a pint of Whitbread. Right now I just want to get a little buzz going and not think for a while.

That's when I see him. He's just a vague blur on a poster stuck on the wall beside the bar, but that image is enough to grip me hard. Over his shaggy head, words in big red print blare: *Fire-eaters! Sword-swallowers! Escape Artists! Magicians! Sponsored by Manchester University LGBT Society.*

"What's all this?" I ask, indicating the poster with a thumb. "I sure like the looks of that boy in chains."

"Doesn't everyone?" George chuckles. "Real cute. That's Mike.

American like you. Comes in here once in a while for a pint. Couple of days ago he showed up and asked if he could put that poster up. Bunch of queer student performers down by the cathedral, an AIDS benefit. Show's tonight at eight. Wish I could go. I'd bend that bloke over my knee for sure." Chuckling, George takes a cloth to the water rings on the bar.

I bend closer, studying the image. The boy appears to be at least a decade younger than I, in his early twenties. He's got a close-cut black beard and shoulder-length black hair, and he's dressed in nothing but gym shorts and chains. The pose is very familiar. It's a deliberate evocation of that famous photograph of Harry Houdini that fascinated me as a kid and inspired my first masturbatory fantasies in my preteens. Mike's lean, nearly naked frame is bent forward, his neck chained and padlocked to his elbows and his wrists chained and padlocked to his ankles. He's smiling, but the look in his eyes—hapless vulnerability—just about melts me.

"Eight o'clock," I mutter. Despite all the work I should be doing tonight, I've already decided. This show is one I simply can't miss.

❖

By show time, I'm sluggish-full, thanks to a big plate of fish and chips I devoured at Via—one of numerous cozy pubs set along the canal in Manchester's Gay Village—and relaxed on a couple more pints, one of Smithwick's ale, one of Strongbow cider. The streets are busy, mainly heteros in their twenties—the boys casually dressed, the girls all tarted up in high heels and dresses that show off as much flesh as legally possible, skin pale and goose-pimpled in the cold spring night. I pass the grand Victorian pile of Town Hall, on past the Ferris wheel, an odd anomaly set amid the city buildings at Exchange Square, and on up Cross Street to the cathedral grounds by the river. The cathedral's small, elegant, ornate—a place I often come for the quiet—but tonight I barely notice it. Eager to glimpse the advertised escape artist, I buy a ticket and take my place among the crowd gathered around a makeshift stage.

The first two acts are so amateurish they're entertaining: a twink-magician who keeps dropping his top hat, a dog-trainer drag queen with a beribboned dachshund so plump it can barely jump through hoops. The fire-eater and sword-swallower are a mite more professional. Still, I'm impatient. I came for that long-haired, chained-up boy. Where the hell is he?

A thin rain starts to fall; the crowd begins to disperse, heading back to the alcoholic entertainments of downtown. By the time the final act is announced, there are only a dozen people in the audience, spreading umbrellas or, like me, cocking a cap against the drizzle. "Mike the Magnificent!" shouts the announcer. It's my long-awaited boy. He steps forward into the spotlight and gives a little bow in response to scattered applause. He's barefoot, dressed in a black T-shirt and a pair of baggy black nylon gym shorts hanging nearly to his knees. His eyes are dark, intense. He's short; can't be more than five and a half feet tall. His hair's a glossy cascade falling around his shoulders. For a second, he looks like a diminutive Jesus, but then he ties his hair back, and suddenly he's just another wannabe-hippie university student. Whatever. Small, sinewy, scruffy men are just the sort that move me most.

Mike lifts the microphone from its stand and says softly, "Thanks for comin', you guys. It's for a good cause. All the ticket money goes to the Manchester AIDS Foundation." His accent is faint but discernible: the northern United States, New York or New Jersey. "I'm an escape artist, so these buddies of mine are gonna tie me up and lock me in a box. Then I'm gonna use my sorcery and get out. Hope you enjoy."

I move toward the stage, hungry for a closer look, till I'm only yards away from the tasty entertainer. Thanks to tonight's mid-March gusts, his nipples are hard beneath his shirt, and the slight swinging of the crotch-bulge between his legs convinces me he's got nothing on beneath those shorts. Behind him, two young men appear. One's carrying handcuffs and rope; one's wheeling a black coffin-like box with silver trim.

Mike pulls his shirt over his head, and the sight of his bare chest makes me swallow hard and cup my growing hard-on through my pants pocket. He's slender but solid; lean muscles line his pale arms and make twin mounds of his chest. A fine coating of black hair circles his nipples and fills the valley between his pecs. More hair trails down his faint six-pack, pools around his navel, and, thickening, disappears into the top of his shorts only to recommence below them, pelting his calves with dense fur.

Nearly naked now, Mike winks at the crowd. For a split second I think he's aiming that shameless wink directly at me. Then he takes a deep breath and clasps his hands in front of him.

Seeing him stripped to the waist already has me hard; watching his friends restrain him has my heart pounding, my mouth dry, and my dick stiff to the point of real discomfort. They cuff his hands before him. They wrap his wiry arms and torso with yards of rope. They tie his feet together, and then his knees. They lift him by the shoulders and thighs, carry him to the box—tilted now so as to expose its interior to the audience—and place him in it. Before they're able to close the lid, Mike shouts, "Wait!"

His friends obey. Mike looks out over the crowd. "I want you guys to believe me when I say these restraints are real and that I'm really tied." He squirms a little, his chest swelling against the rope. His arms flex, muscles bulging to the surface before subsiding. "If you don't believe me, no one's gonna be impressed when I get loose." Another broad smile; another flirtatious wink. "Anybody wanna come up here and see for yourself?"

Before anyone can respond, the boy's eyes are on me. My interest must be more than obvious: I'm standing in the front row, leaning against the stage, staring and open-mouthed. Before I can summon a façade of nonchalance, Mike grins at me. "You, sir? The gentleman with the black leather jacket and the handsome auburn beard. Will you come check the security of my bonds?"

I step back, tremors tickling my calves. "Me? Well, I—"

"Please, sir? We'd all appreciate it. Right, folks?"

Applause ripples behind me. Damn it. The last thing I want to do is get closer to a bound-up boy that beautiful. It's going to take every bit of composure I have not to ravish him right there on the stage. I muster a false smile, nod, and lope up the few stairs to the stage. It seems to take a long time to get to Mike's side, my face stiff with that forced smile, my palms moist with sweat.

I stand by the box, staring speechlessly down at him. For a second it feels like bending over a coffin or an open grave. Mike and I lock eyes. This time the wink is definitely just for me. His beard's glistening. Between the tight strands of rope stretched across his torso, raindrops are winking like tiny diamonds in his chest hair. Now that I'm so uncomfortably and thrillingly close, I could swear his cock's half-hard beneath those clingy-damp shorts.

"Hello, sir. What's your name?"

I clear my throat. Being on a stage in front of strangers is one of my least favorite things in the world. "I'm Alan Wilson."

"American, sounds like. Southern?"

"Yep. Virginia."

"With a beard that big, you *gotta* be from the mountains." Mike gives me a wide grin.

"Yeah. That's true." I can't help but grin back.

"You wanna check these cuffs and ropes, mountain man? Make sure everything's on the up-and-up?"

"Uh, sure. Be glad to." Choking back a nervous laugh, I bend over him, tugging at his cuffed hands. Briefly our fingers intertwine. When I pull at the well-knotted rope wrapping his biceps and torso, I manage to brush a hard nipple. When I check the rope around his knees and ankles, I manage to run a finger through the thick hair coating his calves. Might as well take advantage of the proximity, since I'll probably never see him again. It takes all my self-control not to squeeze that crotch-bulge inside his shorts.

"Secure, right?" says Mike, licking a raindrop from his mustache.

"Yep," I say, stepping back. *Fuck*, he's pretty trussed up like this.

"Thank you, sir," Mike says. "You just wait here. I'll be right out."

The lid of the box descends; the lock clicks shut. New-age music builds; as if arranged for effect, distant lightning flickers over the river. The box jolts and shakes; the music swells; a few minutes pass. Then, with a click, the box opens and Mike leaps out. His hair is mussed, strands falling across his face; his shorts have slipped down on one side, baring a hipbone; his limbs are bright with sweat; the cuffs sway from his left wrist; rope trails from his right ankle. "Here ya go!" Mike yells, pulling his hair loose with a dramatic gesture and lifting his hands to the heavens. The audience hoots and applauds; another spasm of lightning illuminates the sky; the rain grows harder.

Mike adjusts his shorts and wipes sweat-glisten from his belly. With that moist hand, he shakes mine. "Thanks for the help, Mr. Wilson! I better get dressed, and we better get somewhere dry. How about I buy you a drink?"

I manage to keep my enthusiastic *Hell, yes* tacit. Damn, I want to know this boy better. "That'd be great," I say. "How about the Eagle?" I figure a gay guy whose specialty is escaping bondage might like a leather bar.

"Maybe some other time. That's where I usually drink, but tonight, I wanna see the canal all lit up with those pretty blue lights they have strung in the trees. How about Taurus? I'm starved, and I love their steak and kidney pie."

❖

No inside tables free, so we take one outside by the canal, since the rain's finally stopped. By the time we've ordered pints and food—meat pie for him, treacle pudding for my inveterate sweet tooth—Mike's shivering inside his thin sweatshirt, denim jacket, and threadbare jeans.

"Here, kid." I shoulder off my leather jacket and offer it to him.

"No, man." He waves it off. "Then you'd be cold."

"Not me," I say, flexing an arm and patting my burly belly. "I got padding you don't."

"So I see." Mike's glance moves slowly over me, as if I were a meadow he were ambling through. "Muscle-bear, looks like to me. I'm partial to those. That's one magnificent beard."

I stroke my chin and blush. "Damn, you're a flirt. You Yankee boys and your bold ways. Thanks. As for you…a little Jesus, looks like to me. I'm partial to those."

"I could sorta see that during the show. Especially when you checked my bonds." Mike pulls my biker jacket around him. "Warm! Nearly swallows me, but it's really warm. Thanks. You Southern gentlemen and your manners."

Over our meals and frequently replenished pints, Mike and I trade backgrounds. I tell him about my upbringing in Virginia, my grueling days in grad school, my new position in political science at the University of Manchester. In between bites—he's gobbling so eagerly it seems as if he hasn't eaten in days—he tells me about his Italian American parents, their early deaths in a car crash, the wealthy uncle in Belgium who helps pay his bills, his literature studies at the university, his approaching graduation, and his job as a pub cook. By the time we've scraped our plates clean, we've moved on to our mutual bachelorhood, the Brontë sisters, Bram Stoker, and the less-than-exciting local leather scene. Beer and the simpatico nature of the conversation have us both talkative and relaxed. It's been years since I met a man who so effortlessly combined good looks with wide-ranging intelligence. Each smile— so broad, so white, framed by that ebony beard—is priceless.

When the bill comes, there's the usual male battle. I win: professor's salary trumps pub cook's, I explain. "Thanks, man. Next time it's on me, though. Pretty night. Wanna walk?"

Mike stands. Red-faced and swaying, he's clearly feeling the effect of those pints.

Discussing famous escapologists and our mutual lech for Harry Houdini, we stroll along the canal, past the bustling bars, beneath the lit-up trees, then across the bridge and into shadowy Sackville Gardens. Mike presses his face into the blooming boughs of weeping cherry and breathes deep. He bends, picks a white crocus, and offers it to me. "Here ya go," he says, eyes shyly lowered.

I take the crocus and lift it to my nose. It has the most fragile of scents. "Thanks, kid." I slip it into my jacket's inner pocket. Been a while since a handsome boy gave me flowers. "What's this for?"

"I just...I love spring in England. Mind if I smoke?" He sits heavily on a bench and pulls a packet of thin cigars from his denim jacket.

"No. That's fine. Go for it."

"Want one?"

"Sure. I like a cigar once in a while."

For a few minutes, we're quiet, smoking, listening to the canal and traffic edging the park. "Whoa," says Mike, rubbing his brow. "Sorry. I'm pretty drunk. Tried to keep up with you and failed."

"Boy as slim as you should never try to out-drink a bear." I pat his shoulder, hesitate, then seize the moment. "How, uh, how about I drive you home?"

"No need. My flat's just a few blocks away. But you can walk me there, if you'd like."

"I'd like that a lot, actually."

"So, look...you're into me, right, Alan?" Mike exhales a cloud of smoke and clasps his hands in his lap, head lowered again. I can't make out his expression in the dark.

"Yes," I say, trying to sound composed. "Very much. I think you're as beautiful as you are smart, actually."

"I'm feeling the same about you," Mike says, reaching over to clasp my hand. "Which is scary."

"Why scary? I won't hurt you. I'm harmless, kid."

"Forget I said that." He drops my hand. "Guess I'm a little timid. Say, I got some pot back at my place, if you're interested."

"Sure. I indulge in weed rarely, but tonight...Sure. Hey, does it turn you on to be tied up?" I've had just enough drink to say such a thing. "I saw your boner in your shorts when I was on the stage."

"Yeah." Mike hangs his head, as if ashamed. "A lot."

"That's really, really good to hear. So...how about we go back to your place, and, after we get high, I tie you up again? I've had lots of practice with knots."

Mike lifts his gaze to mine. He grins. "Tie me up? You know I'll get loose."

"Is that a challenge?"

"Yeah." Mike chuckles. "You bet. Daddy."

"Maybe you will get loose, though I'm thinking you might not want to. But while you're tied, I'd, uh, I'd really like to make love to you, Mike." I shake my head and take a draw off the cigar. "I'm sorry if I'm being pushy. I'm rarely this forward. But, well, you're really handsome, and it's been a long time since I touched a man as hot as you, and…"

Mike lifts his head, long-lashed eyes gleaming. "No need to apologize, guy. I'd like that. You're super hot too. I love those bushy eyebrows of yours." He lifts a finger, runs it along my brow, and sighs. "Tonight, though, after you tie me, could we just cuddle? I feel kinda fragile, so I'd like to go slow, if that's all right with you."

"Okay," I say, rising. "Cuddling. That sounds real sweet." I take his small hand in mine and lift him to his feet. "Lead the way."

❖

His flat is tiny, his bedroom cramped. Mike lights a candle. We lie on his bed passing the blunt back and forth till it's gone.

"Let's get naked," Mike says, grinding the roach out in an ashtray.

"You first," I say, clasping my hands behind my head. My head's restless, tingling, as if buzzing bees made of pot smoke and blue light were hiving in my brain.

Mike grins. He stands, unties his hair, and lets it fall loose. Off come the sweatshirt, the jeans and tiny black briefs. "Here ya go," he whispers, hands on lean hips. His cock, long and thin, is erect, curling nearly back to his navel. "Your turn."

"Let me see your ass first." Pot always veers my usually soft-spoken nature toward the blunt and lecherous.

Mike turns and bends, hands resting on his knees. His buttocks are small, curvaceous, and white. He reaches back, spreading his cheeks and revealing black hair thick in the cleft between.

"Jesus," I grunt. "You *are* a bottom, right? 'Cause if you're not, you're being a mighty cruel tease right now."

"Yeah. You bet," Mike mutters, spreading his cheeks wider still. "I haven't been fucked in years, but I'm a bottom. Nothing I like better'n to be tied up and plowed by a big bear like you."

"And you're *sure* I can't fuck you tonight? I'll take you real easy, I swear." I lick my lips, staring at that tight rump and that bushy hair.

"No, man, please, let's go slow, okay?" Turning, Mike drops to one knee by the bed. "You're a pretty cool guy, Alan, and I haven't, well, I never do this, invite a guy home, I mean, and I'm afraid if we have sex tonight, I'll never see you again. And I'd like to see you again. Okay?"

I sit up and take his hand. "Sure, kid. I get it. Okay. I don't want just a one-night stand either."

I stand and strip. Mike stares, emitting an audible gulp. "Oh. Wow." He strides over and runs his hands through my chest hair. "Wow. So furry. You're like some wild animal. I love your belly." He runs a hand over its curve. "And wow." He squeezes my biceps. "And wow." He reaches down to cup my hard cock and fondle my balls. "Big, big, big. This is gonna feel wonderful up in me."

I wrap my arms around his narrow shoulders. Mike wraps his arms around my beefy waist. He stands on tiptoe; we kiss for a long time. His body tenses and trembles against me.

"Relax, Mike. You're safe with me. Just cuddling it is. Just relax. I just want to be tender with you tonight. I'm willing to wait, okay?"

Mike emits a little sob and presses himself closer. "I believe you. I'm just…sometimes touching scares me. I'm gettin' over some stuff. Long story. Will you tie me now, and then take me to bed?"

❖

Folded in my arms, Mike slumbers soundly. I wake once, to the sound of shouting partiers on the street below, and pad to the bathroom to piss. When I return to bed, I pull the bound boy close. Mumbling, "Glad you're here, man," he snuggles against me, kisses my forearm, and falls back to sleep. I stroke his long hair, unable to believe my good fortune.

I wake late. Heavy curtains cover the windows, making of the room a dim man-cave, but weak sunlight's spilling through the bedroom door. Mike's still curled inside my arms. When I roll onto my back and stretch, he wakes.

"Hey, man," Mike says, yawning. "Wow. What time is it?"

"Nearly ten." I pat his bare rear. "And you didn't get loose, did you?"

Mike grins. He shifts onto his back and flexes. He's still secured the way I trussed him last night, the same way he was trussed onstage: hands cuffed before him, rope wrapped around his arms, torso, knees, and ankles. "Naw. Feels too good. Feels like swaddling clothes. Like I'm all wrapped up and safe and loved. Like I'm being cared for. You gonna care for me, Alan?" Another endearing wink.

"Damn straight. Count on it. Though, tasty as you look, you're damn lucky I didn't rape you in the middle of the night."

"Yeah? Well, thanks for the restraint. In all senses of that word. Hey, would you put the kettle on? I could do with a cuppa. I'd do it, but…" He wiggles his wrists in the cuffs and gives a mock sigh. "I'm cruelly indisposed, as you can see."

"Sure. If you say, 'Please, sir.'"

"Oh, man. You one of those tops who likes bein' called 'Sir,' huh? Please, sir!"

"Good boy," I say, chucking his chin.

In the narrow kitchen, I heat water, find loose-leaf Darjeeling and a Brown Betty teapot on the counter. "Sugar or cream?" I shout around the corner.

"Both, please, sir."

Tea ready, I return to the bedroom. I gasp, nearly dropping the steaming cups. "You little shit!" I blurt.

Entirely free, Mike's sitting, still naked, on the edge of the bed, rolling rope into neat hanks. He looks up at me and smiles. "Here ya go, Daddy," he says, handing me the cuffs. "Better luck next time."

❖

We spend the day together. It's a sunny Saturday, and the streets of Manchester are full of pale folks luxuriating in light after the long winter. We gobble a full English breakfast near the university, a meal Mike insists on paying for: more tea, bangers, bacon, baked beans, grilled mushrooms and tomatoes, fried bread and eggs. We ride the Ferris wheel and walk along the river. Once, as we're browsing through a little shop in the Gay Village, Mike's cell phone buzzes. His brow creases when he checks the number, but he doesn't answer, a fact I much appreciate. Most kids his age—my students' age—are so addicted to their gadgets that they've lost all sense of manners, but not Mike.

"My uncle checking up on me. He thinks 'cause he helps me with the bills that he can run my life." Rolling his eyes, he stuffs the phone back in his pocket and says, "How about we take your car out to the Shepherd and Child for dinner? You know that pub? Best cottage pie I've ever had. If you don't have other plans."

"Actually, tonight I hope to kidnap a cocky college kid. If he'll let me. But a big pub dinner would be welcome too."

"I think he'll let you. Maybe this time he won't be able to wiggle loose." Mike gives me another adorable wink. "My suspicion is this kid's been lookin' for a daddy who can tie him so well he can't escape."

Throat dry with hope, I can only rasp, "Yeah? We'll see," and squeeze his hand hard.

We have our big pub meal and another night together, this time in my roomier row house. At his suggestion, Mike ends up in my bed naked, with his feet roped together and his hands cuffed behind his back. "Feels wonderful," he sighs as I tug the blankets over us and pull him into my arms.

I wake to wet pleasure wrapped tightly around my cock. Mike, still cuffed, is sucking my prick.

"You sure?" I grunt, clutching his head.

"Uh-huh. It's time," he mumbles around my shaft. "I want you to come in my mouth, man."

"Yeah? Then that's exactly what you're going to get," I say, spearing his taut lips hard. The load I finally shoot is so big he chokes.

When I open my eyes to first light, I find Mike free, grinning triumphantly, one arm hugging my waist, fingers combing my pubic hair. The cuffs and rope are neatly arranged on the bedside table.

"You little bastard." I chuckle. "You think you can get free any time you want, don't you? You think no one can hold you."

"Don't know if I'd say that. Thanks for the load," Mike says, kissing the tip of my limp dick. "I fuckin' *love* to suck cock when my hands are cuffed behind my back."

"Thank *you*. That was one damned fine blow job. God, you have beautiful hair," I say, stroking his head. "So how'd you get loose?"

Mike snickers. "Ain't gonna tell you. Samson made that mistake, and look where it got him. Guy's gotta retain some mystery, right?"

"Yep," I say, grabbing him. "Though I don't think that mystery's going to help you now." We wrestle about on the bed, Mike giggling and struggling beneath me. I'm more than twice his size, though, so soon I have his hands cuffed behind him again. Stuffing his black briefs in his mouth, I tie them in place with the rope I'd used last night to bind his feet.

"My turn to taste you, kid," I growl, stroking his erection. "All right?"

Mike nods frantically. Gripping his balls, I tug them till he's wincing, then take his big cock and soon thereafter his big load down my throat.

❖

Spring waxes; Mike and I spend more and more time together. When our job schedules permit, we meet for lunch, or for pints after work in the Gay Village. Some nights Mike cooks for me, Italian specialties like bruschetta, spaghetti and meatballs, fennel salad, eggplant parmigiana, all washed down with lots of red wine. One weekend, we hike in the Pennines. Other weekends, we drive to Haworth, to visit the Brontë Parsonage; then Whitby, the site of scenes from *Dracula*; then Lindisfarne, to see the ruined abbey and sample mead at the winery. Some nights spent together involve my fruitless attempts to keep him bound; some nights we don't bother with rope and cuffs, instead spending the time till daybreak kissing, snuggling, sleeping, or sucking each other off. When I'm not with Mike and not involved with teaching or research, I'm reading books about escapology and its tricks, trying to figure out a way to bind Mike so he can't get loose. Somehow, unreasonably, part of me thinks that if I can figure out a way to keep him tied, somehow I'll be able to keep him in my life.

To celebrate Mike's graduation, we spend a weekend in Edinburgh, Scotland. That Saturday, we tour the medieval castle, snack on Scotch eggs, and climb the extinct volcano of Arthur's Seat. I buy Mike a tartan scarf; we drink pints of Scotch ale at The World's End and The Jolly Judge. I treat us to a meal at The Witchery—smoked salmon, roast beef, crème brulée. On a professor's salary, it's wildly expensive, but Mike's ebullient enthusiasm over the elegant setting and cuisine more than makes the high price worth it. Afterward, we stroll past the Royal Mile's sixteenth-century tenements, then down a close to our hotel, the Jurys Inn.

By the time Mike's stepped out of the shower, I've poured amber-gold Drambuie in the knotwork-etched shot glasses he bought me at the castle's gift shop today. From the doorway, I watch him drying his long hair with a towel.

"Your butt's downright bewitching," I say, handing him the shot glass.

"Thanks. Speaking of that…" Mike turns, rubbing the moist patch of hair between his buttocks. "I think tonight's the night."

"Really? You mean—?"

"Yeah. I want you to, well, yeah, to fuck me. There are things you don't know about me, things I'm dealin' with, stuff I might tell you about some other day, but...I used to have nightmares all the time, but when I sleep with you, I'm free of 'em somehow. You holding me is like some kinda magic."

Mike fixes his solemn gaze on me. "Look, Alan, I'm feelin' a lot for you. You feel the same, I hope?"

I put down my shot glass and grip his shoulders. "Christ, Mike, you know I do. I know we've only been seeing one another for a few months, but...yeah."

"So I'm not just a piece of ass, right?"

I bark a laugh. "Oh, please. Are you kidding? I'm a busy guy. I've never been the kind to waste time on 'just a piece of ass.' Can't you tell how I feel? I haven't felt such, well, tenderness for a man since I was your age. Jesus, Mike, I thought you knew that."

"Well, I...you never said..."

"That I'm falling in love with you? True. I haven't said it. I've been too scared." I bend, nudging his brow with mine. "But I'm saying it now."

Mike's brown eyes grow bright. "Well, so, I feel the same, so, so, uh, it's time I gave you what you wanted. Even if you can't keep me tied." His grin's impish.

"Speaking of *that*—here's to surprises." I lift my shot glass.

Eyebrow cocked, he clicks his glass against mine. "Yeah? What you talkin' about, mountain man?"

"You'll see, you sexy Eye-talian. I brought a few supplies along. Been reading about escape artists in my spare time."

"Oh, hell." Mike drains his glass. "All right, Daddy. Bring it on."

❖

Contortion; trick locks; hidden keys. Lean and lithe as Mike's limbs are, the first makes sense. Trick locks I avoid by using not cuffs but hemp rope and duct tape around Mike's wrists, torso, elbows, knees, and ankles. As for hidden keys, well, the kid's stark naked, so the only places he could have keys secreted would be his mouth and his asshole. So after I hogtie the boy, I stuff a sock in his mouth and slap a few layers of tape over his lips, then add some tape over his eyes as a precaution. As for his asshole, I grease him up, finger-fuck him a little, then, ignoring his muffled squeals, work a small butt-plug into him.

"That'll open you up for later, boy. *Now* you're set," I say, giving his ass a slap. "Let's see you get out of that."

Mike's still trussed up when I'm done showering, though he's been struggling a great deal, if the mussed bedclothes, unkempt hair, and sweat-shine across his chest and back are any evidence.

"No luck, huh?"

Mike shakes his head and heaves a frustrated groan.

"Need more time?"

Mike nods, huffing hard through his nose.

I stand by the window, watching trains pulling out of the station down the hill. "I'm going to take a walk up to St. Giles Cathedral and back. If you're not free by the time I return, I'm going to fuck you till you're raw. If you *are* free by then, I'm still going to fuck you till you're raw. Agreed?"

Mike rolls onto his side. Muscles pop up along his straining arms. "Um," he grunts, nodding.

I pull on my jacket, leave the room, and lock the door behind me.

❖

When I return, I find Mike limp with exhaustion. He's still bound, and covered with sweat. He emits a long, low moan as I sit on the bed beside him and caress his damp hair. The room's musky with the scent of his struggles.

"Ain't going anywhere, are you?" I kiss his cheek before gently peeling off the tape that blindfolds and gags him and tugging the spit-soaked sock from his mouth. His brown eyes are moist and fierce.

"Oh, *man*," Mike gasps, licking his lips. "Oh *fuck*. I think I finally found him."

"Who's that?" I say, running a finger through his wet chest hair.

"The guy who can hold me. Who can keep me. You wanna keep me, Alan?"

"Ohhhh, yes. Your wrists and ankles look pretty chafed. You want loose?"

"Not yet," Mike whispers. "Not till after you fuck me, sir."

Hands trembling with excitement, I unbind Mike's knees and ankles. Rolling him onto his side, I slip out the butt-plug, only to replace it—slowly but firmly—with my latex-sheathed, lubed cock. When I first enter him, he grunts with pain. Then he goes wild, bucking, writhing, and shouting so loudly I stuff the sock back in his mouth. Soon, though, I've reached some other spot inside him, and he's groaning softly, rocking in a half-tranced state, nodding with rapture as I thrust into him again and again. Right after I've finished, he shudders, spasms, and comes on the sheets. I free him, wrap him in my arms, and fall asleep.

In the middle of the night, his butt bumping against my crotch wakes me. This time I take him on his hands and knees. I don't come, but I tug his little nips and stroke his cock till he's shot again.

In the morning, I wake to his mouth on my prick. "Bareback me, Daddy. Fuck your boy," he moans. "Dump your load up my ass!"

"Mike, I don't think—"

"No one's fucked me in years! I'm clean! Been tested! You?"

"Yeah, but—"

"Please!" Mike rolls onto his back, cups his thighs in his hands, and lifts his legs in the air, giving me a glimpse of his pink hole inside that wild bush of crack fur. "Please! I trust you! Please! Give it to me. Give it to me hard!"

❖

After our weekend in Scotland, I beg Mike to move in with me. He refuses, claiming to need his own space. Despite that disappointment, we spend most of our spare time together. When, once in a rare while, he cancels our plans, because of his work schedule or a visit from his uncle, my distress is so exorbitant it worries me. I've been happily single for years, but now I'm learning to ache for Mike when we aren't together. The depth of my desire frightens me. During those sleepless nights alone, I begin to glimpse the hollow agony my life might be without him, and that glimpse is terrifying.

One summer evening, I'm in my university office, working on my laptop, when there's a tap on my door. It's Mike. He has a black eye.

"Hey, I can't come over tonight. Uncle's in town. I'm really sorry. I'd rather spend time with you, but family obligations, y'know. I woulda called, but my phone got smashed..." Mike trails off, head hanging sheepishly.

I close my office door. "Looks like your phone wasn't the only thing that got smashed. What the hell happened to you?" I ask, grabbing his shoulders.

"Just a little bar brawl," he claims, but when I hug him, he winces. Suspicious, I tug up his T-shirt. Bruises cover his rib cage.

"Hey! Don't!" He pulls away, adjusting his shirt.

"What the fuck, Mike? Who did this to you?"

"Look, I gotta go." Before I can stop him, he's fled.

For hours I wait in my car, across the street from his apartment. He doesn't show up. I call him repeatedly. No answer. Days pass. I report him as a missing person. The cops can't find him. I can barely work, sleep or eat, fearing the worst.

A week later, a cold, stormy evening in June, I'm at home, drinking, trying not to cry, when there's a knock at my door. It's Mike, drenched with rain, dressed as he was the night we met—black T-shirt and gym shorts. His bare feet are bloody; his eyes are both blackened; his pretty lips are split. Without a word, he throws himself into my arms. We hug for a long time before I lead him into the living room.

"I can't stay," he pants. "I'm leavin' town, and I wanted to tell you face-to-face."

"What?" I grip him by the wrist. "Why? What have I done wrong? And who beat you up?"

"Look, Alan, I owe you the truth. We never, we never shoulda gotten involved. I...belong to another man."

"What? Oh, fuck, Mike, no!" Knees shaky, I sit on the couch.

"I'm so, so sorry. I shoulda told you, but things got so good between you and me so fast, I didn't wanna ruin it."

"This guy beat you?" I snarl, fists clenched. "I'll kill him!"

"Look, he beat me 'cause he found out I'm seein' someone else. He gets real jealous. He doesn't know who you are—yet—but he'll have you hurt if he does, so I gotta go back to Belgium with him."

"Belgium? Your uncle?"

"He's not my uncle. I lied to you. He's my, my sugar daddy, and he's been...keepin' me since I was a teenager. He found me on the streets. I don't like it much anymore, bein' with him, bein' told what to do—he doesn't fuck me but I spend most of the time he's in town on my knees, you know what I mean? He's married, a big shot, really closeted; in his world, no one knows about me. I owe him big—he pays for almost everything. I gotta go with him. He won't let me stay in England any longer."

"Christ, Mike. What's the bastard's name?"

"Not gonna tell you that. Not good for you to know. No one can know."

"So why the hell did you get involved with me? If he fucking owns you?"

"I thought maybe somehow I could figure out a way to escape him. Because he's cold, and you're kind. I just needed...the way you touched me...so gentle. Alan, you gotta believe me! I love you! I don't wanna leave you. I wanna stay with you so bad! The way I feel, God, bound up and so warm in your arms...the feeling of you inside me. Oh, *fuck*, I was such a fool to put you in danger. I can't let him hurt you! I've got to go!"

It's not only a sick fear for Mike, a consuming need to protect him, that makes me do what I do next. It's also the thought of that abyss, what my life will be like without him. "You aren't going anywhere. I'm not going to let you run off to some pig who beats you. If you love me, you're staying with me." Grabbing him by the arm, I jerk him to his feet.

"Don't, Alan! No!" Mike's struggles are futile. His diminutive size was one of the things that drew me to him, and it's what allows me to do what I do now. I wrench his arms behind him, clamp a hand over his loud protest, and push him down the stairs to the basement.

❖

Good timing. I'm not teaching this summer. I stay home, watching over my naked captive. The combination of rope and duct tape—yards and yards of both—seems to have conquered his skills at escapology. After a few days of screaming and fighting, Mike grows acquiescent, quiet enough for me to bring him upstairs, peel the tape off his mouth, and let him sleep in my bed. Sometimes he begs me to free him, but those pleas are mixed with obvious dread at the thought of what waits for him in Belgium. More and more, he tells me how much he loves me, how much he wants me to keep him. Then he snuggles close and, in a low, desperate voice, begs me to fuck him. The mutuality of our passion only hardens my resolve. I'm going to keep the boy tied till he agrees to stay. And if the Belgian finds us, he finds us. I'd rather brave that than willingly let Mike go.

He's been my prisoner for a good two weeks when, one gloomy afternoon, I head out for groceries. I leave him gagged and hogtied on the mattress in the basement, napping beneath a warm blanket, his asshole still oozing lube and come. When I return, the basement door's still locked, but Mike's gone. The floor's scattered with his bonds. They look as if they've been cut, sliced with a knife, and they're bloodstained. The clothes I tore off him are still heaped on the floor.

I pace, trembling. I don't know if Mike's been forcibly removed, or if he left of his own free will. I can't call the police and explain that someone might have kidnapped a boy I was holding illegally.

Instead, I drive to his flat, only to find it unlocked and emptied of his belongings. I drive to the cathedral, walk along the river and pray. I drive home, drink too much, bury my face in the pit scents of his T-shirt, the crotch and ass scents of his gym shorts, sob till my sides ache, and fall asleep on the couch.

❖

A Brussels funeral parlor; an October afternoon. This is the abyss I dreaded, and it's darker and deeper than I ever imagined.

I've never seen my boy in a suit. Black and white clothes; black hair, white face. He lies in the coffin as he lay in that box the night we met. I keep expecting him to rise from it the way he did before, like Jesus, like Lazarus, a wild seedling in spring. But of course he doesn't. What chains and tames him now no one can escape.

Drug overdose. Was Mike's despair so deep that he ended himself as the newspapers claimed? I can't believe that. Did he threaten the Belgian with public exposure, causing the bastard, whoever he was, to have Mike killed? Did he leave me of his own free will, to protect me, or was he taken? Was the Brussels banker who shot himself the day after Mike died my rival?

No way to know. Fucking ironic that my criminal behavior— forcibly holding him—might have saved his life. If I'd been able to keep him with me, he might have lived. As it is, he's gone forever. A few strangers gasp as I take his folded hands in mine, caress his hair and beard, and kiss his cold brow. Before the punctilious funeral director can interfere, I've left, stepping out into autumn sunlight.

Incomprehensible, that Mike's gone and I continue. Who knows whom I might love in years to come? I'm only thirty-five. I'm strong still, still good-looking. One day I might find myself lucky enough to be middle-aged, settled down with some sweet guy in a big house with too many cats. But even then, I know without a doubt I'll be haunted by that dead boy in the black box. I bound him; he's bound me. Some part of me he's left chained and padlocked forever. And that's a blessing. Yes, losing him is agony, but I have no more desire to break free of his loss than I did to break free of his love.

From my coat pocket I pull the shriveled crocus Mike gave me in Sackville Gardens and hold it up in the sun. It's more brown than white, but it's all I have left. That, and his clothes, which have long ago lost their precious musk. Carefully replacing the flower in my pocket, I head toward the Grand Place for dinner. *Moules* and *frites*, maybe, or a big Italian meal like my boy used to make me. And some Belgian beer, maybe a lambic. I intend to drink a toast tonight: to what's so beautiful it's inescapable.

AND NOW, FOR MY NEXT TRICK
LEWIS DESIMONE

Harold had a knack for making things disappear. He started with the small, predictable stuff—a handkerchief, a quarter lost in a child's ear, the occasional small animal. It was easy, really—too easy. All you had to do was distract the audience, give them a reason to look in the wrong direction. Harold was a natural at that.

He'd always been fascinated by magic. Not in the way most people were fascinated by it—the ones who audibly marveled at each trick, never questioning why they were called "tricks" in the first place.

The tricks themselves didn't fascinate Harold as much as the tricking. Harold wasn't concerned that a man could cut a beautiful woman in half and then reassemble her with the wave of a wand. What intrigued Harold was the fact that other people would believe it.

He got his first magic set at eight—a deck of marked cards, a jacket with a hidden compartment in the sleeve to hold a string of knotted handkerchiefs, and of course, the top hat and wand. Within a week he had mastered every trick in the manual and had started to design his own. He made his friend Alan's cat disappear one day—dropping a green cloth over her carrying case while an accomplice yanked her, tail-first, out the other side. Harold coughed loudly at the key moment—covering the screeching meow—and his audience was none the wiser.

He didn't return the cat until the next day, when Alan's mother called the house asking if anyone had seen Fluffy. Until that moment—his first shudder of guilt—he'd been planning on ridding the neighborhood of her mewling neediness by dumping her in the woods across town. He lived to regret changing the plan when Fluffy scratched him on her way out of the carrier. At that moment, he resolved never to let anyone else interfere with his act.

Harold had a rare talent. And like all people with talent, he was completely misunderstood. "Magic is all well and good," his father said, "but you need something to fall back on. How about accounting?"

His mother, on the other hand, made no bones about it: "Magic is *not* all well and good," she insisted, glaring scornfully at his father. "It's *black* magic—it's an abomination. Who do you think you are, God?"

He couldn't make his parents disappear, but he could disappear *from* them. And that's exactly what he did. On his eighteenth birthday, Harold packed one suitcase with clothes and another with his magic paraphernalia. And as soon as his mother went off to the bakery—to pick up his birthday cake, he knew, because she was so secretive about her errand—he left. At least he had something real to celebrate that night on the Greyhound bus to New York. He had his freedom—the best birthday present he'd ever given himself, the best he ever would get.

There wasn't much call for magicians in New York. Harold hadn't done enough research before picking a place to live. He'd assumed you could do anything in New York. Since childhood, he'd had Liza Minnelli's voice scatting through his brain, telling him that if he could make it there, he could make it anywhere. But once he'd arrived, he realized he had completely misunderstood the lyric: Liza didn't mean New York was a good place to try your stuff; she meant it was the most difficult. If he'd been an actor or a dancer, at least he would have had ample opportunities to fail miserably, but there weren't a lot of auditions for magicians. His top hat and string of seventeen colored handkerchiefs were useless in the city of the concrete canyons.

But just as he was about to give up, another voice from his childhood obsession with Broadway musicals started chiming in his head. Harold had always wanted a Mama Rose. What he had gotten instead was a Mama Tulip, a spineless flower that bent every which way to find its piece of sun. Mama Rose would have supported his dream. It would have been hers, too. And she would have told him to get a gimmick.

He found his gimmick in Chelsea, when he was hired as the opening act for a demented drag queen who wanted to heighten the contrast to her own show. Trixie Dixie had seen him perform in a run-down bar in Times Square and knew that he was exactly what she needed. He didn't know what she'd meant until he overheard her backstage on opening night, whispering to her dresser that Harold's act was so dull, the audience would be overjoyed to see her take the stage to clean up after him. Putting him on the bill was a cynical way of making herself a star.

But that was just the impetus Harold needed to make himself a star instead. The first night was a disaster, of course, but by the second, he had developed his shtick. And by the third week, people were coming to see *him*. Trixie was beside herself.

Harold thought of his signature trick as Now You See It, but before long, his audience was referring to it as the Tubesteak Tango. And within months he had performed it everywhere from Ogunquit to Venice Beach. The popularity of the trick gave him the confidence he needed to devise an entire show, and before long he had become a rather accomplished entertainer. Nevertheless, at each show, he knew the audience was still there to see one thing, and one thing only—the Tubesteak Tango.

The smart thing to do, of course, was to save it for the end.

"Ladies and gentlemen," he said, and paused. He looked around the room carefully, shading his eyes from the stage lights. Depending on what he saw in the crowd—Provincetown was the safest bet—he would then softly correct himself: "Sorry," he'd whisper to the room full of men, "I meant ladies and ladies." After a titter of laughter, he would then shout, in as close to a basso profundo as he could get, "May I have a volunteer from the audience?"

It was like a bachelorette party, minus the bachelorettes. No one actually volunteered on his own—or at least, no one made it look like he was volunteering. Instead, someone here or there would yank an unsuspecting friend's hand into the air, and, once Harold had nodded approval at the right one, a small coterie of guys would push and pull the chosen one onto the stage, to a chorus of cheers from the audience and feigned protest from the individual.

"What's your name?" Harold asked the latest victim, a mustachioed guy in his early thirties. He made sure always to pick a cute one. No matter how enthusiastic any given table was about hazing their own, there was never a point in bringing some troll to the stage. Not for this trick.

"James," the man said quietly. Harold had to push the microphone under his chin and make him repeat it.

In the audience, he saw an unusual preponderance of gray hair, when he saw hair at all. Just in case he'd forgotten where he was—an occupational hazard for a traveling performer—this was a dead giveaway that he was in Palm Springs. Palm Springs—where old homosexuals go to die. But these days, he thought, the phrase "old homosexuals" was in itself a sign of hope. And magic was about nothing if not hope.

"Thank you, James," Harold said. "Believe me, the questions get easier from here."

James blushed, even his ears turning a bright red. This was going to be a fun one. He was playing it to the hilt.

It was like a seduction. No, Harold thought, similes were inappropriate: it *was* a seduction, just as clearly as the lines he used in chat rooms, or the way his hand casually grazed a stranger's knee in a bar. Only here, onstage, he was seducing the entire audience. Magic was simply a particular case; the general principle remained. Everything, when you came to think of it, was seduction. Seduction was the only way to get what you want.

And the first rule of seduction, of course, was that the person had to want to be seduced. Best of all was when they didn't even know they wanted to be seduced—like an altar boy, too young to label his feelings, who freely bats his eyelashes at a priest.

"What's the occasion?" Harold asked, gesturing toward the table where James's rowdy friends sat, hunched forward and howling. "Is it a coming-out party?"

James's shoulders visibly squeezed together. "No," he said over a nervous giggle.

"Fraternity hazing?"

He shook his head. "No."

"Just on vacation, then," Harold intoned, "endless nights of debauchery."

A hoot went up from the friends' table, overlapping cheers everywhere else.

"Good," Harold said, "that's just what I like to see." He straightened up and addressed his next question to the audience, like the ringmaster in a circus (drag queens had their role models; so did magicians). "Now, are you ready to test the laws of nature?"

More hoots, punctuated by lascivious grunts. The crowd was primed.

"I guess," James said. He was practically quivering. Harold had a sudden image of him as a Dickens character, sheepishly begging for more.

"Excellent," Harold said as he moved toward the back of the stage. The box, which might have been mistaken for an upright coffin if he hadn't had the foresight to paint it lavender, stood imposingly on its casters. Harold pushed it from behind, pretending to strain, and brought it toward the front. "It's time to enter another dimension," he said to James.

James smiled nervously.

"Come on," Harold said, "we don't have all night. These boys want to get out of here before the bars close." He opened the door—silently, thanks to its recent WD-40 treatment—revealing a pitch blackness whose depth could barely be determined from where he was standing, let alone the back of the cabaret.

"Scoot," he said, tapping James gently on the butt and directing him toward the box.

"Go ahead," he added. "I put chocolates inside. See if you can find them."

And, like a good soldier—or at least a drunken one—James made his way into the box. Harold quickly shut the door behind him. He dramatically wiped his brow and bowed toward the audience. They loved that part. They had always loved that part.

But the real focus of any trick was the reveal. It was all about the reveal.

Harold spun the box three times and waved his cape in front of it when it came to rest. He put his hand on the knob and stopped to gaze back at the audience. Most of them—the informed, who knew what to expect—were leaning forward, practically salivating. He had them. He had them all.

Gently, he pried the door open and made a show of peeking inside. As the audience murmured behind him, he yanked the door the rest of the way.

There was a sudden puff of dry ice from a hole in the stage. As it cleared, James was revealed inside the box—sitting in profile, his head turned toward the right to face the audience, knees up, arms folded across his chest—naked.

Two simultaneous sounds emerged from the audience—gasps of surprise and hoots of satisfaction. Harold winked at James and then turned back to the audience with his characteristic leer.

Inside the box, James held his knees tightly to hide his junk, his eyes wide with a coy innocence. He was playing the moment for all it was worth.

Among the cheers, there was a sudden groaning wave when Harold closed the door and spun the box around again for a few seconds. This part always went quickly, this anticlimactic necessity.

He opened the door again and revealed James, smiling more sweetly, standing upright and fully clothed.

The magic was supposed to be in the dazzling speed with which James lost and regained his clothing. But as with any trick, in the end it was really all about the distraction. It wasn't the clothes that this crowd noticed; it was the nudity. For all they knew, the clothes could have been in a pile at James's feet (in fact, they were lying in a heap in the trapdoor *beneath* his feet). The audience didn't care where the clothes had been or how they got there: They had seen skin on a stage. And no matter how many times they had seen a naked man, it never got old. That was another secret to Harold's success: this trick wouldn't have worked with any but a gay crowd. Gay men could never get enough of seeing each other naked.

❖

After a show, he always went to a bar on the other side of town. He couldn't bear having audience members come up to him and ask his trade secrets. In the beginning, he would grab a drink at the very venue where he'd just performed, but he quickly learned that wasn't sustainable. They always came up to him brightly, often laying a hand on his shoulder as if they were old friends. Onstage, across the footlights, he was blind to them all, distinguishing only bare silhouettes. So while they all thought they knew him, he didn't know any of them.

He enjoyed the anonymity of being across town. Tonight, he'd hopped into his rental car and driven as far from the club as he could without venturing out of alcohol territory altogether. He found a small, indistinct bar on the edge of downtown. It was quiet, understated. It would do just fine.

He parked himself at a corner of the marble bar, where the light was dimmer. The bartender, surprisingly chubby for Palm Springs, smiled broadly and wiped a clean patch before him. "What can I fix you?"

Harold preferred Manhattans—the sweet-tooth's version of a martini, he called them; same glass, same amount of alcohol, but they went down much more smoothly. And they were sippable. He could make one drink last for a solid hour if he wanted to keep his wits about him. And Harold always wanted to keep his wits about him.

There were only a few other customers so far: a pair at the other end of the bar, a singleton toward the middle, a few wandering in the back of the narrow room. None of the high-energy chaos he had come to hate in gay resort towns—the pounding music, the pathetically tiny dance floor, the obligatory kitsch of a disco ball casting reflections around the space like a constant reminder of a bygone era. A man could relax in a place like this. A man could have a simple drink and relax.

The bartender made a show of shaking the mixer over his shoulder. "Rough day?" he asked, finally pouring the drink into a glass. Harold stared at the drink, watching the foam slowly dissolve.

"Not especially," he said.

"You just look kind of...intense."

Harold glanced up, into the puffy face, the bright blue eyes. The bartender's smile was genuine. He wasn't like the half-naked pretty boys in those other bars, who made conversation merely to get a tip. This one actually seemed to give a shit.

"I have an intense job," he admitted. "It requires a lot of concentration."

"Surgeon?" the bartender asked.

Harold smiled and shook his head.

"Psychiatrist?"

"That's more like it," Harold said.

The bartender laughed. "Oh, kinda like my job," he said.

Harold raised the glass in a toast. The drink burned a bit, the ratio of whiskey to vermouth a little higher than usual. He liked it.

"Any real crazies today?"

Harold put the glass down and sighed. "They're my specialty," he said.

"Well then, I'd better refill the shaker."

Harold laughed as the bartender moved toward the other end of the bar, where one of the other customers was drunkenly waving a hand in the air.

He fished out the maraschino cherry and plucked it off the stem with his teeth. He never knew what to do with the stem after that. He'd once dated someone who was a whiz at tying knots in them. It was part of his seduction technique, a supposed indication of other talents possessed by his tongue. False advertising, Harold soon found out.

He was beginning to think he'd been at this too long. There were no surprises anymore.

"Hi."

A magician, Harold thought, cringing at the familiar voice, *should never tempt fate.*

"Hi," he said, looking up. "What are you doing here?"

"Did I do okay tonight?" A sheepish look, a young hand gently pulling a flop of chestnut hair off his forehead.

"You did fine, James." Harold looked around the room quickly. "But we shouldn't be talking."

"Come on, Harold," the young man said, taking the stool beside him, "you don't really think anyone believes it's magic, do you?"

"Of course not," Harold said.

"Then?"

"The point," he said—pointedly, he thought, relishing his cleverness—"is that it's *my* trick. Not yours."

"I don't get any credit for taking my clothes off in a confined space?" James said, chuckling.

"No." Harold took another sip.

"That's not what you said the other night."

"When can we do it again?"

Harold rolled his eyes. This wasn't the first time he'd had to put up with this. "James, you can't do it again. What if one of the audience members from tonight shows up again?"

James signaled for the bartender. "I didn't mean *that* trick," he said.

"By definition," Harold told him, "a trick happens only once."

"That's all it was to you," James said, "a trick?"

Harold smiled, as amiably as he could under the circumstances. "Tricks are my life."

They had met a few nights ago, at another bar—a very different bar—darker, with more places to hide. Everyone, Harold reasoned, has his own way of cruising for that special something he's looking for, to fit whatever mood he may be in at the time. But Harold wasn't looking for what the rest of them were. The sex was fun—a lovely fringe benefit—but what he was looking for was an accessory, each evening's own version of Vanna White. James had played Vanna already. It was time for someone else, a new audition.

But first he had to get rid of this one. James was young, impressionable. The only thing to do was let him down easy. "Look," Harold said, leaning forward to create an intimate space between them at the bar. He turned his lips in a half smile, his earnest look. "I'm always a little exhausted after a show—especially one that goes as well as tonight's did, thanks to you. Maybe we can get together on Monday—I'll be much more relaxed then." He scanned James's face for a sign of appeasement; in this light, it was hard to read. "Can I call you?"

James delicately dipped his head to one side. The hair fell again. Some people no doubt found that charming—people who weren't threatened by their own advancing bald spots.

But Harold took it as a positive sign, a nod. "Great," he said. "Now, go back and join your friends. Where are they, by the way?"

"They're out back," James said, "smoking." He gestured again with the hair flip. *Everyone has an annoying habit*, Harold thought. This was apparently his.

"They don't know you're talking to me, do they?"

"We didn't even see you on the way in," James said. "I just spotted you when I came back to use the bathroom."

Harold smiled and nodded. "Good. Well, I'll see you later then."

James slid off the stool and backed obediently away.

Harold returned his focus to his drink, the way the glass reflected the lights suspended above the bar. In the old days, he had practiced hypnosis, trying to get his audience members to cluck like chickens on cue. After a while, he'd decided it was too crass. But the skills were still there: what he'd learned was that it was all in the tone and the choice of words. With the right tone, he could get anyone to do anything.

This bar was going to be hopeless now. With James and his friends hovering, there was no chance of doing what he had to do. He finished the drink with two hard swallows and tossed money on the bar.

"Another?" the bartender asked.

"No thanks," Harold said, smiling. "One's my limit tonight."

"See you another night, then."

Harold debated for a moment. But it was still early. No doubt, the bartender had hours to go before he got off. Another night, indeed.

He was surprised by the cool air outside, the strange way that a desert landscape can become downright chilly when the sun disappears. It was bracing, just what he needed. He decided to walk a bit. The bar where he'd met James was just a couple of blocks away. It was probably safe tonight, with James and his gang settled in. It might be worth another shot.

The music was everywhere, but with the bass turned up, it had a darker tone that he didn't find quite as irritating. The music seemed more like a backdrop, a mood enhancer rather than a distraction. Harold ordered a beer and meandered toward the back, deeper into the darkness.

He preferred standing quietly against the wall, just watching, waiting for them to come to him. And somebody always came to him.

❖

From time to time, he would see a familiar face in the crowd. The repeaters didn't come for the magic, he realized. They came for the beauty. They came to show their friends. They never got tired of it. Harold wished he could say the same.

"What's your name?" he asked as the new kid stepped up, the same hoots following him to the stage.

"Jorge."

Harold customized the banter for each one. Last night, over beers, Jorge had told him about weightlifting. "So what do you do for fun?" Harold asked now.

"I work out," Jorge said, smiling into the audience. He was a good student. "I love to test my strength."

The audience cheered. It was bound to be another successful night.

Jorge stumbled on his way into the box. Harold grabbed his arm and, while he was there, discreetly pointed out the latch in the floor. He never rehearsed with the boys; it was too risky to be seen with them in the club before hand. But the process couldn't have been simpler. No one had ever screwed it up.

Jorge was definitely one of the prettier ones—optimal distraction. A loud groan waved through the room as Harold closed the door. "What?" Harold said with a dramatic sigh. "I'm not enough for you?"

"No!" someone toward the back called out.

Just for that, Harold decided to throw a little extra flourish into the routine. He draped a rainbow curtain over the box so that when it spun, the colors fluttered brightly. Finally, when the box had come to a full stop, he yanked the curtain away and tapped the door three times with his wand.

When he opened the door, the audience burst into laughter.

Harold turned his head with a jerk and saw Jorge standing in the box, still fully clothed. Harold gave him a puzzled look, to which Jorge simply smiled and gave a slight shrug.

"Sorry to catch you with your pants up," Harold said, sotto voce, and glared at Jorge. "Let's try this again."

He abruptly shut the door and gave the box a more delicate and longer spin. Maybe Jorge just hadn't had time to find the latch. Maybe his zipper had gotten stuck. Or maybe the spinning made him dizzy.

Harold rolled his eyes comically to make the audience think this was all part of the show. He was just prolonging the suspense.

He tapped again on the door. "Come out, come out, wherever

you are!" he called and pulled the door open, a bit more cautiously this time.

There was a titter of applause, but still none of the expected giggles or lascivious hoots. Harold continued to gaze into the audience for a moment, before finally turning his attention to the box. The empty box.

His heart pounded abruptly, the rest of his organs seeming to have sunk beyond perception. But, as ever, there was no danger of his emotions seeping through the skin—nothing but calm on the surface, as if this eventuality were exactly what he had intended.

He dipped his head inside the box, playing Jorge's disappearance for laughs. "Jor-ge!" he called out, singsong fashion, as if he were bidding a child to come home for dinner.

The audience laughed along with him, and Harold shut the door once again and spun the box a few times for good measure. He tapped it again—three times, the agreed-upon signal—and carefully opened the door.

This time, he peered inside immediately, not bothering with the ritual of watching the audience instead.

A gasp erupted behind him. The box was still empty.

❖

He expected it was just a joke. Someone was playing a trick on him, and smirking at the pun.

In his dressing room, he searched every corner, out of instinct as much as anything else. He hardly expected to find Jorge hiding behind the drapes or crouched under the vanity, but it served some purpose, if only psychological, to look. There were no signs of him anywhere.

He rifled through his bag, his wallet, the pockets of the pants he'd been wearing that night. Finally, he found Jorge's card. They called them "trick cards"—a simple design, just a name and number printed on a white background. He grabbed his cell phone from the table and dialed.

He heard five rings and then a computerized click. "Hi, this is Jorge. Apparently I'm doing something more interesting at the moment, so please leave a message."

Harold shut the phone and stared at the wall.

He waited until everyone was gone—the audience, the backstage crew, the waiters cleaning up the tables where wine and rose petals had been spilling all night. Most of the lights had been turned off. He had to search in the dark for the first switch, then lit his way toward the wings, bulb by bulb.

The box was in the corner, where it was always stashed between shows. It looked more like a coffin than ever, a lavender black hole, a place where things got lost.

Harold approached it cautiously. He actually felt afraid to touch it. The box, he thought suddenly—in the dark, in the fever of anxiety—was haunted. Something inside it had snatched Jorge away.

He creaked the door open. The darkness inside was deeper, pure black. There was nothing there—no ghosts, no goblins. And no handsome young man.

But he had to be somewhere. He was probably watching Harold from the flies, a hand cupped over his mouth to smother the laughter. Jorge was playing with him, that was all.

Harold reached into his pocket for the phone. Trembling slightly, he pressed the redial button.

The ring was louder, not just in the ear pressed against the phone, but outside, in the room—the familiar opening chords of "Addicted to Love." He was right: Jorge was out there somewhere, spying on him. All he had to do was follow the music.

It sounded like he was hiding behind the box. Harold ran swiftly around the box, and found nothing but more darkness. The sound got louder when he rounded the door again. The music, jerkily repeating, was coming from inside.

Frantically, by touch, Harold found the latch to the trap door. It was just a compartment, barely the size of a cabinet drawer—no room for a man. It was intended only for—

His clothes. The fabric was cold on his fingers—the silky shirt

Jorge had been wearing, the black cotton slacks that now vibrated in his hand. He pulled the phone from the pocket and saw his own number flashing on its screen.

It didn't make any sense. The only trick to the box was the secret compartment. There was no escape hatch beneath that, no hole in the stage, no back door. Jorge couldn't just disappear. It wasn't possible. It wasn't supposed to go like this.

Harold held his cell phone out, lighting up the darkness of the box. He rummaged through the secret compartment, but couldn't find anything beyond the clothes he had already removed. Slowly, he crawled inside. Maybe if he actually tried to stand in Jorge's shoes, he could figure out what had happened.

He laid a hand against one wall of the box, the other lighting it with the phone. The wood was smooth and surprisingly cool to the touch. He rubbed it gently, searching for holes, a latch he hadn't known about. He still couldn't rule out that someone was screwing with him. Some stagehand, or perhaps an envious performer tired of Harold stealing the spotlight, might have cut a door in the wall and persuaded Jorge to slip through it, to humiliate him.

Harold approached his work methodically, sliding his hand slowly across the wall from one side to another, then down a bit and back the other way. He imagined a grid superimposed on the dark wood, his hand quite meticulously catching each square. When he had assured himself that the left wall was clean, he moved to the back. He reached up to the top of the box and had just begun to slide his hand across when a draught of air struck him from behind, followed by the sudden slamming of the door.

He turned around and struck the door. There was a tiny latch on the end, for emergencies, but it wouldn't budge. He banged against the wood, but it refused to give. He caught the panic rising in his chest and stopped for a moment to breathe. There was a way out of this. There was always a way out.

He was fine until the box started to spin. Harold had always been a rational man. You couldn't be an effective magician without being a rational man. A superstitious person wouldn't be able to handle this job. Magic was all about controlling the environment. You couldn't do magic if you weren't certain of your control. You couldn't perform magic if you actually believed in it.

But when the box began to spin, the rational gave way. Harold was no longer a magician, in command of his world. Inside the spinning box, the box that he had spun so many times to distract and mesmerize his audience, he was simply a man—a man who grew increasingly terrified with each revolution in the dark, cramped space.

He pounded at the wall, not sure anymore which one was the door. He heard himself whimpering, felt his throat constricting, his heart beginning to race. Someone was out there, someone who had it in for him. The same person who had made Jorge vanish was now going to do the same to him. And he would never understand why or how.

As the box spun more and more quickly, Harold fell to his knees and pressed his hands against opposing walls to steady himself. He was becoming nauseated, and he closed his eyes, concentrating on the breath that, despite his best efforts, was growing more and more shallow.

For a moment, he even considered praying.

And then—quite suddenly, without warning, without any winding down—the box jerked to a stop. It was only the extended arm against the wall that kept his head from smashing into the wood. He slumped against the wall and waited, not fully trusting the stillness, fearing what might be on the other side of the door.

He didn't have to push against the door. Now that the spinning had stopped, the latch abruptly clicked and a sliver of light peeked in. The door creaked open slowly.

Harold stumbled out, into a shadowy spot surrounding the box like an inverse halo. He righted himself at center stage and stood still, waiting for his legs to stop shaking.

He was looking down at the floor, the thick dark planks of scuffed wood. At the edge, he could see that the footlights had been reversed, facing outward now and leaving the stage itself dim, sketchy. Finally, he lifted his head and gazed out at the audience. It took his eyes a moment to adjust. He wasn't used to being in this position—the watcher, rather than the center of attention.

He couldn't make out the tables. All the telltale signs were gone—wine bottles standing upright against white tablecloths, women in sparkly dresses, men in sport coats or shirtsleeves, leaning into each other for a whisper while their eyes stayed riveted on the stage. There was none of that now: all he could see was a blur, a pinkish swath of light, gently undulating before him.

He peered carefully at one spot, the table where Jorge had been sitting earlier, before Harold had called him up to enter the box. Gradually, the pink blur shifted and became more distinct. An arm emerged, reaching up into the air, into the light, before settling back down onto what he could now tell was a wide, smooth back, a man's back.

And suddenly it all became clear. Once he knew what to look for, he could see it in every corner of the room—men in clusters of two or three or more, bodies gently writhing, backs arching, faces leaning in for a kiss. The room was surprisingly silent, only the faintest murmur rising in the air. Harold watched, mesmerized. Here, a hand grazed a stubbly cheek, there a pair of naked legs clenched tightly around someone else's thighs. Necks curled around necks, lips opening to lick, to bite.

Directly in front of him now—at that table—a face turned toward him, and he recognized Jorge's distinctive smile.

The vision was only momentary, as Jorge arched his back and his head dropped, eyes closed. Harold moved his gaze along Jorge's chest, toward the face that was kissing his nipple, the hand that was caressing his skin.

The other man looked up, as if bidden by Harold's glance.

"Hello, Harold," James said, smiling mischievously. He maintained eye contact with Harold as his hands gently rode along Jorge's side, tickling the skin above a delicate scar on his hip. He watched Harold as his tongue carved another path along Jorge's chest, down across the smooth expanse of belly, dipping into the crotch. As his mouth closed over Jorge's cock, James's eyes held onto Harold's, forcing him to watch, staking his claim, a claim that Harold was denied.

Harold moved forward, toward the lip of the stage, but as he reached out, beyond the footlights, he felt a pressure pushing him back—an invisible barrier, a fourth wall made only of warm air that kept him in his place.

And beneath him, Jorge gyrated slowly. Though his eyes would not leave James's, Harold still felt Jorge's staring at him. Together, their eyes possessed him. Their eyes held him imprisoned in this spot, burning in the heat of the footlights, tormented by their pleasure and his own impotence.

A voice resounded through the theater—slightly muffled, perhaps Jorge's, the breath growing shorter. "Is this all we are to you?" it asked. "How many of these men"—and suddenly Harold saw the familiarity in the other faces; he scanned the room and discovered that he knew them all—"how many offered you more than this? A conversation, a shoulder for your troubles. But all you wanted was this, your little trick."

"I gave you all the chance to be onstage," he said, the words stammering forth awkwardly.

"Onstage?" The voice laughed. "Who said we wanted to be onstage? Fifteen minutes of fame, standing up there naked for someone else's amusement?"

"You knew what it was about," he said. "You all knew."

James's head kept bobbing even as a dark arm came to rest upon his shoulders, as another one stroked the smooth curve of his ass.

"We're not props, Harold."

"I never treated you like props."

And suddenly someone laughed. Somewhere in the room, a chuckle erupted.

Harold looked up, toward the back, where a man suddenly stood amid the writhing crowd—Tyler, his name was Tyler; they'd met in Saugatuck—and pointed at the stage, laughing.

Down in front, James was licking Jorge's thigh, his hand gently stroking his cock. And his eyes watching Harold.

"Is this all you think there is?" James said between licks. "People appearing and vanishing at will, when you wave your wand?"

"It's magic," Harold said, his voice suddenly cracking with defensiveness. "It's an act."

"Yes, Harold," said James, "we know." His hand drew tiny circles on Jorge's chest. "Love is magic for you, Harold. But for some people, it's real."

More laughter, in the other corner now—a sudden burst, derisive, oddly sad. And within seconds, the laughter began to ripple through the room, like waves in a bathtub, back and forth, back and forth. Around the room, naked bodies stood up and pointed. Harold pressed against the air at the edge of the stage, but still the wall held him back. He couldn't move through it. He couldn't even fall.

With the laughter swirling, surrounding him, drowning him, Harold turned his back on the room. Behind him, in the shadow, the box stood, yawning at him, promising the comfort of vanishing.

In Through the Out Door
Rob Rosen

Wagon pulled up through the middle of town, cloud of dust rising in its wake. Two giant mares pulled her, snorting as the wheels came to a halt. We all broke from work to have ourselves a look-see, seeing as strangers through those parts are about as rare as a snowfall in June.

I wiped my hands on my apron, hung it on the hook and ran outside, eyes taking in the large wagon, the equally large horses, and the rather large man that soon emerged from a side door, his hands held up high as he greeted the crowd that quickly gathered. He was dressed all in black, from his black boots up to his black slacks and black vest covering a black shirt and right on to his spiffy black top hat, which rose a good half foot above his black mane of hair. Only thing not black about him was the white of his skin and the blue of his eyes, which sparkled like the lake at the edge of town, blue enough that you just about wanted to take a dip in them.

"Friends!" he shouted, a wide smile forming beneath his thick, black mustache. The crowd hushed, all faces expectantly staring up at him. "I am the Great Waldini!" A murmur swirled around the crowd, the horses stamping their hooves at the sound of it. "And I bring to you today the magic of the Far East, spells as ancient as the hills that surround this splendid town of yours, powerful prestidigitation that will amaze and stun you right on out of your very socks." I grinned and thought, *and the coins out of our very change purses, more than likely.* Still, the thought of something other than work was appealing. As was the Great Waldini himself. A real stunner he was.

Enough to make my crotch twitch from inside my britches, a thick bead of sweat suddenly trickling down my cheek.

The crowd moved in closer, clearly eager for the show that was about to take place. I watched as Waldini rolled up his sleeves, muscular forearms covered in a black matting of wiry hair, his smile growing even wider on his handsome face as the tricks came and went, lightning fast. Coins appearing from behind ears, rings that were locked becoming instantly unlocked, water burbling up from an empty cup held in his hand, doves flying out of his hat, each trick getting him a loud round of applause, gasps from the ladies, shouts from the gents. Me in the back, I stood staring, transfixed. Though not by the magic. No sir, no how.

Flowers sprung out of his pockets and he handed them to the women in front, a rabbit followed the doves, the hat floated above his head, all while the crowd, not to mention my cock, grew and grew and grew some more.

Waldini then grinned so bright as to put the very sun to shame and wheeled out a colorfully adorned casket, which he pressed up against the side of the wagon. "And now, friends," he hollered, the crowd hushing once more, "I will saw one of you all...*in half*!"

Well, boy howdy, that got the crowd to cheering even louder, me included. Not every day you get to see someone sawed in half, I figured. Then he asked for a volunteer, and, well, I reckon I got carried away and yipped and hollered the loudest, seeing as he spotted me in the back of the crowd and pointed my way. "Ah," he said. "A brave young man we have here." He waved me forward. "Step right on up, sir. Step right on up."

The crowd parted as I made my way through, though, watching the casket lid get raised as I approached. I climbed the stairs he produced and hopped inside. He stood behind me, just for the briefest of moments. "Play along and I'll fill your pockets with coins," he whispered, not knowing, of course, that there was little room left for anything else inside my pants besides my tree limb of a swollen prick. Still, I nodded and crouched down before sliding in, realizing in a jiff that the casket was already halved, me on one side, fake feet somehow pushed on through and out the other. *All in the name of magic*, I thought, my eyes suddenly locked on to his, so much blue that the sky all of a sudden paled in comparison.

He glanced from my face down to my tenting pants, his grin widening, a wink cast my way. "You got a rabbit hidden in there, too?" he whispered as he lowered the casket's lid.

"*Jack*rabbit," I whispered back. "And it's itchin' to break free."

He turned and reached for the saw. "All in good time, sir," he murmured before turning back around. "All in good time."

And then the saw came down on the casket, my head moving back in forth in well-acted agony as Waldini talked to the crowd, cracking jokes at my expense, the saw moving ever downward. And then, with a flourish of his hands, he parted the casket in two, half of me on one side, the other, apparently, pushed a few feet away. My ears were greeted to a thunderous shout of approval, coins flinging their way toward Waldini, who scooped them up before joining me back together again.

"And now, friends, my last trick!" he shouted, a large drape appearing from out of nowhere before settling down over both me and that casket of his. "I will make this man...*disappear*!" The crowd again fell silent as I listened beneath the drape, Waldini's spell pushing forth from between his lips, while his free hand released a latch on the back of the casket and I tumbled in through the out door of his wagon before crawling out of sight.

Then I heard the crowd erupt in the loudest applause yet, with more hootin' and hollerin' than even at a roundup. I smiled, picturing the small wealth the magician was collecting at that very moment, and then before I knew it, we were riding our way out of town.

"You okay back there?" he yelled from up front a short while later.

I chuckled. "Considering I just been sawed in half and then disappeared, I suppose I can't complain none," I yelled back, having a look around the wagon, at the pictures of the Great Waldini taken from all over the country, at the small bed nestled in the back, which I promptly hopped on, waiting for my eventual release.

And then, twenty minutes or so later, the horses came to a

slow stop and in he walked, smiling brightly as he nodded my way. "You're a born actor, sir," he told me, tossing me a handful of those promised coins.

I blushed and grabbed for them before pocketing them in my work britches. "Just following your lead, is all," I replied, meeting his gaze as my cock stirred yet again.

His wink returned, his finger pointing at my midsection. "That *lead* to the aforementioned *jack*rabbit, sir?" he asked, a beguiling leer joining the wink.

I leaned back against the wall of the wagon and spread my legs, the tenting in my pants even more noticeable now. "That it does, Waldini," I replied, my voice suddenly hoarse. "Where you gonna make it disappear to next?" Seems he wasn't the only one who could do that fine bit of double talk.

He coughed and moved forward, closing the gap between us until his hand rested on the thin material, his hand gripping the wide head within. My eyelids fluttered shut and a soft moan got pushed up from my lungs. "I think I know just a place for it," he replied, voice equally raspy, thick as molasses now.

"Magic again?" I asked, eyes popping open. "Nothin' up your sleeve?"

He laughed and stood up, staring down at me, those eyes of his sparkling like diamond dust. "Up my sleeve?" he replied, with a tilt of his head. "Let's see now." Slowly, he removed the vest and set it on the bed, then, button by button, worked his way down the black shirt, a thick down of hair revealed, then a flat belly as the shirt got pulled out of the slacks, pink nipples jutting out from swirls of black as the shirt parted before joining the vest. Then he stood there, chest rapidly expanding and contracting. "Nope, nothing up my sleeve, sir," he proclaimed, arms held out.

I nodded, gulped, wiped the sweat from my forehead. "Down your pants, then?"

He grinned. "Now then, what kind of magician do you think I am?"

I grinned back up at him. "I'll show you what's down mine, if you show me what's down yours."

That mischievous grin of his widened, a nod thrown in for good measure. "Seems fair, sir."

My nod echoed his as I kicked off my boots and unbuttoned my pants, the material pushed down before I slid on out, underpants tenting something fierce by that point, and with good enough reason, I reckoned. "Guess I got me my own wand to do some magic with, Waldini," I made note, and then released said wand as it swayed to and fro before coming to a standstill, raised up stiff and strong as a flagpole.

Again he moved in closer. "Gonna be hard to make *that* disappear, sir."

I shrugged. "They don't call you the *Great* Waldini for nothin'." Then I pointed to his pants, the material barely able to hold what he was hiding within. "And now that I done showed you mine…"

The nod returned. "Like I said, fair is fair." He bent down and removed his black boots, then unhooked his slacks, which dropped to the wood floor, his cock springing out, no underpants for the magician. "Whoops, guess I had something hidden in there after all."

Thing was huge, too. Horse hung, we call it, the head thick as a plum and slick with spunk, balls swaying as he moved in even closer, until he was standing at the foot of the bed, gazing down at me, a hungry look on his face that must've mirrored my own. I grabbed my stiffie and shook it at him. "Now then, where we gonna make this thing here disappear to?"

He crouched down and took a hold of it, sending a warm eddy through my belly before he took a lick of the tip. "Abracadabra," he fairly groaned, taking it in before a tear streamed down his cheek. I grabbed a hold of his thick, black mane of hair and pushed him further down, watching my pink flesh slide deep within his throat.

I moaned, staring down at him as he stared up at me. "Nope," I grunted. "I can still see it. Ain't disappeared just yet, I'm afraid."

He popped my prick out of his mouth and again stood up, the chuckle returning. "Well, no, sir, I'm not done with all my tricks just yet. Gotta save the best for last."

I watched as he got on all fours, hairy ass pointed my way, hole winking out at me, ringed as it was in a halo of black hair. He spread his legs wide, balls dangling low. Truth be told, a prettier sight I ain't never seen before. "Think it'll disappear in there?" I asked, hopping off the bed before kneeling behind him, my fingers tickling the silky center.

"I believe so, sir," he replied. "Like you said, they don't call me *great* for nothing."

I shook my head. He had me there. I bent down further, nose to hole, taking a deep whiff of him, the smell of musk and sweat wafting up my nose, nicer than any flower I done ever smelled. And then I took a lick, a suck, a slurp, my tongue traveling through all that soft, black down of his, while my fingers played with his heavy nuts, twirling them around. Still, there was *magic* to be done, if'n that stiff prick of mine meant anything.

I spat into the ring and gently slid a finger up and in and way to the back. Waldini moaned loudly, his back arched, head thrown back. Moaned even louder when a second one joined on in. Heck, that wagon of his got to rockin' when the third one joined the fray. Then again, like he said, you gotta save your best tricks for last, and mine was slapping up against his hole in no time flat, replacing those spit-slick fingers in a jiffy.

A rumble rode down his body and out through mine as I once again slid in through the out door, so to speak, my cock moving in and out, in and out, more and more with each shove. "Mmm," he moaned, jacking that great big cock of his as he shoved his mighty fine ass into me.

"Mmm," I echoed, staring down, watching the progress unfold. And then, "Ta da!" when my pole of prick at last disappeared altogether, my balls slapping up against his rump, a swarm of butterflies suddenly set loose inside my belly. And then I slid it all the way out, *pop*, my cock hovering in midair before it again got crammed all the way in again, getting the loudest moan from Waldini yet as the trick was repeated, and then repeated again and again and again.

The last time, Waldini rolled over on his back, legs up and out, furry chest glistening with sweat, those blue eyes of his just about on fire now as I buried my cock deep inside his ass. Then I leaned down and did something I ain't never done before, adding a new trick to my growing list. I brushed my lips against his, his against mine, our tongues joining before our mouths did, until it fairly felt like I'd landed on a cloud. And then I reached down and grabbed his sausage-thick prick in my hand and jacked that prick for all it was worth, all while I fucked his ass silly.

Still, I wanted to catch the end of the act, so I got all vertical again and stared down, his cock swollen and throbbing in my grip before it finally shot. Thick streams of come came a-flyin' out, one after the other before landing on his belly and chest, and all while he bucked beneath me, moaning up a storm. His asshole clenched good and tight around my cock, too, and then I came right along with him, my groans even louder than his moans as I shot that hefty load of mine up his ass, filling it up until it gushed back on out again, gobs of it dripping down onto the wood floor a minute later.

Huffing and puffing, I slid my prick out and collapsed on top of him, my mouth finding his again, his eyes open, until I was lost in a pool of blue. Then I pulled an inch or so away and said, "That was…great."

He chuckled. "Well now, sir, how do you think I came by that name of mine in the first place?" He stroked my cheek and shot me that mesmerizing wink of his. "Guess I need to make you reappear, though, huh? Back to work for you?"

"About that," I replied, with a wink of my own. "The way I hear it, a *great* magician always has himself a nice-looking assistant, right?"

He nodded. "That's mighty true, sir. And can't get any more nice-looking than you."

Then I nodded. "Yep, I reckon so." My lips again pressed up to his, those butterflies of mine taking wing yet again. "If'n you think there's enough magic in this wagon for two, I mean."

Waldini wrapped his arms good and tight around me and grinned, lighting up the place as sure as sunrise. "Feels, all of sudden, like there's enough to go around," he replied, with a heavy sigh. "Way more than enough indeed."

THE MESMERIST'S ASSISTANT
JAY NEAL

The door to my cell flew open and the screw threw my clothes in, making a pile on the floor. "Best get dressed, boy," he snarled. "Mr. Magistrate is coming to visit and I don't think he'll want to see you naked."

Shows what he knew. I'd put my clothes on, sure, but as for Mr. Magistrate not wanting to see me naked—well, odds are more than one magistrate has seen me naked in my time.

Now, as for how I came to be here, staying in this poorly appointed room of Tothill Fields Prison as a guest of Her Royal Majesty, Victoria Regina, without my clothes on—well, that was a bit of bother.

It didn't start out anything special. Mr. Mornay and I were visiting Biddle's Club for one of our demonstrations. There were eleven old gentlemen there to see us that night, scattered about the room in their leather wing-back chairs. Mr. Mornay had already worked through the preliminaries of the demonstration, so we were starting my part of the evening. I hadn't got my clothes off but a minute before we heard a set-to and a lot of noise in the hallway outside the room containing all of us.

Next thing we knew a bunch of rozzers poured into the room, rather embarrassing several of the old gentlemen who, even if they didn't have their trousers around their ankles at the time, might as well have had. Mr. Mornay made to escape out a side door, but his way was blocked by the sudden appearance of some more blue bottles. I would have followed him, too, if not for the impediment of an arm around my neck with these stated intentions: "You're coming with me, boy."

He threw me in the back of the Black Maria and that's how I ended up here. How my clothes came to be here, now in a heap on the floor, I'm sure I can't say, and to be honest I didn't really notice for a while that I didn't have a stitch on. Odds are the rozzers got a buzz from carrying a naked boy about, my willy wavin' around for all to see, since I got a bit of a buzz from it myself.

I had my few clothes back on by the time the screw came back to take me to talk to Mr. Magistrate.

"Come on, boy, time to see His Nibs and no time to waste." He grabbed my ear to drag me along; they like to do that for the illusion of power and control it confers. I did my part by exclaiming "Ow! Ow! Ow!" as we walked hurriedly down the corridor.

We reached the interview room, where he opened the door and marched me to a chair set before a table, and pushed me down onto the chair. "Now, you answer Mr. Magistrate's questions right sharp, and none of your smart mouth, neither, or I'll knock that smirk off your face."

I gave him my best stink-eye look, since he expected it. To Mr. Magistrate he said, "You sure you'll be okay? He's a crafty one, this one is."

"I think I can probably manage."

"I'll be just outside. You call me if he gets out of hand." Exit the screw.

Mr. Magistrate, not nearly as well dressed as I expected him to be, sat serenely behind his table. With his left hand he smoothed the tips of his mustache before he spoke.

"My name is David Turner. I'm a magistrate at Bow Street Station." He made this statement and then waited patiently, maybe even respectfully.

So I responded, "My name is David, too. Davey Scuttle, from someplace near Spitalfields."

"How old are you, Mr. Scuttle?"

"I was born in 1862 or 1863, so I'm at least seventeen, but we always tell the old gentlemen that I'm fifteen. I know I don't really look fifteen but they would believe it because they wanted to. I think being short and ginger helped. Freckles, too."

"How long have you been associated with"—he looked at a sheet of paper he had on the table—"Mr. Edouard Mornay?"

"About a year, I guess."

"How did the two of you meet?"

"I was doing a spot of dippin' one night on the street when I came to his attention."

"You mean he caught you picking his pocket?"

It seemed smarter to keep quiet on this detail, so I didn't answer.

"This was when he recruited you for his scheme?"

"I don't know about any 'scheme.' He told me he needed an assistant for his project, and he said I'd do nicely."

"I'm sure he did. And how did he explain his 'project' to you?"

"He said he was planning to make a tour of the gentlemen's clubs in London, giving 'Scientific Demonstrations for Discerning Gentlemen.' He's a mesmerist, see, and I was going to be his subject for revealing the surprising mysteries of the new science of animal magnetism."

"And what transpired when Mr. Mornay revealed these 'surprising mysteries'?"

"He always warmed up the old gentlemen a bit with some simple demonstrations of his powers in mentalism, some simple mind-reading or identifying objects one of the old gentlemen gave to me to hold in my hand, something like a pocket watch, or a locket, or a coin."

"Are you asking me to believe that Mr. Mornay determined the nature of these objects by using only his mental powers?"

"How bloody likely is that? No sir, it was a bit of a gaff. We had a group of code words so I could tell him what I was holding. 'Something dear to the owner' was the locket, and coins were usually 'items' or 'things.'"

"How then would you convey the denomination of the coin?"

"Number of words in my sentence. 'I hold the item now' would be a shilling, or 'I have a thing from the gentleman's left vest pocket' would be a crown."

"Didn't this require a great many code words?"

"No sir. There's not so many things a gentleman keeps in his pockets."

"And what would happen after these amazing feats of divination were completed?"

"Mind-reading or messages from the spirit world. Last night at Biddle's he had a particularly good session."

"Did Mr. Mornay have such mind-reading powers or the actual ability to contact the spirit world?"

I couldn't help it. I snorted. "What do you think?"

"So, last night at Biddle's…?"

"He closed his eyes, held his hands up high, and talked in his slow, spiritualist voice. 'I'm getting an image. I see a young woman—a beautiful young woman—who experienced great pain and suffering. Her name…her name…I see the letter *M*, or perhaps *E*'…

"One of the old gentlemen cried out, 'It's my daughter Elizabeth!'

"'Yes, Elizabeth,' Mr. Mornay said. The old gentleman said, 'Our dear daughter Elizabeth, taken from us last year during the birth of her first child. How is she?'

"Mr. Mornay said, 'She loves you very much and all is forgiven.'"

Mr. Turner raised an eyebrow. "How did Mr. Mornay know these things? Did he have prior knowledge?"

"'Course he didn't, but it's not hard to figure. Most people know some young woman who's died in childbirth—and every one of 'em's beautiful! You'd be surprised how many are named Mary or Elizabeth. People always feel guilty about something and are glad to hear they're forgiven."

"So the mentalism was all fakery?"

"It was an honest, scientific demonstration of the power of suggestion."

"Very well. And what came next in the course of this 'scientific demonstration'?"

"Mr. Mornay would hypnotize me to reveal the wonders of animal magnetism."

"Why you?"

"I'm a very suggestible subject."

"I'm sure you are." He didn't even smile when he said this, but I could hear the smile in his voice. "And how did Mr. Mornay accomplish this?"

"With his pocket watch. The watch is popular with the old gentlemen. He'd hold it up by its chain and swing it gently back and forth, like a pendulum. 'Concentrate on the motion of the watch, see it swing left, see it swing right, then left, then right,' he'd say, using his dreamy voice. 'As you watch you feel yourself growing sleepy. You cannot keep yourself awake. It is impossible for you to keep your eyes open.' After a minute of that I couldn't stay awake and I fell into a deep hypnotic trance."

"And then what would happen?"

"I wouldn't know, would I? I was in a deep hypnotic trance. You don't remember anything that happens when you're in a deep hypnotic trance."

Mr. Turner pondered this silently for quite a little while before he spoke again. He tapped one of his fingers on the table while he thought.

"Mr. Scuttle, let's be clear about this. Mr. Mornay was no more a mesmerist than I am the Queen of England. I know it, you know it, and he knows it. To this point we have had an honest conversation with a truthful exchange of facts. I want to continue in that fashion. For that, I need your complete cooperation. What transpired while you *pretended* to be in a 'deep hypnotic trance' was contrary to Her Majesty's law. The Crown wishes to prosecute Mr. Mornay for these transgressions and for what he forced you to do."

"'Ere, I never did anything I didn't want to do."

Mr. Turner lowered his voice, as though someone might be listening. "Listen to me carefully, Davey Scuttle. To prosecute Mr. Mornay we need your testimony. In view of your tender age and self-evident innocence, it will be the Crown's position that Mr. Mornay seduced you into participating in activities that are most definitely contrary to your nature, so no blame will attach to you. Do we understand each other?"

"Yes, Mr. Turner, that seems clear enough."

"Good. Let us proceed, then, with your deposition, Mr. Scuttle, in a frank and forthright manner. I ask again, what occurred at Biddle's after you were placed in the apparent hypnotic trance?"

I told Mr. Turner the whole story this way.

So they'd know I was in my trance I kept my eyes closed, like I might be asleep. I stood motionless while Mr. Mornay explained some things about my deep hypnotic trance.

"Gentlemen," he said, "Davey is now in a deep, hypnotic trance. I can speak directly to his subconscious mind, his most deeply hidden animal self. This is a highly suggestible state, as we will demonstrate. He will do anything I command because his conscious self is powerless to refuse me while I control his subconscious.

"Davey, can you hear me?"

"Yes," I said in a slow, dreamy kind of voice, "I can hear you."

"When I snap my fingers, you will open your eyes and be under my command. You will obey my every order until I snap my fingers again to end this deep hypnotic trance, when you will remember nothing of what has happened. Do you understand?"

"Yes, I understand."

With a flourish, he snapped his fingers and I snapped my eyes open. But I didn't move, and I stared straight ahead.

"Davey, raise your right arm in front of your body." I let my stiff arm float up until it was straight out from me.

"Observe how, if I suggest he feel pain, he feels pain. Davey, I am holding a lighted candle beneath your hand. Can you feel the warmth of the flame?"

"Yes, I feel it," I said.

"Careful! It's burning your hand!"

I jerked my hand away as though I was burned. The old gentlemen chuckled.

Next, Mr. Mornay took out his pocket knife and opened it. He held it up for the old gentlemen to see. The sight of it always made them a bit restless and uneasy.

"And now," Mr. Mornay said, "we will see that if I suggest he feel no pain, he will feel no pain whatsoever. Davey, I hold in my hand a feather that I will now draw across your arm. You will feel only the sensation of the feather's tickle."

He slowly drew the knife across my forearm, causing the old gentlemen to gasp and groan like they felt the cut on their own arms. Sure, the knife really wasn't sharp, as they could see because there was no blood on my arm, but they were too busy feeling the pain themselves to notice that detail.

These demonstrations had the old gentlemen well warmed up and ready to accept and enjoy what came next without feeling guilty. This was the goal of the evening, the best part, the big finish, what they were all there for.

"The human mind," Mr. Mornay explained, "has depths science is only beginning to explore, potentiality we are only beginning to understand, powers that we have yet to exploit. The subconscious mind is an unusual and unexpected landscape that puts us in touch with our most basic animal instincts and impulses, as we are about to explore. Do not be startled or shocked by anything you are about to experience."

Mr. Mornay paused to let the tension cook some. When he judged the moment to be right he commanded, "Davey, remove all your clothing."

This always caused quite a stir, but it was no surprise. This is what all the old gentlemen were there for. Word got around, and this was the real reason why Mr. Mornay got invited to all the gentlemen's clubs in London to give our scientific demonstration.

I wore only a shirt and britches with nothing else underneath since I don't have drawers anyway. They liked watching me take off my clothes, but wearing too much complicated things and took too long to get off.

So it wasn't long before I stood there, stark naked for everyone to look at, and looking was something they really liked to do. I was still in my deep hypnotic trance, so I stood still with my arms at my side and looked straight ahead, but still enjoyed watching the old gentlemen shift around in their chairs and try to rearrange themselves without being seen because their own willies were getting hard.

I wasn't hard myself yet. My willy was still soft because that was part of the demonstration. Maybe the best part.

"Gentlemen," Mr. Mornay said, "even the depths of the mind that are normally beyond our reach are within my grasp in the hypnotic state. Observe: Davey, produce for us your erect member."

And I did. It didn't take but a few seconds before my Richard stood straight up, stiff and proud. And the truth is that this part of the demonstration was easy. What was not easy was keeping my willy soft until Mr. Mornay said to make it stiff. You try stripping off in front of all those eyes staring at you with all their longing and lust and you'll see what I mean.

"So," Mr. Turner asked me, "do I take it correctly that the unspoken but widely understood purpose of this 'scientific demonstration' was to display your naked body for the salacious pleasure of the audience?"

"No sir," I said, "you do not. I mean, it is not true to say that we stopped at that."

The Magistrate's eyebrows raised slightly, and he waited for me to continue telling my story.

"Lookin's good but touchin's better, and that's what the old gentlemen paid for, so that's what they got."

Mr. Turner's eyebrows shot up as high as they could go.

"Gentlemen," Mr. Mornay explained, "shocking though it may seem, during the hypnotic state, the usual barriers of social convention are pulled down and the usual behavioral strictures of society are totally banished! In a moment I will command our test subject—unwilling, perhaps, yet unable to refuse—to pass among you, which he will do without demur. In this state he is totally compliant, a slave to our desires. Observe, if you will, that you may touch him, feel his smooth, young flesh, even stroke him, and he will not—indeed, cannot!—deny you. And yet, I remind you, he will remember nothing of what has happened when I awaken him from his deep hypnotic trance."

This was all a bunch of guff since I was really awake the whole time, but it gave the old gentlemen an excuse to do what they'd paid for, which was to feel me up and play with my Richard so that they could have their own pleasurable release.

"Davey," Mr. Mornay commanded, sweeping his arm out in a dramatic gesture, "walk now among our guests and let them experience firsthand the truth of our demonstration."

So I did. I stepped off our little stage and walked slowly between the chairs the old gentlemen were sitting in. I paused near each one so that he had a good chance to look and touch me. It took a bit for them to get over being shy about it and reach out, but they always did, usually rubbing their own Richards through their trousers while they did. Some just liked to feel how smooth my skin is. Some would stroke me a few times, but never for very long unless they had a special arrangement. Some seemed particularly eager to feel up my arse.

Mr. Turner raised a finger to stop me. "Did anyone ever violate you from the backside?"

"No, sir," I said, "we never did no buggery."

Mr. Turner thought about that for a moment, tapping his fingers on the table. "What happened next?"

"That was when your plods barged into the room and started cartin' everyone off to jail."

Mr. Turner looked a little put out about that, but it was the truth. "Tell me, then, what would usually happen at this point in the 'demonstration.'"

Like I said, I made sure to stop at each old gentleman's chair so each one had a chance to feel my arse or hold my Richard. Most of them pretty obviously were hard by then and they'd be rubbing themselves through their trousers, but trying not to be too obvious about it. When they were all good and warm, it would be time to give the special treat to the Designated Daddy for that night.

The Daddy was one of the old gentlemen who'd paid extra to get the special treatment, and that's what we called him. One night it was a birthday surprise paid for by the Daddy's friends, who were all there to watch. I bet he still remembers that birthday party.

"How would you know who this designated person was?"

Mr. Mornay always knew who it was and we had some code phrases he would use as he guided the demonstration, but usually he could just use the particular code when I stopped earlier by that night's Daddy. Then, after I'd been felt up by everyone, Mr. Mornay could say something like "Davey, it is time for you to find your Daddy and express your appreciation for this evening's fine audience," and I could go right to him. It made the mind-reading effect stronger.

"What did you then do for this 'Daddy' to show your 'appreciation'?"

I started gentle by sitting down in his lap. Wiggling around like I was really happy to be there always stiffened his willy if it wasn't, or stiffened it even more. Always. I did that until he started moaning, and that always got the other old gentlemen going. They liked to watch, and the Daddy liked to be watched, but they were shy at first about watching even though they'd all felt me up already. They all got over that soon enough and started rubbing themselves through their trousers without trying to hide it anymore. It excited them to be doing it in the same room with each other.

This is when I leaned back against Daddy's chest so I could whisper in his ear, "I want you to rub my Richard. Please rub my Richard." That always drove 'im crazy! He'd groan with anticipation and hesitate—but not too much. No sir. In no time at all he'd have his big, Daddy hand wrapped around me, stroking up and down like he'd been aching to do it all evening, because he had.

Usually, the way I was sitting, I could feel Daddy's own Richard through his trousers right along the crack in my arse, or I could wiggle a little bit to make it that way. That was the best because then I could wiggle back and forth and clench my cheeks and help Daddy get to his own peak. It didn't hurt that all the other men in the room were that close to their peaks, too. The air was pretty warm and heavy with the smell of sex.

I tried to hold off on my own peak until I thought Daddy was right at the edge, then I let go, making some noise to help push Daddy over the edge, too. Seeing and hearing me spilling my cream on Daddy's hand pushed the rest of the old gentlemen to do the same, which they always tried to do without making any noise, like they were trying to pretend that they weren't all creaming in their own trousers. No matter, there was a lot of satisfied heavy breathing going on when we finally got past this part of the demonstration.

You know how men are after sex, so everyone had lost interest by now in anything more to do with our scientific demonstration of the wonders of Mesmerism, so Mr. Mornay tried to finish us up as quickly as he could. He got me back onstage and into my clothes without much talk, snapped his fingers to wake me from my deep hypnotic trance, demonstrated that I remembered absolutely nothing about what we just did, and then got me and him out of the room as quickly as we could, so no one felt embarrassed.

"That is quite a story you have to tell, Davey," Mr. Turner said to me.

"Do you think I'll have to tell it in court? There's some things I wouldn't feel comfortable describing in front of a judge."

"We'll see about that, but I think we'll be able to shield you from testifying. Now, tell me honestly, Davey, were there any other activities Mr. Mornay involved you in beyond what you've told me so far?"

"Other activities, Mr. Turner? I don't know what other activities you might mean."

"I have nothing specific in mind, but it strikes me that you and Mr. Mornay, for instance, would be quite well situated to blackmail some of your audience."

"Blackmail! Mr. Turner, I don't know how you could even imagine such a thing. The old gentlemen trusted us—they *believed* what we were doing, even if it was a bit of a gaff. I could never betray that. I mean, they were all like real fathers to me. You couldn't do that to your father, could you?"

"No, Mr. Scuttle, I take your point: I could not." He thought quietly to himself for a little bit more, then he stopped tapping his fingers on the table. "Given that, I think we're done here." He stood, so I stood.

He called out for the screw to come in and he came in so fast you knew he'd been trying to listen through the door. He must not have heard much because he looked like he expected to get to rough me up some. Shows what he knew.

Mr. Turner might have smiled just a little when he said, "Mr. Scuttle, you're free to go."

"Free to go?" I said.

The screw almost squeaked in indignation. "Free to go! You're lettin' this little pile of dung go free?"

"Yes, I am," Mr. Turner affirmed. "You are free to go about your business. The guard will, I am certain, be delighted to show you safely to the exit."

"Thank you, Mr. Turner, sir."

"Mr. Scuttle, one last thought: It's probably best if we don't meet like this again."

"Yes sir. I mean, no sir."

I was out the door before Mr. Turner had a chance to change his mind—and before the screw had a chance to grab hold of me. I hadn't even been inside a full day, but it was good to feel footloose again.

Besides, there was work to do. If I was going to keep working this gig, I needed to find a new assistant to replace Mr. Mornay and get him trained. That takes time, and there wasn't much to waste. I mean, I wasn't getting any younger, and I wasn't sure how much longer I could convince the old gentlemen that I was a young boy wiggling innocently in their laps.

SONS OF ORION
XAVIER AXELSON

*W*hen will I see you?" I whispered the words against his throat, *my lips moist and my breath hurried. "Will I see you again? I must..."*

My fingers traced a line down his throat. I felt him swallow, felt his want in the return of his touch. We had just made love, we still smelled of our sex; furtive and urgent. Had we known it would be the last time? Did we know?

Did we...

The mirror reflected my dismay, my loss; our love, the touch of our bodies lost in time, held together in stray pieces of my memory.

I asked again: *Did we know?*

I watched my lips move in the reflection and was shaken by the reality. I had been sitting reveling in the past when I was to perform in less than an hour. Perform; that's what it became. Through time and the descent of disbelief among the masses, I was now a performer. *A magician.* I would have spat the word from my mouth before saying it. I would never believe it, never accept it as truth. I knew the truth. This was illusion, a mirage; the way I managed to survive and live a pleasant life. If doing tricks was the price I paid for living well, then I would do it. And hate it. The torment of losing him was a high price. It seemed only fair I grieved for him in a nice house, filled with nice things; but I would trade them all to bring him back.

Did we know...

I shook my head angrily. It was done. Over and forgotten. The brotherhood had disappeared. Were there any left? I didn't know and stopped caring, searching, lamenting the loss of our society, our legacy of true magic. None of us *were* magicians. We *were* magic.

My anger stirred the animals. The large brown rabbit I let roam freely in the house stopped moving, ears erect, listening. The black and white doves fluttered from their elaborate perches in the aviary attached to the garden atrium. I could hear the beat of their wings, feel their unease at the force of my anger. The wind picked up. I could feel it, and for a moment I was tempted to give in to the rage that swelled inside like a river pushed back behind a dam. I am NOT a magician, a performing seal! Must I endure humiliation on top of the loss of him? *Must I...*

"Sir?"

Then it was gone.

I saw the Djin in the reflection, his small body a mere trifle of his true size. He had come to me as a gift from the brotherhood, a gift of great reverence and of the highest regard. I had just been made a full Son, a full member. I could hear the High Cleric's somber voice:

"To you, Niram, who is now a Son of Orion, I bestow a prince of the sands of time and intuition; may he serve you well."

"How long have you been with me, Djin?" I asked as I stood and took my eyes from the mirror that held nothing but memory.

"A thousand years, but a day," the Djin answered, his voice like wind across the desert.

I nodded, paused to reach down and scratch the top of the brown rabbit's head. Its ears flattened under my touch; eyes closed, its heartbeat slowed.

My anger had passed. The wind fell back, the beating of the doves' wings ceased.

"A thousand years," I said slowly and straightened up.

"You mustn't think of what is gone, you mustn't—"

"Who are you to say what I must and mustn't do? You forget

your place, Djin. True, I love you as brother and magic deity, but you were a gift of Orion, God and great hunter of the stars."

The Djin bowed and took a step back, head down as he lifted his left arm. My black gloves were draped across his wrist.

"I meant no harm. I only sense your troubled thoughts and wish you a successful performance. May the magic be with you tonight."

I came up to him, could smell the exotic spice of his skin. The winds of the desert blew through his being and stirred passions of wanderlust inside me. How long my passions lay dead, how long I stifled them behind the doors of my strapped heart. Would I never know the freedom of the winds like the Djin?

I took the gloves.

"You think me a fool, harsh and unloving, but you know my pain. I envy your wandering heart, your freedom of sky, vast knowledge of lands beyond the human. Forgive my harsh words, Djin."

The Djin bowed lower. "I know you meant no harm. I too know the pain of loss, the night the fires stole the brotherhood, when Orion vanished into the sky and took solace in the stars. I am a trifle next to his Son."

"Ahh well," I said moving past him, "we are doomed to want what is no longer." I turned and looked at him. "I must finish dressing. You may go, Djin."

He vanished, leaving only the smell of spice behind him.

I undid my pants and tucked my shirt in, cream white against almond-colored skin I inherited from my parents.

"Must I never know you," he whispered as his lips pulled away from the succor of my nipple, "but taste you." He licked slow circles across my chest. "Like plum, ripe in the sun of Sicily."

"A poet, you are," I said and lifted my arms back behind my head, giving him full access to the expanse of my chest.

"Smell you," he said, and pressed his nose to the soft thatch of hair under my arms, "like straw in the barns, warmed by a thousand suns."

"Mmm," was all I answered, enthralled by the seductive timbre of his voice, the feel of his mouth on me. It was when he stopped that I said more. "Is it not enough?"

"To one who sees, it is an easy question," he answered sadly. "I live with magic at the cost of my sight, born into the world of shadow, never knowing the sun, the plum, the straw but only imagining. Is it enough?"

Is it?

I had been staring out across the lawn. My mind lost. Was it enough? I shook my head and made my way from my rooms. The Djin stood by the door, my hat and jacket in his hands.

I took them, opened the door, and was about to leave, but turned back and called, "The plum trees are in need of harvesting. See to it and bring me a dozen of the fruit." I knew, even though the Djin had gone, he heard my request. "Thank you, Djin," I called again as I left. The only answer was the door closing behind me.

My driver, a beautiful woman called Miriam, stood by the car, smartly dressed in a navy suit tailored to fit the voluptuous curves of her body. Wild, black licorice curls hung to her shoulders. Her eyes were hidden behind sunglasses, and a smile spread across her lips.

"All right then?" she asked as she opened the door, her English accent clipped, but kind.

"Yes, thank you, and yourself?"

"Can't complain. Reggie's sick is all, right misery when he ain't fit."

"Then I must fix him something when I get back," I answered, and got in the car.

"Mighty kind of you, sir," Miriam called out before closing the door. "To the Winterain, then?"

"Yes, and only one show tonight. Please be there at ten p.m. sharp to pick me up."

"Will do, sir," she said cheerfully, then turned on the car and edged it down the driveway. Once the wheels met the road, she took off like a shot. I enjoyed Miriam's ability to drive fast, maintain control, and manage to get me where I needed to be on time.

"You mind a bit of music, then?" she asked, her voice buoyant.

"Not at all," I answered, hoping the sound would drown out my thoughts.

I leaned back and closed my eyes. Miriam found a station that played standards and she sang along. I smiled in spite of myself when I found myself joining her.

"You know this song?" she asked.

I opened my eyes and saw her smiling at me in the rearview.

"Who doesn't?" I called back.

"My mum and dad lived for American songbook stuff, and I got the ear for it from them."

I nodded and closed my eyes again.

There had been music before the fire, before we were separated.

"How did you learn to play?" I asked, coming upon him sitting cross-legged, a strange stringed instrument on his lap.

He had been naked, his skin like the inside of a ripe peach, the hair on his body golden-red.

"I would paint you if I knew how," I said, not waiting for an answer, only hungry for closeness and the touch of his hands.

"I learned by the nuns. They taught me after the High Cleric bestowed the instrument to me as my gift of initiation. There was one in particular—Sister Magnificat. She was a strange woman." *He smiled when he said it.*

"Magnificat? And she was a nun?" I asked, stifling a laugh.

"We called her Sister Maggie for short," he replied.

We both began to laugh.

"Sensible," I managed over a chuckle.

He began to play, and his smile didn't fade.

At first, I stood and stared at him. My eyes lingered over the curve of his shoulder, the way his muscles twitched under the strain of concentration and the fluidity of his fingers across string and wood.

"I believe you are a satyr," I said when my lust rose to an

uncontrollable height and I had to interrupt his playing with my kiss.

"Then you are wine that I thirst for above all other." His hand moved the instrument.

"Will you be near me during the initiation ritual?" I asked, our lips parting long enough for the words to fall from my mouth.

"I will," he answered and then pressed his mouth against mine. The feel of his tongue, wet and insistent, made me want him more than air. His naked skin warmed by the sun and his strong, woody smell intoxicated me like wine.

"Alaric," I whispered, hoarse with need, "say you'll be with me after Orion blesses me."

He pulled away from my embrace. "If I could look you in the face," he said as his hands reached up to caress my chin and lips, "I would look into your eyes and swear on Orion himself; no allegiance, his to the stars, or otherwise, is stronger than my devotion to you."

"Alaric." I said his name aloud, but he was gone. That day was long gone.

"Sir?"

I stirred from my reverie.

"We're here," Miriam announced. She was coming to open my door even as my memories of my lost lover faded.

The Winterain Theatre was owned by two longtime lovers, men devoted to the old theater and the performers who showed there. I had been performing at the Winterain for years and was equally fond of both Henry and Matthew—Matt to his friends.

Matt greeted me at the stage door.

"You look tired," he said before we embraced.

"I am tired, a little," I answered when we parted.

"You need more of a break?" Matt asked as he ushered me to my dressing room.

I shook my head. "No. More sleep, less thinking."

"And who's thinking?" I heard Henry call out from the hallway.

"Did you see what Angie left you?" Henry came rushing in, flamboyant and radiant in a stylish suit and huge smile.

"What did she leave me?" I looked at Matt uncertainly.

Angie was a cabaret singer Henry and Matt booked between larger engagements. She was a notorious gift giver, and when Henry pointed to a large covered cage pushed into a corner, I again looked at Matt.

"What—" I started to say, but Henry cut me off.

"You'll never guess!"

I walked over to the cage hesitantly.

Is it enough...

"Open it!" Henry cried excitedly.

I lifted my hand and let my fingers caress the fabric: a heavy brocade, dark and rich.

Is it?

Alaric...

I pulled the cloth off and was stunned to see a beautiful black bird staring back at me from behind the bars of an old cage.

For a minute, I didn't know what to do. The fabric fell from my hands. I heard someone rush over and pick it up.

"Niram?"

The bird was beautiful, and I was stunned into silence.

Henry came to my side, "Niram, it's a raven, Angie found it in her backyard with its wing broken. All this time she's been caring for this bird so she could give it to you."

"Niram?"

Is it enough...

I felt Henry was about to touch me, and I pulled away.

"Can he fly?" I asked, my voice harsh, almost cruel.

Both men were taken aback.

I asked again, "Can this bird fly?"

"I don't know," Matt said over Henry's dismayed groans.

The show would begin in fifteen minutes. I could hear people moving around outside the dressing room.

"Niram," I heard Henry plead but couldn't stop myself. I went to the cage and looked at the raven, its eyes wide and black—mirrors of flight, wide-open space and sky. I grabbed the cage. It was heavy, but I managed to steady it with minor discomfort to the bird.

Hadn't the raven been the bird of Orion, the god, my god of the midnight sky, of the wild hunt, of the constellations?

In a cage?

A pet?

Never.

I moved past the bewildered men.

I didn't see them coming after me until I was at the stage door pushing it open with my back.

"What are you doing?" Henry called out. Matt stayed silent.

"If its wing is healed," I said as I stepped outside and opened the cage, "then the raven should fly."

I watched as almost instantly the bird leapt from the cage. It looked back at me with eyes blacker than Orion's skies, and it cocked its head as if waiting.

"Will I never know you?"

"If I could look you in the face...I would look into your eyes..."

The raven spread its wings. It was not uncertain. It had done this before. It knew the wind, the air, and would soon know the sky again.

"I would tell you I am more devoted..."

The bird rose into the air, suspended in the coming night winds.

"I would tell you I loved you..."

"Alaric?"

Matt and Henry joined me in time to see the raven disappear into the sky.

"You're on in five minutes!" a stagehand called out from behind us.

"Then let the show begin," I said and brushed past the stunned couple.

❖

"Let them see the night," I whispered to myself as I stood waiting for the curtain to rise. I saw the raven taking flight behind my eyes, its wings outstretched, feeling the air, sensing freedom, a return to instinctual bliss.

"Let the night come to me," I intoned before I slipped my hands into my pockets and pulled out my gloves. I slid them on, relishing the cool feel of the soft leather.

The curtain rose and the applause rushed forth like a wave, but I let it flow past me, never touching me, but warming me just the same. What would I show them? What would they see?

The night sky, I thought as I looked not at the audience, but above them into the dark reaches of the ceiling. *Let them see the night, The night of my initiation. The last night I saw Alaric.*

"Ladies and gentlemen," I said, raising my voice and forcing the words from my mouth with dramatic emphasis, "I give you," I paused for effect, enjoying the hushed silence that fell on the theater, "the night sky." I thrust my right hand up and twisted my wrist so my palm faced the ceiling. I closed my eyes, and even as I brought the illusion to them, I could hear their sighs, gasps, and cries.

I could smell the night air of long ago, feel the tempting arm of memory reaching down from my illusion and ache to touch me. It was not their night sky they saw, but mine, from that last memory just before the brotherhood was destroyed by fire, by fear. I reached further into the memory and drew my initiation to life behind my eyes. The High Cleric's voice began to call down the sky to bear witness to the sacred ritual.

"Niram, brother, tonight, night of all blessed nights, you are the embodiment of Orion; the stars…"

"The stars." I intoned his invocation to the audience and, hearing their astonished voices, knew the stars appeared and twinkled brightly in the sky above them. In my memory, the High Cleric's voice rose with expectation.

"Orion the hunter, who alongside the goddess of the moon..."

"The moon," I said aloud, adopting his expectant tone. I twisted my hand further up until I felt the cold white light of the moon fall upon my face. As my memory became more realized, my heart began to pound, my pulse quickened. I could smell the fire. The people with torches would soon burn our sacred structure to the ground and we would lose our faith, our brotherhood, and I, my lover, by the hands of disbelievers.

Was it enough?

"Reaps the clouds, sows the sky with his seed, the planets..."

"The planets," I said louder, raising my voice over the growing frenzy of the crowd. They were seeing and believing the illusion, and I was sacrificing a memory.

"The constellations..."

"The constellations," I said, cold beads of sweat rolling down my back, raising bumps along my spine. Could I push further? Could I bring the illusion even closer? Could I make them feel what I felt?

"Niram, you are a son of Orion. May you be blessed with the slow burn of a bright star..."

"The stars," I repeated. This time I raised my other hand and thrust it high above my head, making the stars shoot wildly across the sky. I thought I heard a woman weep. The High Cleric's voice was loud in my head. I felt myself being touched by his hand, felt his gifts flow into me.

"Beauty and youth beyond time, beyond the measure of earth but the eternity of the stars, the moon, and the sky—you, son of Orion, who has taken the god into your body, will be given these gifts..."

I could make them see more! I thought wildly as I fought between memory, illusion, and reality. I could do it. I ached for release. If I could not see him, if I could not give myself wholly to him again, then why not surrender to the magic? Why not give myself truly to Orion and become one with the night sky? It was my only death, my only way to escape an eternity of longing. I reached higher and felt my feet leave the floor. Would I combust like a dying planet? Flicker brightly, then vanish into the cosmos? I heard shouting and cries from the audience. A man cried out, "Quiet!"

But then, just as the heat of star fire began to burn through my fingertips, I saw the black mirrors of the raven's eyes and heard the echo of its call. A tear fell from my face.

Was it enough?

I could give them this final show of amazement, blaze, then die. I tried once again to gather the illusion, strengthen my resolve, but it was gone. My feet touched the floor.

"The raven," I said with finality, the memory of my last night in the brotherhood gone.

I opened my eyes to see the celestial beauty I created fade. But before disappearing completely, each star, planet, and constellation turned into a raven. Fear ensued as the birds cried out above the audience. I watched in fascination as people covered their heads and shrieked as if the birds were real. It was during this black winged tumult that I saw him.

Alaric.

I smelled him, dry straw and sun. He stood in the middle of the theater among the masses of hysterical people like a beacon in a dark sea. I saw him, and again his smell hit me, and where once I was the enchanter, I became the enchanted.

It can't be, my mind screamed.

NO!

"Enough!" I shouted, and the birds vanished. Slowly, the people settled and a tense calm eventually returned. I rushed from the stage, ignoring Matt and Henry's pleas. I had to know. But when I arrived in the place where Alaric stood, he was gone and so was his smell. Had I gone too far? Had I brought him out of memory and into my illusion? Was I so desperate to believe my own fantasy?

I looked around, but I did not see him. I called out his name. A woman said something, but I silenced her with an old trick I learned while training in the brotherhood. I rushed back and forth among the rows of people.

"Where is he?" I shouted.

By now Matt and Henry were upon me, gesturing and calling for ushers to evacuate the theater.

"Where?" I shrieked as my legs gave way. I shook my head against helpful hands, but betrayed by my physical limitations, I fell to the floor. Why hadn't I been brave enough to give in and dissolve into my night sky? Why hadn't Orion taken me into his father's embrace?

Was he here?

I sniffed the air, desperate to recapture Alaric's warm scent, but was rewarded with Henry leaning down and pressing a flask beneath my nose.

"Drink this." He thrust the lip of the flask against my mouth and spilled the contents down my sweat-drenched tux shirt until I opened my mouth and accepted the burn of the alcohol. "You were magnificent tonight!" he whispered enthusiastically close to my ear. "Magnificent." When he tried to force the flask on me again, I pushed his hand away.

Struggling to sit up, I refused Matt's hand and leaned against a nearby seat, hoisted myself onto unsteady feet, and looked around.

The theater was empty. I could hear the murmur of voices and looked to the closed entrance doors.

"I got the crowd out to the lobby bar," Matt said, his voice full of concern.

"I need to go home," I said weakly as I walked hesitantly to the back of the theater.

"What happened in here tonight?" I heard Matt ask Henry as I stumbled away from them, "I never saw him do anything like that before."

To which Henry answered, "He's the best and the best, are always the most complicated."

I didn't wait to hear more but made my way as quickly as I could out into the night air, grateful Miriam was there waiting. When she saw me, she rushed forward, but I waved her way.

"I'm fine Miriam, just tired." I got in the car, closed my eyes, and didn't open them until I got home.

❖

The Djin was waiting for me when I opened the door, a frown on his face. His golden eyes were bright. He knew what happened at the theater. Being of ancient magic, he was well aware of my abilities and his sight was far reaching.

I held a gloved hand up in an attempt to dissuade his disapproval, but the gesture was of no avail.

"You dare," he started to say as I walked past him.

As I began to undress, I could hear him behind me, feel the burn of his anger and smelled spice, heard the whir of wind.

"It is not for you to decide when a god takes you into his embrace."

I shook my head; I wanted to say something but couldn't think of a reply. I pulled one glove, then the other from my hands and winced as the air touched my still magically charged fingers.

"Orion will take you when he deems it so. If you killed yourself, gave yourself to the illusion, it would be your soul's oblivion for all time. You would be beyond his embrace, in an eternity of suffering. Surely the brotherhood taught you such things, I know it so."

I pulled my shirt from my body and let it fall to the floor. Released from this sweat and booze-damp cage, I took a deep breath. I knew of the oblivion, the endless chaos of a magical soul in the depths of the universe, beyond the call of one's savior. Could it be worse than being beyond the arms of one's only and truest love?

I stopped walking. The great hall that led to my bedroom seemed endless and echoed with the Djin's reproachful tongue. The brown rabbit had fallen in next to me and, sensing both my unease and the Djin's anger, began stomping its powerful legs in warning. I reached down to stroke it. Gathering it into my arms, I held it close, feeling its alarming heartbeat. I relished its wild smell a moment before I turned and confronted the Djin.

"He was there tonight," I said, my voice hopeful, desperate.

"You speak lies. You are still enraptured by your own memory.

You are no better than the fools you trick for money," the Djin said angrily, though I could hear his tone had softened.

"No, it is not a lie." I stroked the head of the brown rabbit and murmured into its ears.

"Niram, you gave too much to them tonight. I have warned you against using your own memories for illusion. It is a gamble with your own sanity."

"It is not," I said, unintentionally raising my voice. The rabbit squirmed and I bent down and let him go. He raced away from us.

I stared a moment after the creature and then at the Djin.

"I am tired, Djin. Come in my room only if you wish to ease my nerves. I am no longer interested in being harangued."

I undid my pants, let them fall from my body, and entered my bedroom. Moments later I heard the Djin follow. He carried all my discarded garments and silently put them away.

The first thing I saw when the Djin turned on the lights was a large woven vessel containing a number of dark purple plums at the foot of my bed. The smell overwhelmed me. Had it only been an illusion, my memory, and the want of him that drew him from my mind at the theater?

No. I saw him. I know I did.

The memory of his golden presence in the audience was beginning to arouse me, and I put on a robe that hung in my closet as I felt my cock grow hard.

I went to the basket of fruit and, after close inspection, picked a rather large, heavy plum and pressed it to my nose. Its skin was taut as if it barely contained the flesh of the fruit and might burst in my hand. I knelt down and wrapped my arms around the basket, the fruit still carefully held in my right hand. Would the pain never stop? I thought again of the oblivion I could find if I so chose.

"Niram." The Djin had come up behind me.

"Call me sir. Certainly I've allowed enough disregard for one night," I said, still holding on to the basket.

"I call you by your name because what we speak is not of this arrangement, but of our time before this. You know it." He came closer as he spoke until I felt both his hands on either side of my head.

My skin prickled under his touch. His magic was strong, and my cock strained beneath the robe to be released and stroked by such a power. It wasn't that I wanted the Djin sexually—such things were forbidden—but his power was electric and arousing.

"Let me take him from your mind, sir," he added, the last in a soft comforting tone. "Let me ease him from you as simply as you can ease the skin from the ripe plum."

As he spoke, I felt his fingers press harder against my temples, I envisioned him walking down the halls of my mind; full-sized, powerful, not on two legs but a tornado of memory-erasing strength.

"Let me take him," he intoned and pressed harder.

My cock bobbed and I arched forward until I felt it press against the side of the basket. I gasped at the intended friction and rubbed back and forth, savoring the pleasure it sent rippling through my body.

The Djin would find Alaric. He was a persistent and pervading detective. He could find where I hid my most secret needs and wipe them away as if I never knew Alaric's touch, his mouth against mine, his cock in my mouth, the feel of his insides, velvet and tight. I wanted release from the pain, and yet…

"Stop!" I shouted, lurching away from the invading hands of the Djin. I sent the basket tumbling, and the black-purple fruit rolled across the floor. I spun on the Djin in anger.

"You must never do what you tried to do again or I will be the one who banishes you to the oblivion. I have allowed for your many freedoms out of love and connection to the greater magic of the night and Orion, but you have taken a step past what you ought."

The Djin struggled to regain himself and moved toward me, hands supplicating forgiveness.

"I meant only—"

I shook my head. "Say no more and leave me at once. Come back only when I call you."

The Djin turned to leave.

Before he reached the door, I called to him, "Miriam's husband is ill. Make him something and give it to her in the morning."

He nodded slowly and was gone.

Alone, I looked about the room. Fruit was scattered across the marble floor, and in my hands the remains of the fragrant and ripe plum, now a mass of pulp and broken skin, the stone the only solid thing left to hold on to.

❖

It had started to rain a fine soft pelt of water. It was not a shower, but the temptation of a storm; a night Alaric would have deemed perfect. After I cleaned my hands of the destroyed plum, I turned off the lights. The room was bright with the silver glow of a storm moon. I went to the great glass doors that looked out onto my lawns and opened them to the night. I savored the caress of the warm wind on my body. I undid the belt of my robe and let the breeze pull it open. I was exhausted physically and mentally but was restless. I stood in the doorway and took in great breaths of the rain-scented air. To my left I could see the outlines of the aviary where the doves roosted. If I listened carefully, I could hear their endless cooing. They were at peace. The dark lawns before me resembled a great black sea; the moon's light evaded great patches that held mystery. I felt the eyes of animals upon me, hidden from the rain but awake.

"Alaric," I whispered. My hands searched my body, seeking comfort and the ease of human touch. My nipples grew erect under my attentions, and I pulled on them until I cried out his name into the empty night.

"Must I never know you?"

My hands traveled down over my stomach, which quivered beneath my urgent touch. I felt the soft trail of dark hair and pulled on it longingly, wishing his fingers were searching me, bringing me pleasure. I let go, consumed by an angry need. I pushed my robe from my body, stood naked in the arms of the night and began to stroke my swollen cock with the want of one long denied.

But as I ran my clenched hand over my cock, I felt something alive call out to me.

"Niram!"

My eyes snapped open but saw nothing. I looked at the aviary and willed the moon to shed more light. The doves began to stir. I heard the wild beat of their wings, and soon the aviary was alive with their chaotic stirrings.

"Niram!"

Again the voice called, this time closer, more intent, more present. It had to be real. I stepped out onto the grass, knowing it was not the eyes of animals I felt, but his eyes. I wanted to shout his name but I couldn't. The doves grew ever more unsettled and I ran toward the great glass enclosure.

Damn the moon, my mind shouted, cursing its still-inadequate light. "Show me!" I finally managed to shout as I rounded the aviary. There standing on the other side was Alaric.

He was searching, his unseeing eyes not a hindrance, but his unfamiliarity with the house grounds had him at a loss. He pressed his hands against the glass of the aviary, all the while trying to calm the doves with an ancient chant.

I went to him and stood close until his fingers found me.

"You," he whispered. "I could hear your voice but couldn't find you, only glass."

"Alaric," I said. The name that had been so painful to say aloud now fell from my lips like a salve over a wound.

"You," he said again as fingers roamed my face, then neck, "so long ago. I've looked for you over seasons, years and hours." He shook his head. "And for one who cannot see…"

I could stand it no longer and pulled him into a crushing embrace. Both of us began to shake, but I didn't care, I only wanted him as close as was possible. The soft rain that fell only made him smell better, feel more real.

We parted only far enough for him to reach up and finger my lips with a trembling hand. "A mouth I have hungered for," he said, his other hand reaching for the back of my head. In a second we were kissing with such ferocity, I felt blissfully overwhelmed. Our lips were abandoned for tongues, deeper need and deeper satisfaction. We both groaned with relief, pleasure, and long-deserted hope.

The doves above our heads had settled into a restless unease, their fervent cooing a symphony to our lust.

"Wait," I breathed as I pulled away from his mouth. "Inside, let me take you inside."

I led him around the aviary, our hands clasped, fingers digging into each other's palms, both afraid the other would vanish.

Once inside, I stared at him in the moonlight. "How are you here?" I finally gasped after several minutes of silence. "Are you really here, or am I crazy?"

Alaric smiled then laughed. "I am here, after a long and"—he stopped and shook his head as if remembering something terrible—"painful journey, I have found you."

"How?" I repeated, moving closer to him.

Alaric sensed me, reached out and touched my bare chest, pressing his hand against my heart.

"I sensed your magic. I was traveling and stopped only to ask directions to my next destination when I felt your illusion, the great call of Orion and the dark drawing down of the constellations." He stopped speaking and pulled me close. "Were you abandoning yourself to the oblivion?"

"I couldn't take it," I said hoarsely, my face pressed against his neck. "The illusion promised release from my torment."

"And the raven?" he asked softly, his lips close to my ear, his hands stroking my back.

"A gift I set free. How did you know?"

"It returned the favor and guided me here. It sits in the tree at edge of your lawn."

"I felt it," I said. "I felt its eyes, although I thought them more beast than bird."

"Your magic was strong enough to stop me, but the raven was my true guide. Orion chose wisely when he chose his messenger."

"You are wise," I said, pulling his mouth to me. Once again we kissed.

"I must have you," he said, pulling away from me. "It has been too long."

"Have me and possess me," I returned, tearing his shirt from him, "and I, you."

I fell to my knees and hungrily grabbed at his pants as if I were plagued with famine and he, a banquet. I ripped his pants down and was rewarded with the naked, hard swing of his cock. I wanted to relish him but my greed overwhelmed my patience, and I swallowed his cock with the fervor of a praying zealot.

He filled my mouth completely and I trembled at the fit of my lips around his smooth, pulsing flesh. His moans were deep and guttural. He had waited as I had, wanted and longed as I did. His fingers laced through the hair on the back of my head and he pushed himself deeper into my mouth and throat. If I gagged I didn't care, I only wanted more of him and deeper. I tasted the salt of his pre-come, felt the tickle of his pubic hair against my nose, and inhaled his masculine scent. Memories threatened to flood my fevered mind, but I held them back. It wouldn't do. We would create new memories. The time of languishing in the past was over, and with every thrust of his cock into the back of my skull, I felt each painful thought slide away.

"You," he said through a pant, "it's you." He pumped harder. I let one of my hands drop to his thigh and caressed his leg. His muscles began to tighten and shake. He would come if I didn't stop, and I knew neither of us was ready for this to end.

"Niram," he said, hoarse with anticipation, "I need you inside me."

"Get down on the floor," I demanded, no longer in control of my body, voice, or mind. I had given up not to oblivion but to desire.

He did as I commanded, and I was on top of him before his head touched the floor. I pushed his hands above his head and let our bodies rest against each other. His pleading groans told me he enjoyed the weight of my body on his.

The plums scattered earlier were around his head and hands. I watched as he found one and pressed it quickly to his nose.

Recognizing it, he pushed the tender fruit against the punishing bite of my mouth. I bit hard into the fruit, my teeth just grazing the stone. Its succulent juices ran down my lips and chin and filled the room with the smell of plum. Alaric knew the scent aroused me, so he heightened it with his own magic. Upon feeling drops of the juice fall on his face, he arched up from under me and kissed me deeply.

"Now," he grunted when I let his mouth go from our kiss. He parted his legs, and I lifted them over my shoulders.

I looked down and could see my cock hard, thick, and dripping, the tickle of the fine hair on his body making it bob with anticipation. He handed me another plum. I grabbed it and squeezed the ripe fruit right below his balls until the juices ran thick and sweet against his opening. I threw the fruit aside once it expelled all its sweet and fragrant fluid.

"Now," he said again.

I plunged in, tentative but unafraid. I pushed past the velvet tightness within him and found his juice-slicked opening a welcome relief to my angry and engorged cock.

Alaric bucked and called out but soon found his way around my invasion and began to ride me, if not by his own driving need then by a memory of my motions. His body remembered, and so did mine.

"Harder," he begged as I plunged deeper. Sweat dripped off me and fell onto his belly. He stroked his own swollen cock until his strokes met each of my furious thrusts. "Niram, harder. I know you can go harder." The last word was a gasp as I pulled out and then thrust back in, making him writhe in unrestrained ecstasy.

"I'm going to come," he cried out as I withdrew, this time not all the way, and went deeper and harder.

I felt him tighten against my thrusting cock, and his legs spasmed over my shoulder.

"Fuck," I heard him gasp and knew he was coming.

I watched as the first spurt hit his chin. I arched his body up so the next hit his chest and ran down over his sides. Seeing him explode sent me careening into the depths of orgasm. I lowered his shaking body in time to pull my cock from the constricting hold of his insides and spill my seed onto his still-twitching cock and balls. I cried out as rope after rope of come sprayed from my long-denied cock. "Alaric!" I shouted, other words falling incoherently from my mouth until I collapsed, spent and trembling, on top of him.

Neither of us spoke, but we clung to each other like shipmen afraid to be tossed from their ship by a tremendous wave. Only after Alaric found another errant plum, bit into it, and swallowed did I feel daring enough to believe he was truly with me. I buried my head in his shoulder, enjoying the feel of his muscles moving under my chin. "Did you know that last time…did you know…"

"That we would see each other again?" he said after he swallowed another bite of plum. "I knew the brotherhood was scattered, the walls of our sacred place burned to the ground. On the last night, the night of your final initiation, I knew nothing except loss."

He handed me the half-eaten fruit and I took a thoughtful bite.

"I didn't know," I said as I chewed. "I thought we would have found each other right after, but somehow we didn't."

"No, we didn't," he added. "My blindness became real that night, almost as if the collection of our magic kept me from ever being truly blind, but when I stepped out of the sacred space into turmoil, I felt lost and I was afraid."

"And now?" I asked, tossing the stone of the plum and looking down on his handsome face. His eyes had grown more opaque and his mouth more sumptuous.

"I am a blind man who knows some magic, nothing more. I do not have your fame or prowess."

"I had nothing, until now."

Alaric smiled. "Do you still have the Djin?"

I laughed. "Ahh yes. And you, your instrument?"

It was his turn to laugh. "Of course. The gifts of the brotherhood are not tossed so lightly away."

"Then you must play for me!" I cried, "I long to hear that music again!"

"I will play for you tomorrow, Niram, for what is time but an illusion?"

LET'S JUST KISS AND SAY GOOD-BYE
TODD GREGORY

That's got to be the most original pickup line I've ever heard—and I've heard a lot of them." My voice sounded bemused, because I didn't know whether I should feel insulted, amused, or afraid of this good-looking young man with the enormous brown eyes and incredibly expressive face standing next to me.

"It's not a line." Every inch of that oh-so-expressive face, from the thick black eyebrows knit together over the wide-open spaniel-like eyes and the strong nose, to the thick lips and the dimple in his chin, was working together to convey *please you have to help me.* "Look, I know how it sounds." He swallowed. "I know I sound crazy. But you have no idea—no idea how important this is. *Please* come home with me." He shifted his weight from one foot to the other, anxiety radiating from him in waves.

He certainly believed it was important to convince me to leave the bar with him. His voice rang with urgent sincerity, and everything about his body language—the way he stood there, the slight hitch in his shoulders, the tilt of his head to one side—was a further indication he was being honest.

He wasn't feeding me a line.

He couldn't have been more than twenty-five at the most, since his tanned skin had yet to lose that wonderful soft, fresh glow of youth. The lashes framing his oh-so-amazing eyes were long, black, and curled. He was slightly shorter, maybe an inch or two, than I. The baggy jeans several sizes too big were hanging low on his narrow hips, so I could see the black waistband of his underwear with *Calvin Klein* written on it in red, just below the flatness of his stomach and the trail of wiry black hairs leading down from his navel. His nipples were hard and visible through the black cotton tank top he was wearing. His arms were muscular and lean, little veins snaking over the muscles of his upper arms and expanding in thickness as they road-mapped over his hairless, tanned forearms. His fingernails were ragged and bitten down to the quick—so far down it had to have bled and hurt. His shoulders were also round and well-muscled, stretching the cotton of the tank top. He'd missed a spot on his right cheek when he'd last shaved, a small, barely perceptible patch of wiry long hair along the line of his strong jaw. His thick bluish-black hair was cut short—almost so short I would have thought he was in the military. He clearly wasn't—he didn't have that ingrained rigid posture I'd come to associate with servicemen.

I felt a smile tugging at the corners of my mouth. He was quite adorable in the way all young men in his age group always were, his olive skin almost glowing with vitality and hydration and youth. There was a small scar on the side of his nose, probably from chicken pox or the measles.

There was a time when I wouldn't have questioned him, when I would have just rolled my eyes inwardly at his bizarre pickup line but it wouldn't have stopped me from leaving the bar with him. He apparently lived nearby—which would have been another plus for me in my own horny youth. But I wasn't young anymore—hadn't been in quite a number of years—and now thoughts like *he could be a serial killer* or *he could turn into one of those crazy stalkers* danced through my mind as I fought my attraction to him, no longer driven by an all-consuming need for orgasm that overrode everything else, every thought about personal safety or communicable diseases.

That time was far in the distant past, when desire was what brought me into gay bars.

But desire wasn't why I'd stopped at the 700 Club after work this evening.

The truth was I couldn't face walking into the silence and emptiness of my house again. I'd had yet another shitty day at work—something which seemed to be happening with more and more regularity these days—and so the thought of walking into my empty house and facing the silence alone was too much for me to consider. I didn't want to flick the television on while I warmed up leftover Chinese food to eat while wasting another evening of my life watching a marathon of one of those horrible *Real Housewives* shows that seemed to be all Bravo broadcast anymore. I managed to find a parking place in front of my house on Orleans Street and sat there for a few moments, staring at my front door and drumming my fingers on the steering wheel before deciding I couldn't go inside yet. I didn't even go into the house to change first—I locked my briefcase in the trunk and walked down to the corner in my shirt and tie and dress pants and black dress shoes and plopped down on a bar stool and ordered a pomegranate martini from Joe the bartender. I loosened my tie and relaxed, listening to ABBA playing through the speakers and sipping my martini.

The last thing I expected to happen in here was to have a sexy young man come up to me and say *I need you to come home and have sex with me. It's really important—the fate of the world could depend on it. I need you to help me with my magic.*

"I know it sounds crazy, but it's true," he went on, his tone still urgent, determined to be believed. His right hand picked at the label on his brown bottle of Budweiser, tearing it off the sweating glass a little piece at a time before flicking the flecks of white and red into the metal ashtray. "Please?"

He was adorable, really, and it was so tempting to just say yes, so I could watch his face relax into happiness and relief and an enormous smile.

But I was also old enough to be his father—and the significant age difference just gave me the creeps. I didn't want to be *that* gay man.

"I just live across the street," he added, as though the convenience would somehow convince me, when the suggestion of knowing his lithe body carnally had not.

"Why me?" I finally said, looking into those enormous eyes, hoping I wouldn't get lost in their depths. I gestured around the room. There were at least ten other men in the bar. Granted, I was the only one sitting by myself, the only one not laughing and having a good time with a group of companions. "Why not someone else? Does it really have to be me?"

"The window is very short," he replied, his eyes remaining locked on mine. He placed his left hand on my leg, twirling the tip of his index finger on my inner thigh. "I don't have a lot of time. And it has to be a mature man, a man who's lived long enough to have the knowledge and intelligence that comes from experience." His eyes swam with tears. *"Please."*

I thought about pushing his hand away, but the light, delicate touch of his finger tracing circles on my leg felt kind of nice. How long had it been since another man had touched me, anyway? Since Talley moved out after eight years together, out of our apartment in the Quarter, and bought a house uptown on Constantinople Street, a house for him and his new boy to live in?

I bit my lower lip. Six months—it had been six months since Talley decided I couldn't give him what he needed and the boy— Dylan—could. It was all bullshit, anyway. Talley was freaking out about getting older, saw his youth slipping through his fingers, and thought somehow Dylan could give it all back to him, like having Dylan shove his twenty-two-year-old cock up Talley's ass and shoot some young loads up there was some kind of magic talisman that would ward off the impending fiftieth birthday, stop the hair loss, and keep his chest hair from turning gray. He wanted a young man to make him feel young.

Idiot.

I wasn't going to make a fool out of myself, losing my head over a young man, the way he had.

And this young man, this beautiful young man-boy with the amazingly pretty eyes and the adorable face, the hard nipples jutting through his black cotton tank top, with his weird sense of urgency— going across the street to his apartment wouldn't change anything. It wouldn't make me feel young, or desirable, or like I still had what it took to attract a hot young man. It wouldn't change anything. It wouldn't make me thirty again, or even forty.

"What's your name, anyway?" I asked, lifting the martini glass to my lips and taking another sip of the sweet, fiery liquid.

He glanced at his watch and sighed in impatience. "It's Barnabas. Does it matter?"

"Barnabas." I finished the martini and put the glass down. "You go by Barnabas?" I couldn't mask the astonishment. The only time I'd ever heard the name before—outside of the Bible—was on *Dark Shadows*. His mother had obviously been a fan of the show.

"It's my name, and no, I'm not a vampire." With another sigh he sat down on the stool next to mine and finished tearing the label off the beer bottle. "You're not going to do it, are you?" The expressive face went from desperate pleading to bitter disappointment in just a matter of seconds. A hint of sadness tinged his voice. "It's going to be too late in a little while, anyway." He put the bottle to the full red lips and drank. "Sorry I bothered you."

"You weren't bothering me," I replied, not wanting the conversation to end, starting to already regret not taking him up on his fervent invitation. His pants had crept down a little farther when he sat, and his underwear had slid down a bit as well, so I could see the start of the deep crevice between his round, hard butt cheeks, and the soft downy hair just above.

"Just because your partner betrayed you and broke your heart doesn't mean every guy is going to," he said in a pouty tone. "And if you don't get over it you're going to wind up alone for the rest of your life. Is that really what you want?"

I could feel my cheeks starting to burn, and I opened my mouth to say something snotty but shut it again as I wondered, *How did he know that?*

How did he know about Talley?

Maybe—maybe he *could* do magic.

"Of course I can," he said without even looking over at me. "You really thought I was nuts?" He shook his head.

I felt a chill go up my spine. Who—or *what*—was he?

He turned his head and looked at me. "I'm a witch, and I need your help." He made a face. "Needed your help—the window is going to close soon."

He sounded convincing. He certainly believed what he was saying.

And he was starting to convince me.

Or it was the erection starting to stir in my pants?

"*So*, it's not too late?" I heard myself asking, waving Joe away when he noticed my empty martini glass. "There's still time?"

He nodded and gave me a knowing half smile. He glanced at his watch. "If we get started within the next fifteen minutes…yes, there's still time." He slid down off his bar stool and extended his hand to me. "So, you've changed your mind?"

I nodded and stood, not sure if I was doing the right thing, or the smart thing. But he had read my mind, hadn't he? How else could have known about Talley?

As I followed him out the front door onto Burgundy Street, I couldn't figure out an angle for him to be working that made sense. Sure, if he lived in the neighborhood—which he seemed to—he could have known about me and Talley. The French Quarter is a small village where everyone knows everyone and their business. But how could he have known I was thinking about Talley and his boy-toy? He couldn't have. He'd answered me when I'd thought about something else, too. I wasn't sure if I was ready to believe he was a witch who needed my help with his magic, but I was willing to play along.

Besides, it wouldn't hurt me to get sexual release with another human being—it beat watching porn and yanking my own dick.

He led me to a building just on the other side of St. Ann from the Rawhide Bar. Dusk was falling, and lights were coming on all over the Quarter. He went up a short flight of steps and slid a key into a lock. I followed him into a dark hallway, in an old building that smelled slightly musty and of rot and decay. He unlocked a door at the rear of the hallway, just past a flight of dusty wooden steps with peeling brown paint and a banister that didn't look trustworthy. He opened the door and smiled at me, waving me inside to a studio apartment that desperately needed to be cleaned from ceiling to floor. Everything seemed dusty, and cobwebs hung from the ceiling in the corners. When he flipped the light switch, I could see the wrought iron chandelier was festooned with cobwebs and dust. Several of the bulbs were blown. Books were everywhere, books and clothing. There was a mattress shoved against a wall, and there was a tiny little kitchenette in one corner, next to a tiny little bathroom. The wallpaper was faded and water stained, peeling in places to show yellowed plasterboard underneath. The sink was piled with dirty dishes, the garbage can overflowing with Styrofoam takeout containers, banana peels, and rotting apple cores.

Just being inside the place made me feel dirty, like I needed a shower.

Christ—get over yourself, Queen, I thought as he started lighting white tapered candles. The candles were everywhere, melted wax making strange designs on the sides of the slightly warped candles. There were spots of wax on some of the tables, and on the floor. Once the candles were lit he slipped his tank top over his head and tossed it into a pile of other clothes in a corner.

In the bar I'd thought he was attractive—but I'd had no idea just how beautiful until that moment.

His bare torso was perfectly formed, his pectorals thick and round, and every movement of his arms made muscle fibers stand out against the olive skin. Other than the treasure trail leading from his navel to the Calvin Klein waistband, his skin was completely smooth. Some black hairs were evident under his arms, and he smiled as he walked toward me until he was standing less than a foot away. He took my right hand and held it to his silky-smooth chest. The skin under my hand was warm, and I could feel the pounding of his heart.

He smiled as he loosened my tie and unbuttoned my shirt. "You're in really good shape," he whispered as he slid my shirt down my arms. He folded my shirt and placed it on a chair, rolling up my tie and putting it on top of the shirt. He leaned closer to me, and I felt the wet warmth of his tongue as it traced a line from the hollow at the base of my throat down the cleavage between my own chest muscles to dart in and out of my navel. As his tongue licked at my navel he was undoing my belt, loosening my pants. I somehow managed to kick off my shoes as he worked my pants down, and

I stepped out of them. Again, he gave me that knowing half smile as he carefully folded my pants and set them on top of my other clothes.

My cock was hard, but he seemed uninterested in it. He took me by the hand and led me over to the mattress, pressing both hands against my chest until I sat down on the cool sheets. He backed away from me and slid his own oversized jeans down without undoing them. I could see an enormous, thick erection inside his black underwear, but he turned his back to me so I could see the perfect shape of his amazing ass as he switched off the chandelier. The soft glow of the white candles now provided the only light, and I could hear my breathing becoming harsher and more fevered as he help up one of the candles, his back still to me, and began chanting in a low voice in a language I didn't recognize or understand.

He smiled at me when he turned and walked over to the mattress. He held the candle up over my nipples. Some of the hot wax spilled, and I gasped as the drops hit my erect nipples, burning yet arousing at the same time.

Still chanting, he reached down and grasped my cock with his free hand and I flinched, gasping as he toyed with the head through my underwear, the wax cooling and hardening on my nipples.

He set the candle in a holder and straddled me, pushing his hard ass down on my erection and rocking backward and forward, still chanting in that strange language, and I closed my eyes.

It felt so good.

It had been far too long.

And in my mind, the chanting took on a soothing, calming rhythm mirroring the gentle grinding of his beautiful hard ass against the shaft of my cock.

I opened my eyes and looked up into his.

And somehow found myself looking back down at myself.

I want him I want him so badly I want that big dick inside my ass.

I started and tried to get up, but he was strong, so very very strong and he was holding me down. "Relax," Barnabas whispered, a string of drool hanging from the corner of his mouth as he kept grinding his underwear-clad hard ass against my aching erection, "Don't be afraid, just go with it, you're going to be fine."

And he started chanting again as he flicked the round dried wax from my nipples, the now-exposed skin tender from the all-too-brief heat.

Somehow, his underwear had disappeared.

Magic, I thought and almost started giggling, but before I could start I gasped as my cock slid into him.

His ass felt velvety and warm, welcoming to my hardness, like it was where my cock belonged. It felt better than any ass I'd ever entered before, warm and loving and caring. It had never been like this with Talley or any of the countless men who'd come before him, names and faces lost in the mists and fog of time passed, but I knew with certainty it had never felt this good, ever.

He slid down, taking all of me inside him, and his own gasp of intense pleasure interrupted his chanting, the chanting that never seemed to stop, and I wondered what this was all about, this ritualistic fucking—

It is a ritual, it is the great rite I need to perform to enhance and build my own power, it is the feast day of Hecate, and I needed you inside me before the night fell and her time ended.

—I looked up into his eyes and he was smiling down at me, his eyes half-shut yet somehow glazed with his pleasure and I knew he was enjoying this as much as I was, and even the chanting, which had seemed so strange to begin with, now seemed a part of it all, it would seem weird to fuck someone in the future without the sound of the chanting in the background, and I could feel him riding me, riding up and down on my cock, slowly and gently so that he could savor every inch of it, every second increasing his own pleasure, and when he settled all the way down onto it the next time, he took his own big, thick cock and slapped it against my stomach, and I felt dampness, a long string of pre-come stretching from the slit of his cock to my stomach as he moved back up, stroking his big, thick cock with one hand as he kept riding me up and down, chanting—

—and I realized I could understand what he was saying.

"O Great Mother, I beseech thee, release the shackles in my brain as I open myself and my soul to you, as I make this offering of this man's seed mixed with my own, and allow me to continue my learning of your ways and your power as you work through me to achieve the perfection of this world as has always been our plan, your mighty plan, thwarted over the centuries by the patriarchs and the selfishness of men—"

And I could feel my load start to rise, that exquisite moment of pain and pleasure when the ache in my lower belly began, the clenching of my balls as the ache grew and spread as my own seed, the seed of my power, the seed he needed to commune with his goddess, began making its inexorable way up the shaft of my cock, and I could feel myself start to breathe faster, desperately wanting the ache to give way to the explosive pleasure of my orgasm, of my come spurting out of me inside his magnificent, magnificent ass and that was when I was realized, remembered that I wasn't wearing a condom—

"You needn't worry about disease I am clean the goddess protects me, I know you are clean as well, I need your seed planted inside me, and—uh—uh—uh—"

He half screamed, his entire body stiffening as his own orgasm began—small warms drops of come squirting out onto my chest and stomach, bigger shots of his liquid landing on my face as he convulsed, groaning with each eruption of his own fluids; his ass tightened almost painfully on my cock, halfway down, and I could feel my own urgency growing, and I grabbed his hips with both hands as he kept shuddering, his own orgasm seeming to be endless as it rained down on me, soaking me like a rainstorm, and his convulsions tugged on my cock but I grasped his hips with all of my strength and shoved my own hips upward, forcing his ass to unclench and my cock went up into him, my lower back aching from the arching necessary to force myself all the way inside him, and he screamed again as I managed to get inside and he relaxed, bringing himself back down on top of me with all of his weight and we slammed back down into the mattress and his eyes were wild, wild with sated pleasure and need and desire, and his lip twisted, his eyes taking on a determined lusty look, and he started riding me again.

Slamming down into me and going up, taunting the head of my cock, teasing it with his opening, moving his hips from side to side to increase the tension and teasing of the incredibly sensitivity of the skin on my cock—

And I couldn't stop it if I had wanted to, although why I would have wanted to stop anything so amazing and pleasurable was beyond me, and I could barely stand the feeling of the first drops exploding out of me and splashing inside him, coating his insides, and I kept crying out as load after load exited through the slit of my cock and my whole body shook and trembled as he clenched on me again so I couldn't move, my body shaking and trembling and goose bumps rising up all over my skin, everywhere, and I couldn't bear it anymore, and just when I thought my heart would explode in my chest I finished, it was over and I fell back, gasping.

"Thank you," he whispered, moving so that I slid out of him.

I couldn't speak.

I slowly sat up, got to my feet, and staggered over to where my clothes rested on the chair.

My mind was dazed.

I felt drained—but not the way I used to after an intense fuck fest with a hot guy back before Talley came into my life—it was more than that.

I felt like a piece of my soul was missing.

But that was crazy, wasn't it?

"I'm sorry," he whispered. "But you wouldn't have come here with me if you'd known that."

I knew I was right—somehow, his ritual had taken a part of me away, that was what was needed on the feast day of Hecate to increase his power.

"You're just a soul vampire," I whispered as I pulled my underwear back on, one hand resting on the back of the chair so I wouldn't fall down.

He came up from behind me, still naked. I could feel his semi-erect cock pressed against my own ass.

His hand came around and pressed against my forehead.

"There must always be payment for what we take, and my payment to you will be this."

Images started flashing through my mind: images of the first time I ever laid eyes on Talley, when we met, when we first fucked, when we dated, and everything. My entire relationship with Talley flashed through my mind, and the pain, the hurt, the agony was so intense I could hardly stand it, it was like my heart was breaking all over again, and then—

It was gone like it had never been there in the first place.

And the drunken, woozy feeling was gone, too.

I finished dressing, not saying another word to him until I had slipped my tie into my pants pocket and slid my feet into my shoes.

He was watching me, sitting naked on another chair, magnificently beautiful, the long semi-hard cock hanging down between his muscular legs, his eyes wide open and almost pleading as he watched me.

The pain I'd been living with since Talley had left was gone.

All I felt was a nostalgic happiness about the joy I'd found with him while we were together.

I wanted him to be happy.

"Did you get what you needed from me?" I asked as I walked over where he was sitting.

He nodded.

"This won't happen again," I said, knowing it was true as the words came out.

He shook his head.

I leaned down and kissed him on the cheek.

"So this is good-bye?"

He nodded.

"Good luck to you, then, Barnabas," I said as I closed the door behind me.

I walked out the front door and down the front steps.

I felt—*good*.

I started whistling as I walked home.

TRANSPOSITION
'NATHAN BURGOINE

"Check us out. Twins!"

My great-uncle's eyebrow arched. "Hardly."

I gestured to my suit, which mirrored his. It was a vintage design, and I'd spent more than I should have on them. They were made to resemble a faded photograph I'd found of him in one of his many albums when we'd been getting him ready to move into the seniors residence. Packing him up from the lovely Suffolk cottage he'd lived in by himself his entire adult life had been a long and sad process. The break we'd taken with those albums—despite his failing health otherwise, my great-uncle had a whip-crack memory—was one of the best moments I'd had in the last year.

"That was taken on a cruise," he'd told me. "Everyone dressed up on cruises back then, even just for dinner. It was taken at a magic show." Then his eyes had grown soft, and he'd smiled at me and told me to put that album in the "keep" pile. I'd snuck the photo out and hatched the idea with my mother over the next two weeks.

When I'd showed him the cruise tickets, he'd stared at them a long time before thanking me in his usual reserved manner.

"I'm sure it will be good to smell the sea again," he'd said.

The *Proud Empress* was a rarity. Most cruise ships didn't last thirty years, but this one had been restored twice, and lovingly so. It was a sister ship to the one he'd ridden all those years ago, and when we boarded, he paused, leaning on his cane heavily, and looked about with wonder.

"You'd think it was the same ship," he said. "Except all the curtains are red, instead of blue." Then he'd looked at me, nodded once, and said, "I need to get off my feet. Where's our cabin?" I was rooming with him. My parents had another room on the other side of the ship. My mother had claimed it wasn't done on purpose, but I had my doubts. My great-uncle wasn't the easiest man to get along with, though I adored him.

The suits had been my second surprise, and once he'd changed and I'd come out of the tiny bathroom—breathing a little heavy and trying to fight off the claustrophobia—in my own version of the same outfit and proclaimed us twins, he'd sat on his bed and smiled at me. From my great-uncle, those smiles were rare unguarded moments.

"Are you ready for the magic show?" I asked.

"Did I tell you about the magic show?" he asked in return. "The first one, I mean. Back then."

I shook my head. "No."

"It was scandalous." His lips turned in a sly smile. "Back then, I enjoyed a good scandal. The magician, you see, was a woman. Her assistants were men."

I raised my eyebrows, not getting it. "Okay."

He laughed. "Wouldn't matter to you these days, but back then, it bothered some folks. She wore a kind of tuxedo—with trousers!—and her assistants were the ones in the white shirts and sequins." He shook his head. "People were funny back then. My sister—your grandmother, rest her soul—thought it was a disgrace. No sense of propriety, she said. Can you imagine folks these days getting upset about a woman in a suit?" He chuckled. I loved him so much when he told stories like this. His eyes had lost focus. I could tell he was remembering everything vividly. "She was also Russian or Yugoslavian or something—she had a thick accent. The audience was, well…hostile is too strong a word, but they weren't going to be easily amused, that was for damned sure. When the poor woman—Tatiana! That was her name. When the poor woman asked for a volunteer for the cabinet trick, no one moved a muscle."

I winced. "That must have been awkward."

He nodded. "So I raised my hand. Your grandmother could

have died on the spot. One of Tatiana's gents came down and led me into a cabinet. There were two of them on the stage." He gestured now, holding up both hands. He closed one. "I was to go in one, and she'd pop me out of the other." He shook his head. "They put a blindfold on me, but it turned out it was just a trick. You see, the fellow, he put me in the first—"

"Don't!" I said. "Don't ruin the magic."

He looked at me. "Winston, there's very little I've learned in my years, but something I can be sure of is this: the only person capable of ruining the magic in life is yourself."

I felt a kind of ache in my chest. "Sorry. I like illusions."

He nodded. We sat in silence for a moment. I wondered if he was going to go on. He took a deep breath and spoke again.

"For a little while, I was...well. Somewhere else." His voice was amused, and I knew he was humoring my desire not to have the trick spoiled. "With another one of those gentlemen—someone I hadn't seen on the stage at all. It was all very trusting. I could have ruined it, you know. It seemed to me that it was such a big risk. But the gentleman—his name was Kosta, which I guess is another Russian or European name or whatnot—was charming, and did little magic tricks for me while I waited for my big reveal. Tatiana drew it out, you see, and we were alone for a good while."

Again, he paused. He pulled a 1965 Churchill coin out of his pocket, one I'd seen many times before. It was large and silver, and I'd watched it skip across my great-uncle's knuckles many a time. I knew it had been a gift from my grandmother, a kind of punny joke. He put the coin on his knuckles and then began weaving across his hand with gestures that were a little shakier than I remembered. Still, the coin danced.

"He started teaching me how to do this," my great-uncle said. "Though I was pants at it at the time. He offered to help me practice, though. Of course, I couldn't say yes." A ghost of a smile appeared and vanished. "Well. I'm sure he was just being kind and keeping me busy while Tatiana did her show." The coin went back into his pocket.

Something in his voice made my chest ache again.

He looked up. "You know, you shouldn't be stuck in here with me." He shook his head. "Why aren't you out making friends? You could take one of those pretty girls we saw at the pool to this show, instead of me."

"Uncle Winston, I'm gay."

It just burst out. I froze, feeling my gut clench, and waited. What the hell had I done that for? My mother had cautioned me against telling my great-uncle. "He's from a different age," she said. "His family was so different, love. Aristocratic. He's so...proper and... difficult." She'd hugged me. "I can't tell you what to do, honey, and I know you love him very much—though he's a difficult man to love—but I don't know if it would be a good idea to tell him."

My great-uncle regarded me for a long while. His lips tightened.

"Your generation is much braver than we give you credit for," he said.

I started crying.

"Oh, now, don't do that," he admonished, patting my shoulder with his shaking hand. "It's a compliment, for God's sake."

"I know," I said, swiping at my eyes and regaining composure. I smiled at him. "Thank you."

He regarded me with damp eyes, and I knew it would cost his pride dearly if he were to join me with tears. I redoubled my efforts not to snivel.

"When your fool mother gave you my name, I told her it was a bad idea," he said, and I laughed. Winston hadn't exactly been the greatest name to have as a child, but I had grown to like it. "I thought my name would be a bad enough inheritance. It turns out we have more in common than nomenclature."

I stared at him. My mouth opened. Closed. Holy flying crap.

"Do you mean...?"

"It was a different time," he said, dismissively waving his hand. "We didn't have very many opportunities. And the ones we did have...Well." His eyebrow rose, and he squeezed my shoulder. "Do you have someone...in particular?"

I shook my head. "No." My voice cracked a little, and I cleared my throat. "Not yet. I don't like the bars—they're so crowded, and…" I shrugged. He knew I was a bit claustrophobic.

He looked at me. "Well, if you can stand some more advice from an old man…"

"Of course I can, but where are we going to find an old man?"

His lips quirked. "If you feel that…spark…for someone, you take your chance." He let go of my shoulder and smoothed his jacket. "Not that you're not one to speak your mind. Your generation is better at that sort of thing. But believe me when I say this: if you've got an opportunity with someone, you take it. You take your chance, Winston. Propriety and consequence be damned. The world can change in those moments." He pulled his watch from the jacket pocket and opened it with a shaking hand, ending the conversation with the gesture. "We should go. It's almost time for the show."

❖

"You two look lovely," my mother said. She and my father looked spiffy themselves, but I had to admit that wearing the period-designed suit made us stand out. Neither of us was tall, but the cut of the suits made me look trim instead of small, and the gray color flattered what my mother called "the Winston blue" of my eyes.

"*He* looks lovely," my great-uncle grunted. "I look like a shriveled old man in a nice suit."

I hid my smile but pulled my camera out of my pocket. "Would you take a picture of us?" I asked.

She took the camera, and my great-uncle let out a put-upon sigh, but stood beside me. The camera flashed, and then we took our seats. The ship's theater was just a table or two shy of being full, and the great red curtains that fell across the stage were still closed. A waiter paused at our table, and we ordered drinks.

When the lights dimmed, the murmurs of conversation fell away. Spotlights lit, and the curtains pulled open.

Center stage was a woman in a tuxedo jacket, tie, and a top hat; but instead of trousers, she wore fishnet stockings, though a modicum of modesty was maintained by a very high-cut leotard that covered her while still revealing her shapely thighs. She also wore a black cape.

I leaned over to my great-uncle. "At least she's not wearing tuxedo pants. Grandma would be happy."

He snorted.

With an accented voice, she introduced herself as Karianna, which I assumed was a stage name, then she raised her cape high with both arms to introduce her assistants. When she lowered the cape on both sides with a flourish, she was flanked by two identical men bowing. They raised a hand each and straightened. They were obviously twins.

Maybe in my great-uncle's day, they would have worn white shirts and dress pants with sequins, but I was pleased to note that in the glorious present, the shirts had been replaced with deep blue vests made of a shiny material decorated with some gold embroidery, and the matching blue leggings they wore were much tighter than dress pants. There wasn't much about the two men left to the imagination, and that was fine by me. They had definitely spent some time at the gym. When they raised their arms, the vests rose just enough to show off their stomachs, which were firm and tanned and obviously shaved smooth. They were dark-haired and handsome, and I missed their names completely in the applause.

I didn't dare look at my great-uncle, but I could feel myself grinning. This audience was far more eager than the one he'd told me about.

Rings were twined and untwined with graceful ease, objects vanished into Karianna's top hat and were reclaimed, Karianna wrapped herself in her cape and, when she unfurled again, had inverted her tuxedo from black to white. Each illusion seemed a bit more dramatic than the last, and I caught myself applauding as loudly as anyone else. Her two helpers moved constantly, bringing her the next prop or taking away the previous one, and the whole event was so fluid it was impossible to ponder a trick before another was performed.

I loved it.

When the twin assistants—by now I'd learned their names were

Amin and Zoran—wheeled in two cabinets, I turned and grinned at my great-uncle. He leaned forward, looking at them, and shaking his head just a little, he glanced at me and smiled. There was nothing reserved or melancholy in that smile, and I turned back to the stage with a contented sigh.

"My next trick I learned from my mother," Karianna said, "who learned it from her mother, and so on. A piece of magical intrigue passed through generations." She gestured at the two cabinets with a flourish, first the left, then the right. "These cabinets have been in my family for as long as we can recall, but now this transposition I only do on this stage. The cabinets have a special connection, a path between them, that I can conjure for your enjoyment." She smiled. "But first, I'll need a volunteer."

I raised my hand.

The only person more surprised than my parents was me. When Karianna looked around at the audience, her eyes found me even through the glare of the lights. She gestured.

"There, the young man in the lovely gray suit."

One of the twins came down off the stage to our table. I rose as he arrived, and he walked me back up to the stage, his hand at the small of my back. Up close, the magician's assistant was physically imposing. The stage makeup made his eyes seem severe, and he was on the edge of being too muscular. He was a little bit intimidating, and easily six feet tall. No wonder he'd had to bow down behind Karianna's cape when he'd been introduced with his brother.

He smiled at me, but that only made me more nervous. By the time we'd walked to the stage, which had seemed to take ages and yet no time at all, I climbed the stairs with a nervous grin, coming face-to-face with Karianna. Those damned cabinets didn't look so large from up here. What had I been thinking? I hated small spaces.

She winked, and all my tension vanished. This was an illusion, I remembered. It would be fun.

While Karianna spoke of the cabinets again, the twins had returned, each with a long strip of black cloth. They tied one around my eyes and the other around my hands, which I held in front of me, binding my wrists together. Then, with strong hands leading me to the right side of the stage, I stepped inside the cabinet, was turned around by their strong hands, and then heard the cabinet door close.

❖

It was incredibly quiet in the cabinet, and with my eyes blindfolded, I could tell myself I wasn't trapped inside something small. Except I was. My body shook, and I could hear my own breath much louder than it should be.

I barely heard Karianna's voice as she announced she was going to turn the cabinet around twelve times. When it moved, the reality of my confined space—even unseen—hit me all the harder, and I started to sweat. I held still, feeling myself turning without any real sense of how far I'd turned or how many times I'd already gone around. Nausea rose in my stomach. I felt like I was dropping somehow. I couldn't breathe fast enough. I panted, and my head spun more and more.

I have to get out of here!

I reached forward, and then a hand took my shoulder. I jumped, but I managed not to yelp. Someone guided me forward a few steps, and I hesitated before I put each foot down. Shouldn't the cabinet door be in front of me?

"Have a seat," a voice said. I sat, trusting there would actually be a chair behind me. There was. Someone undid my blindfold.

I blinked, and the face before me smiled. Handsome in a classical way, he had lovely dark eyes and black hair just long enough to curl. His smile was infectious, and I caught myself grinning back, despite how unsettled I felt. Instead of a blue vest and the sequined pants, he wore a snug white shirt and classy-looking dress pants, with a red sash tied through the belt loops.

"You okay?" he asked in a subdued voice as he untied my hands.

"Claustrophobic," I admitted, feeling stupid. The tension in my chest loosened, and I looked around. "Where's the cabinet?" We were in a fairly large room with all the walls hidden by blue curtains arranged in a circle, obscuring any doors. A series of chairs lined the edge, each facing in, with a small table in front of each.

"I can't give away the trick," he said, winking. "Do you need some water?"

I nodded, feeling pathetic. "Sorry. I guess I shouldn't have volunteered, but…" I wasn't sure where to go with the thought, so I let it drop off.

He put a white handkerchief on the small table beside him, lifted it up by two corners, and shook it. When he snapped it away from the table, a glass of water appeared.

I smiled. "You do magic."

"I'm Kosta, the apprentice. I'll entertain you while the show goes on." He gave me another wide smile.

I started at the coincidence of names, but then remembered the stage names of everyone involved. They were distinct and European and likely as much a part of the act as the cabinets themselves. They probably recycled them.

"I'm Winston," I said.

Kosta drew me to my feet while I drank the water, my hand still trembling. He walked me around in a circle, from table to table, making objects appear or disappear. Finally, once I was sure we'd gone all the way around the tables at least once, he bowed and told me to sit again. He pulled out a coin and danced it across his knuckles for me, then snapped his fingers and it disappeared. When he reached forward and pulled the coin from behind my ear, his fingertips brushed the side of my cheek, and I noticed again how handsome he was.

"I like that one," I said, feeling myself blush. I shifted in my chair. It was ridiculous that a mere graze of his fingers had me feeling so fluttery.

"I can show you how to roll the coin," he said, taking my hand. He had a gentle touch, but his hands were rougher than I thought they'd be. I imagined he worked hard for a living, even if he did work as a magician's apprentice. I needed to shift in my seat a second time—partly to lean forward while Kosta put the coin on my smallest finger, but also partly to conceal the effect his touch was having. One thing about vintage suits I hadn't planned on was their lack of generous give in the crotch of the trousers.

"Now, roll your fingers like this, and you'll feel the coin balance tip. Go slowly right now…"

I tried to mimic the motion he made, and the coin tipped toward my next finger. I was just about to offer a self-congratulatory laugh when the coin slipped between my fingers and dropped to the carpeted floor.

I leaned down for it, as did Kosta, who crouched before me. Our fingers brushed on the coin. I looked up at him, pulling my hand away, and his eyes flicked down, then up at me. I realized with a start that his angle of view was pretty much directly at my crotch. My arousal was obvious.

"Try again," he said. This time he knelt in front of me, pressing a bit closer against my knees as he put my hand back into position. I sucked in a breath—he smelled like soap. When he put the coin on my hand, I was so distracted by his touch I barely began the motion of my fingers before it slipped back off onto the ground.

This time, Kosta didn't move for it. He leaned in and kissed me.

His lips were softer than his hands and the kiss itself was very hesitant, almost nervous. It charmed me, and I kissed him back.

He leaned back, a blush rising on his cheeks.

"I'm sorry," he said. "That was…"

"It was very nice," I said. My head spun again. It felt like the room was turning. I met his gaze, and he smiled, nodding once.

"It's almost time to get you ready again. If you'd like…" Kosta said in a soft voice, looking slightly away as he picked up the coin again. "I could teach you how to do this later? After the show?" He wiggled his fingers and the coin disappeared. His confidence seemed to be returning. He picked up the blindfold.

Would it really be appropriate to hook up with a magician's assistant when I was on a cruise with my great-uncle and my parents? It would certainly surprise them, and it seemed sort of a heartless thing to do to my great-uncle. Kosta tied the cloth around my eyes. I felt dizzy again. I should turn Kosta down. He tied my hands with the black cloth, and once again I felt his rough fingers against my skin.

I shivered. Kosta's hand rested on my shoulder. "If you don't want to, I understand."

Thing was, I wanted to.

If you feel that spark with someone, you take your chance. You take your chance, Winston.

"I'd love to, Kosta," I said, and then he was helping me stand, and the wave of claustrophobia and motion overwhelmed me, and I tipped sideways. A dull roar filled my ears, and then I was falling.

❖

"Hey guy, you okay?"

I opened my eyes, but I was still wearing the blindfold. I was only barely on my feet. Someone was holding me up, arms wrapped around me awkwardly, my tied hands pressed against my stomach by the grip. The voice wasn't Kosta's.

"Sorry," I gasped. "I think I passed out. I'm a little claustrophobic. Bloody hell. Did I ruin the trick?"

"Never mind that—can you come with me? I'll get you into a chair, okay?"

I went in the direction I was pulled and sat down gratefully. A moment later, the blindfold was removed.

I stared in confusion.

It was a curtained room, just like the one I'd just been in with Kosta. Except the curtains were red, and the guy in front of me this time was wearing an outfit like the ones the twins were wearing onstage. He was taller, a bit broader than Kosta, and he wore his hair cut almost military short. Unlike the twins on the stage, he hadn't shaved his chest.

"Is this part of the trick?" I asked as he undid my wrists.

"Normally there's no fainting," he said, and winked. He crouched down in front of me. "Did you need a glass of water?"

"Are you going to pull it out from under that handkerchief?"

He smiled. "Have you done this before?"

I looked around. "Apparently not." I shook my head. "When… When did I get here?"

He leaned forward. "Are you sure you're okay? We have some time before you're due to go back up."

"Up?" I said.

He smiled and put his thumb in front of his lips. "Sorry. Trade secret."

"I think I just had a hallucination," I said, shaking my head when he looked alarmed. "It's okay. I guess it was just being in the small space. Like I said, claustrophobia." *And the stories of a great-uncle*, I added mentally.

"If you're sure you're okay," he said, flourishing the handkerchief from the table. Again the glass of water appeared. He handed it to me, and I took a drink before putting it back on the table. I rose before he asked, which surprised him, and as we walked around from table to table, I felt myself grow calmer. Once we'd done the circuit a while—he did some of the same tricks I'd "seen" Kosta do, but most were different—I sat back down again. Only this time I wasn't sure I was back where I'd started. Watching him move was more than enthralling. He had nice arms, not too muscular, but obviously strong, and the cut of his tight pants made admiring his lovely butt not exactly a challenge.

Also, the hard-on I'd gotten from my hallucinatory visit with Kosta was not abating.

"The little walk around the tables is to put me somewhere else, isn't it?" I asked, glancing up from his chest when I caught him looking at me with a sly smile on his face.

He waved his hand, and a coin appeared between his fingers. He danced it across his knuckles, and then—with a snap of his fingers—it vanished. When he reached behind my ear for it, I held my breath, and the slight grazing of his skin against mine had the same effect it had had with Kosta. He pulled out the coin with a smile.

"Can you show me how to do that?" I asked.

He nodded and crouched in front of me. "Sure."

He took my hand and demonstrated the motion, walking the coin on his fingers once more, then balancing it on mine. I tried to concentrate on something other than his hand touching mine and failed. When the coin dropped, he managed to catch it in midair.

I clapped, and he gave a mock bow, still crouched in front of me. He glanced at me, a smile tucked in the corner of his mouth.

"You might want to calm down a bit before it's time to go back."

I felt my face burn. I hadn't managed to hide my hard-on after all. "Vintage pants," I said.

"Whatever turns your crank." He grinned.

I laughed. "No! I meant...Never mind. Wow. Uh, this is awkward."

"You're cute when you're awkward," he said. "Cuter than when you're fainting."

I looked at him. Was he flirting? Again, I thought of my great-uncle's words. *You take your chance, Winston.*

"Well, you're the magician. Make it disappear!" I said.

He grinned and reached over to cup my crotch. I let out a little moan when he squeezed. He leaned in close to my ear. "Stand up," he said.

I rose shakily, and his deft fingers undid my belt and unzipped my fly while his lips lingered at my ear. He flicked his tongue a little, and I shivered, my back arching. He tugged at my underwear and the heat of his hand against my cock was a jolt. His other hand slid around my waist, and he moved slightly behind me, pressing himself against me while his hand began to pump.

I could tell *he* was enjoying himself, too. That or he had a wand in his pocket.

I leaned back into him, and his voice was low in my ear.

"You're definitely the best thing to happen on this show," he said, jerking me a little faster. I breathed heavily and turned my neck until I could kiss him. His tongue entered my mouth and his free hand slid up to the center of my chest, pulling me hard against him. I reached awkwardly behind me and gripped his ass with both hands.

He stroked me a moment more before I cried out into his mouth and burst across the carpeted floor.

We stayed locked like that, his tongue exploring my mouth and his hand still working me for a few more moments, then he broke off the kiss and laughed.

"Stay put for a second," he said, and reached awkwardly for the handkerchief, still holding my softening dick. He wiped his hand and my cock and then nodded. I stepped back and managed to tuck myself away and zip up again.

He glanced up, and then back at me.

"Come on," he said. "We need to get you blindfolded again."

He tied the black cloth back on my eyes, and when I felt the strange turning and rising effect, I realized I had no idea what his name was.

I was willing to bet it wasn't Kosta.

Once again locked in the cabinet—the sound quality had changed, and I could hear Karianna's muffled voice through the wooden walls—I took a deep breath and waited. Being inside the cabinet wasn't so bad this time. Apparently the cure for claustrophobia was a hand job. I nearly laughed, but I heard loud applause as the door to the cabinet was opened, and my confused and blindfolded face was revealed.

One of the twins took my shoulder and walked me onto the stage, then undid the blindfold and untied my hands. I looked at the other cabinet, all the way across the stage from where I was now, and grinned.

"Our brave volunteer has been transposed through the mystical cabinets!" Karianna said, her hands raised. The applause continued, and she gestured to the stairs at the edge of the stage. "Thank you very much, young man."

"Thank you," I said—meaning it—and then went back to join my family.

My great-uncle wasn't at the table. My mother gave my shoulder an affectionate squeeze, and I sat down, eyeing the empty spot where my great-uncle had sat. He must have gotten tired, I thought.

I leaned over to whisper to my mother while the twins onstage helped Karianna set up a pair of chairs. Someone was about to be levitated.

"Where's Uncle Winston?" I asked.

"By now?" My mother frowned at me. "Suffolk, I assume."

I blinked, but she'd already turned back to the stage. *Suffolk?* I must have misheard her. We watched the rest of the show, and when it was done—and the genuine applause had died down—my parents smiled at me.

"How did the trick work?" my mother asked.

I just smiled. "I have no idea. I was blindfolded at the time." And hallucinating. And getting a hand job. We all rose. I was a little giddy.

She shook her head. "Fine. Be that way."

"Hey, about Uncle Winston," I started.

"Honey, just enjoy the cruise," my mother said. "If he wants to send us on a trip, let him do it. He doesn't have kids of his own to spoil, and he loves you."

I frowned again, and my mother shook her head. "Go. Go have fun. Your father and I are going to turn in."

She kissed my cheek, and they were gone.

I walked back to the cabin I was sharing with my great-uncle, frowning. The cruise had been my idea, not Uncle Winston's. I shook my head, unlocking the door, and stepping inside.

My great-uncle wasn't there. Neither was his suitcase, his toothbrush, or anything else. There was, however, a small package on my pillow, with my name on it. It had obviously been delivered while I was at the show.

I frowned and undid the envelope. It was a card, written in my great-uncle's graceful penmanship.

Winston—Enjoy the cruise! Was grand seeing you off—we hope you have as much fun as we always do. Take lots of pictures, so we can see them when you get back.
Love, W & K.

I stared at it. I tore open the package and saw that my great-uncle had gifted me his Churchill coin. I held it, and then reread the note, confused.

"Take lots of pictures?" I said. Then I remembered my camera. I pulled it out of my pocket and turned it on. I pressed the review button and saw the last picture that had been taken.

It was me, in my suit, just before the magic show.

I was alone.

I skipped back through the photos, but I wasn't sure I'd taken any of my great-uncle other than the one before the show. Then I saw the first picture I'd taken. It was the dock where we'd boarded the cruise ship. I'd snapped a shot of the people waving good-bye, just because it seemed like the thing to do, but now...

I frowned and zoomed in as much as the little camera would let me. There, on the dock, was my great-uncle Winston, waving good-bye. And beside him, arm in arm...

He'd aged well. But I could still recognize the smile.

Kosta.

I stared at it until the camera screen went into power save mode and blanked. I picked up the note again. *Love, W & K.*

"He's in Suffolk. With Kosta," I said, trying the words out loud. My fingers closed around the coin. *The world can change in those moments.*

But how...?

"Winston," I said, smiling to myself. "Don't ruin the magic." I turned off the camera, hung up my jacket, dug through my suitcase for something, then left my cabin.

They were still cleaning up when I got there, and all the lights were on. The twins and Karianna were working at one end of the stage together, though they'd changed out of their costumes into jeans and T-shirts. I looked about, biting my lip, and then saw my friend from the curtained room near the stage, thankfully packing away things on his own. I wouldn't have had the guts to go talk to him if the twins or Karianna were nearby.

He'd changed into shorts and a white T-shirt. He didn't notice me approach until I dropped the handkerchief I'd taken from my suitcase on top of the cables he was bundling.

He glanced up.

"Hydraulics under the stage and false bottoms in the cabinets?" I guessed. "That's why the trick is only done on the ship."

"Not telling," he said, but his eyes sparkled. He picked up the handkerchief. "What's this for?"

"Thought I should give you a new one," I said. "Also, I'm Winston. What's your name?"

"Jack."

I burst out laughing. Across the room, the others looked at us.

"Apt," I said. I tried to stifle my laughter.

He smiled, blushing. He folded the handkerchief. "They do wash, you know. You didn't have to bring me a new one."

"I know," I said. "But I wanted to see you again and thank you for the, uh, hands-on demonstration. Do you believe in magic?"

"I make a living with magic," he said. "Or, well, I make a part-time summer bonus with magic." He leaned against the stage. I took his hand and squeezed. He linked his fingers through mine, glancing down at them, then back up at me.

"You're forward," Jack said, but I noticed he didn't let go.

"It's a strength of our generation."

He smiled.

"I really want to learn how to do the coin thing," I said.

"It's going to take a while for us to pack everything away," he said. "But if you're willing to wait…"

"I'm not. I'll help you tidy up." He smiled at that. "Then you can teach me."

"You're not gonna faint on me, are you?"

I shook my head. "I'm claustrophobic. I assume there's room somewhere on the ship."

His smile grew. "My cabin is pretty small."

I leaned in. "Mine's pretty big."

Jack winked. "I knew that already."

MANLY MAGIC
DALE CHASE

Dodge City was a revelation. Big town with fine buildings and so much window glass it fairly sparkled. Sidewalks were crowded with people, though I quickly saw most were cattle drovers like me, in off the trail from Texas. Our stock had been delivered to the pens, we had money in our pockets, and Dodge was our reward. After washing off a pound of trail dust, my partner Dan Fitch and me set out onto Front Street, where our step was light, as there was much to see. Men's hoots and calls accompanied as we went along while music from saloons added to the festivities, making it more than the biggest barn dance ever.

Dan, who had taught me cow punching and some other things on the trail, had ridden two prior drives and, being older than me, twenty to my eighteen, knew the town. He had also been to theaters. "Saw a trained monkey once," he said. "Did tricks of all sorts."

I had never seen a monkey but then I had seen little compared to Dan. Life on my family's hardscrabble Texas ranch had offered little promise, which led me to driving cattle. Had I stayed home I would never have gotten anywhere, and I saw I wanted to be somewhere. Once I had signed on with the J-bar-G outfit, Dan took me under his wing, showed me about riding drag behind the herd, and when not doing that, showed me how a man could please a man. Now, that was a revelation, but Dodge was too.

"Looka there," Dan said, nudging me toward an alley. There stood a man with his dick out and a woman kneeling before him as if about to pray. We watched her take him in hand, at which I drew a breath, and when she got her mouth onto it, I grabbed Dan's arm, as he had sucked my cock out on the trail. We remained fixed in our tracks as the woman did her work while the man stood with hands on hips, lower part thrust forward. Dan had to pull me away because I would have stood there until the man came or I did.

"Girl gets paid to put out," Dan said as we moved on, and I wondered if boys did that. I didn't ask Dan, though, as I did not wish to appear ignorant.

"Want to see a show?" he asked. "Up there is the Lady Gay and next door to it the Comique Theater. Let's see one tonight, the other tomorrow."

We looked at signs telling who would play each place, but I let Dan decide since he had seen shows before. "I don't know," he said when as we stood before the Comique. "I like these *Happy Hottentots Doing Grotesque Dancing, Leg Mania, and Contortion Feats* and the comic is well known, but the Lady Gay has a wizard. Let's go see that."

"Wizard?" I said, not knowing what that was. The colorful ad showed a man in dark suit and high hat. He had a fine mustache, spit of beard, and was looking right at me.

"Magic," said Dan. "He makes things disappear before your eyes and he conjures from up a sleeve. I once saw a white bird pulled from a hat. Close your mouth, Billy. I am telling the truth. And look, they've also got a singer and a comic."

Well, I could not imagine any of it, so I agreed to that show and we paid fifty cents and went into the Lady Gay.

I do not know what I expected, but it was still more. Just inside the door was the most ornate bar I had ever seen, with fine gold scrollwork and big mirror behind. Beyond this were rows of seats and at the end an elevated stage below which some musical men were seated. Chairs were filling fast, but we got seats not too far from the front. The men were noisy, as many were already drunk, but I did not care. I kept wondering how anybody could make things disappear.

A sign was set out that said *Noble Keyes, Comedian*, and there came this fellow in checkered suit and funny hat. As he strode onstage he tossed three little red balls into the air, all the while talking up a blue streak about us cow punchers and cattle stink and then our stink, which got us to laughing. He cut up something awful on city folk, getting bawdy at times, which caused me to nudge Dan more than once, and when he got into privy humor, I thought I would bust a gut. I had not laughed that much in some time, but at last he thanked us and said we had best settle down for the wonderful Miss Marla Grimes.

This was a beautiful woman, dark curls piled atop her head and red dress tight upon her body. The men carried on at sight of her, but when she started singing they quieted right down, for she had a wonderful voice. Again I nudged Dan and he nodded, for it was most pleasant to hear her melodies. Then the sign changed to read *Montague the Wizard* and I became most excited. A big box was brought out, a fine red cloth placed on it. Then the wizard came out.

He was better-looking than his picture, slick in his black suit, and he wore white gloves, which he began to remove. His expression was steady, never taking his eyes off us. When his gloves were off, he waved them about and suddenly they were gone.

"Did you see that?" I asked Dan. "Where did they go?"

"Disappeared. Magic."

This I could not understand. "Where?" I demanded. "Disappeared where?"

"Nowhere. Now shush and watch. That was just the start."

Next the wizard took a length of rope from the big box and held it up. He took a knife from his pocket and cut the rope in two, then set aside the knife. He held the two rope pieces for us to see, then did some work with his hands and showed us one piece again.

"Well, I swear," I commented, and again Dan shushed me.

The wizard then took out a blue scarf and tied a knot in the middle, and with no more than a shake had it undone, though I could not see how. He put this away in his box and took out a red scarf and gave it a shake and there appeared a knot in one end. He shook it again and the knot disappeared. After this he played around with the scarf and suddenly it was gone completely, but he then reached behind his head and found not the red scarf but the blue one he had put away. The crowd went wild at this, which caused the wizard to smile and bow. I had now stopped nudging Dan.

When people had calmed down, the wizard showed us his empty hands, then pulled a fan of cards from behind his knee, after which he did all manner of tricks with them. After a while he acted like he was done with cards and put them away, but his empty hands soon filled with them again and he began to sail cards one by one into the crowd. This set the men leaping and falling about and it took some minutes to restore order.

Now the wizard said he needed to borrow a hat from someone. Here he looked down at me and I sucked in a breath, as I thought my heart would stop. The wizard kept his eyes upon me as he came down off the stage and held out his hand. I took off my hat and gave it to him. He smiled beneath that stripe of mustache, and I thought I would come in my pants. Then he took my hat up onto the stage. Dan now nudged me.

Once my hat was up there, the wizard began to produce silver dollars from thin air, holding each one up for us to see. He did this over and over, each coin going into my hat until it was nearly full. He then poured them into a paper bag, which he wrapped tightly. Moving to the edge of the stage, he threw the package to me, which brought me to my feet to catch it. I could not wait to get my hands on all that money, but when I opened the package, it was a box of candy. I held it up for all to see and the place roared while the wizard fixed his eyes on me. I was hard down below due to his attentions, although I was not sure he was a real man, even if he did look like one.

The wizard, still having my hat, made it part of his show and took all manner of things out of it: flowers, a yellow ball, a red ball, a glass, you name it, it was all in my hat. Everyone else was laughing at this, but I sat mute as I was so taken with this fellow. When he was done he brought my hat down to me and said, "A fine hat you have," before returning to the stage. I looked into the hat, though I knew it would be empty.

From then on, the wizard had me. He did magic linking and

unlinking three big brass rings. He made flowers appear in an empty flowerpot. More things disappeared, more things reappeared, and then he said he would do his final presentation. "I need a volunteer from the audience," he called, looking past me. The drover who went up onstage wore a black coat over white shirt and we could see he had cleaned up like the rest of us. He was made to stand facing us while the wizard stood behind, and I wondered if he could make an entire man disappear. I sat forward on my seat, as did Dan, and the place grew quiet. Then the wizard took hold of the man's collar, gave a yank, and away came his entire shirt from beneath the coat. The man stood bare-chested, the buttoned shirt in the wizard's hand. My mouth dropped open and my hand slid to my crotch, as I was further aroused by such a move. As the crowd hooted and hollered, I wondered if the wizard could get pants off like that and what he would do with the naked man, for surely this was some sort of manly conquest.

The drover was handed his shirt and went offstage to the back, where I supposed he would put it back on. How lucky he was to be part of the magic. All I had managed was my hat. "I would like to be that man who lost his shirt," I told Dan as the wizard began to bow.

"You'd want him to take your pants," Dan remarked, and I had to agree.

I did not want to leave, but the show was over. Everyone stood and started walking out. Dan had to pull me from my chair but agreed to a drink at the bar. The crowd there was thick, but we finally got a whiskey. "That was something," I told Dan.

"Told you."

"How did he do all those things?" I asked.

"Magic."

I liked the sound of that word. It was new to me, as was Montague the Wizard. "Montague," I said to Dan. "That is some name."

"Foreign."

"He didn't sound foreign."

"How would you know?"

He had a point. Only foreign I knew was Mexican, and he

surely was not that. As we threw back the rest of our drinks, there came a commotion and up strode the wizard. "It's him!" I cried, clutching Dan's arm.

"Let go of me," he said, shaking me off. "You are acting silly."

I pushed past the others because I wanted to know more of the wizard, and when he saw me, he smiled. "The man with the hat," he said.

It was atop my head and I took it off as it was now special, but I found myself unable to speak.

"What is your name, boy?" the wizard asked.

"Billy Barrow, up from Texas."

"Well, Billy, I would like to buy you a drink for helping me with the show."

Just then Dan pushed forward. "This is my partner, Dan Fitch," I told the wizard.

"Charmed, Mr. Fitch," said the wizard. "I am Montague, but you may call me Monty. Now let's get our drinks."

The crowd parted for the wizard and he stepped to the bar with us alongside. I was now puffed up beyond imagination, as a heat came off him. Whatever magic he had inside him was like a furnace and it occurred to me, as he handed me a drink, that I might warm myself.

"That was some show," Dan offered.

"Well, thank you, Mr. Fitch. I enjoyed presenting it to you."

"Call me Dan," said my pard. "And call me Billy," I chimed in.

"Dan and Billy. Good names. What are you boys up to now?"

We looked at one another and shrugged. "Don't know."

"How would you like to join me in my room? I've had enough of crowds and would enjoy your company."

"Sure enough," I said, nudging Dan, who swatted me away.

Monty finished his whiskey, bid good night to the men, and walked out with us, which puffed me up even more. If I kept on, I would soon float away without any magic. "I am at the Dodge House," said Monty, and Dan said we were too.

His room was bigger than ours with probably twice the furniture. A fine settee, soft green chairs, big dresser and wardrobe, and the finest bed I had ever seen. "Try it," Monty said when I eyed the thing. He tossed his hat onto the dresser, removed his coat, and folded it carefully over the back of a chair while I sat on the bed, feeling my bottom sink into heaven. "It is like a cloud," I noted.

Monty took off his tie and opened his shirt and I saw he had nothing underneath, for there was dark hair in the open part. "How old are you boys?" he asked.

"Eighteen," I said proudly. "Dan here is twenty. This is my first trip to Dodge, but Dan has been before and seen shows. I am most impressed with your magic."

"And I am most impressed with yours."

Here I paused, as I was lost to his meaning. I felt myself flush as I could not hold up my end of the conversation. Finally I said, "I have no magic. Wish I did."

"Nonsense. All men have magic, and young men the most."

I glanced at Dan, who raised his eyebrows with puzzlement. I then looked back to the wizard, who came and sat beside me. "Innocence," he said, his hand squeezing my leg. "I have a magic you enjoy and you, Billy, have a magic I seek. A special magic, that of youthful innocence, although I would venture you and Dan have imbibed on the trail."

I looked to Dan, whose mouth was now open. He had sunk into a chair but was leaned forward, hands on knees as if ready to leap. "Imbibed?" I said.

"Fucked, dear boy. You do fuck one another."

"Oh," I said, feeling foolish. "'Course. Did it all up the trail, every chance we got."

"Wonderful. Then you know a man's special magic."

"Don't take no wizard to fuck," Dan said, which caused Monty to chuckle.

"You are right, Dan. It does not take a wizard, but I will tell you, a wizard can take it far beyond what is done on the trail."

Monty's hand now slid to my cock, which, already throbbing in my pants, began to spurt. When I gasped, he began to prod and I enjoyed a release of good proportion. "Wonderful," he said and he continued to prod me even after I was done.

"Couldn't hold back," I told him.

"I would not want that. Now, why not get out of those soiled trousers. You too, Dan. Let us all get comfortable for our manly magic."

I sat fixed as things were moving in a direction not anticipated. Monty got up. "Don't you want to feel more of that?" he asked, to which I had no argument. I looked at Dan, who grinned and stood, began to undo his belt.

Dan and I had fucked on the trail by getting the necessary parts free and then buttoning up after. Only time we shed our clothes was when bathing at a river. Now we were to strip naked for a wizard. I glanced his way and saw his shirt off, his broad chest covered in dark hair, and then he was undoing his pants and pushing them down. He sat to remove his shoes and socks, after which he stood in just drawers. "Come on, boys, strip," he urged when I gaped.

I put a hand to my coat, then stopped as an idea came to me. "Pull off my shirt like you did that fellow in your show."

He laughed. "Dear Billy, what you saw was a trick. I will be happy to show it to you later on, but right now, I want you naked. Take off your clothes."

This confused me some, but I dared not argue and so began to shed everything while my thoughts scurried about. A trick? Like fooling? I had been fooled some on the trail, sent to fetch things not existing which got me laughed at, and I had seen a man do tricks with a lariat. As I stole glances at Monty's drawers where bulged his cock, I could not get a handle on what he meant, but then I was down to my drawers and stopped because of the sticky mess in them. I glanced at Dan, who stood bare and holding his hard cock like it might start up without him.

"All of it," Monty said, motioning for me to drop the last, which I pushed down to reveal my stiff dick. "Magnificent," he remarked. He then stood Dan next to me and ran his hands over us for a while, but he did not touch our cocks. He fingered our tit nubs, caressed our faces, but held off going for what I thought he wanted. Instead he stepped back and dropped his drawers.

His dick was more than either of ours and sprouted hard from a thick dark patch. His balls were big and low hanging and my first thought was of all the spunk he must carry, my second of taking such a rod. Dan's was big enough, but not thick like this one. I had been in Dan's butthole too, as we liked it both ways, so I wondered at Monty's backside, all this wondering in about two seconds.

"Now, dear boys, if you think you've seen magic this night, you are mistaken. I shall take you to places you cannot imagine, but first you must put on a show for me. You have seen me perform, now it is your turn. Dan, get onto the bed and give Billy a good fuck."

I looked at Dan, wide-eyed and holding his cock. Nobody had ever seen us do it, but I liked the idea of a wizard of magic watching, so I told Dan, "Come on," and I hopped onto the bed onto all fours. "Fuck me," I added, at which Dan got behind me and put it in.

"Magnificent," called Monty. He pulled a chair alongside the bed and sat with hand on his big cock while Dan began to pump in and out of me. "I ain't gonna last," Dan announced after about a minute and Monty said, "No matter, give it to him."

Dan rode me hard and unloaded in no time while I thought of other things, weather and such, to avoid coming into the bedding. Soon as Dan was empty, he pulled out and sat back. "Now, Billy," came the command, "you change around and fuck Dan."

We reversed and I got into Dan, which left off all thought. I began to plow him with all I had and managed a good minute before letting go a gusher. "I am coming," I called out so Monty would know, although my dick work probably showed him. When done, I pulled out and fell back. Dan rolled over and we lay on the bed, dicks soft for once. Monty stood up to look at us. "Delectable," he said and he leaned over and took my soft prick into his mouth. I held back a squeal as he began to suck.

Now, Dan had sucked my cook a good many times, but never like this. It was like some snake had me and I felt it run up and down, try to wrap around, felt it squeeze and tickle and, of course, I came again. Monty swallowed my stuff and kept on. In fact, he ran a hand under my bottom to put a finger in me and prod while his other hand pulled Dan's cock. Finally, he released us and stood, big prick drooling.

"Both of you, on all fours, bottoms facing me."

We did as told, Dan and me lined up for him. I looked back to see the wizard put his thing into Dan, who let out a gasp, and I saw my friend's mouth fall open. Monty pumped his rod into Dan awhile, then pulled out. "You want the magic prick, Billy?" And with that he put it to me.

Holy God, a bigger snake was inside me and plunging into places Dan never went. I clamped my jaw to keep from crying out, then after a bit Monty withdrew and got into Dan again. This I welcomed as my butthole, had it a voice, would have been screaming. But I wanted the magic dick in me and not my friend, so I issued some moans and Monty got the idea and came back to me. He gave me a good long reaming until he roared and gave up his juice.

When he had finished, he pulled out and said, "Billy, get down here and lick me," and I saw I dared not refuse. He seemed more bull than man, making me feel more colt than stallion, so I kneeled to lick him. As I did this, I saw from the corner of my eye him taking Dan's dick in hand to pull, and I liked the way he kept at both of us at the same time. My jaw ached by the time we were given a rest. Monty poured us drinks, his big thing relaxed for once. He downed two whiskeys while Dan and me had one.

"Now, Billy, the shirt trick," Monty said, setting aside his glass. "Get me your shirt and coat."

He laid the shirt on the bed and buttoned up the front and the cuffs. "Stand up," he said and I did. He then draped the buttoned shirt over my front and down my arms, said to hold still while he put my coat on me. By the time he had it all secure, I saw the trick. He could pull it off because it was not really on, it just laid over my front under the coat.

He stood behind me. "Montague the Wizard," he declared as he took the shirt collar and yanked. The shirt slipped off me, sleeves pulled right out of my coat's arms, and there I stood, naked but for the coat.

Dan clapped his hands. "Never had any idea how it was done."

"You now have my secret," said Monty as he tossed aside the shirt and removed my coat. "Never before have I revealed the trick to anyone, so you see how special you are. Now, boys, I want you to get onto the bed and suck each other's cocks. Dan, you lie back and, Billy, you climb over in reverse and drop your dick into his mouth while you take his into yours. Yes, like that."

He settled back into the bedside chair as I got over Dan to round up his soft morsel. Dan began to suck my dangling dick and we worked until things rose up for Monty's viewing pleasure. From my spot on top, I could see him sitting with legs wide, hand on his prick, stroking himself almost gently, like he meant to play some, which I understood, as having a hand on a cock, your own or another's, was always welcome.

As I sucked Dan, I tried to make my tongue do snake tricks, but Dan squirmed so I got back to what we usually did and soon had a stiff rod in my mouth while Dan had my pole. When Monty rose from the chair, I ran my eye that way and saw him pumping himself, sweating and breathing hard, and then, as he kept on, spurting big gobs of spunk, which he directed onto us. Sight of him coming pushed me over and I let go into Dan's mouth. A second later I was swallowing his cream. Once done, I got off and sought my drink, which I took right down. Monty, dick still in hand, poured me another.

Things then quieted. I found I wanted to ask about the shirt trick but could not as I did not understand my own question. He'd shown me how it was done and I saw that was special, so why didn't it feel that way? Could I ask that? I was thinking on how to say such a thing when Monty said we must leave, as he needed his sleep. Once we were dressed, he said, "Billy, would you like to do the shirt trick in my show?"

I lit up clear through. "I would like that very much."

"Good. Be at the theater an hour before show time. Come backstage and we'll get you set up." He opened the door and stood naked as we left. Anybody could have seen him, but maybe he liked that idea.

Next morning I got into Dan something fierce, awakening stiff like usual and not wanting to piss it away. He was asleep and swore some when I climbed on but soon as I shoved in, he was begging me to give it to him and thrashing out a come. I rode out a gusher, all the while thinking not on my pard but on the wizard's big snake. Once done, we both fell back asleep until around noon, when we went out to eat. We spent the day looking round town, having ice cream one place, whiskey another, but I thought more on the wizard's show than on what we were up to. Finally, after supper we went to the Lady Gay and I left Dan at the bar while I sought Monty backstage. I was directed to a small room where I found him bare-chested as he arranged things in his coat.

"Body loading," he said. "Coat is as much a prop as the rings and scarves and even your shirt."

I stood mute, as he seemed more like a grocer stocking shelves than a magic man. He caught this, for he turned and smiled. "Illusion, Billy boy. It is all illusion, but tell me that is not part and parcel of life. We see what we want to see."

Here he came over to caress my cheek. "You, dear boy, may be the sole exception. Such beauty amid the rank multitudes. An angel's golden hair, the fairest skin, dancing blue eyes, and cherub's pink lips. God has granted you many gifts, Billy. He has bestowed true beauty upon you." Here he paused as if catching himself and went back to his coat. "Now," he said, putting it onto a chair, "let us ready you for the performance."

As he had in his room, he fixed my shirt so it lay across my chest and along my arms under the coat. Except this time, of course, I had pants on.

"Now take your seat in the audience, and when I call for a volunteer for something special, you raise your hand. I will choose you and you then come up, acting like you do not know me, and we do the trick."

"That what you did with the other fellow?" I asked.

"Yes."

I wanted to ask did he fuck the other fellow but could not manage that, so I let myself be scooted from the room and found Dan. We then took our seats.

The comic told some of the same things as before and added new stuff on drunkenness while the singer did all different songs. Then Monty came on and I found myself thrilled to look upon him. He was a sight to behold as he put on his show, and I thought on what lay beneath his fine black suit. I also found knowing I would take part in his show made watching different this time, but it was the other knowing, the trickery, that laid heavy on me. I looked around to wonder if the men believed the magic, as I had, or did they know about trickery? I was thinking on such things when Monty called for a volunteer for something special. I was chosen from among many raised hands.

I had not noticed before that there were lights in back but, looking out from the stage, I saw how they shone upon Monty and me to make us special. I stood still as I awaited the shirt pull, thinking I had liked it better before I knew how the trick was done or that it was a trick at all. I was now part of fooling the men and not sure about that, but then the pull came and I stood bare-chested while the crowd whooped and hollered. Monty ran a hand under the back of my coat to squeeze my bottom while everyone clapped. He then urged me off the stage while he took his bows. I hurried to the little room and soon he joined me where I stood holding my shirt.

"Magnificent," he declared as he swept in. He seemed breathless and I saw how the show excited him. "A superior performance, Billy. You did exceptionally well. Now put on your shirt while I change and we'll join your friend at the bar." He seemed to have it all planned, which I liked, as it would surely lead to more fucking.

At the bar Monty slapped Dan on the back. "Your friend is quite the performer," he said, to which Dan agreed. "You looked good, Billy," Dan said, "and nobody knew the trick."

Monty got us whiskey, and as we drank, his hand slipped under my coat to again squeeze my bottom. Fingers prodded my crack and got my dick stiff, which I knew he wanted. I could see Dan was also up for something, so he was disappointed when Monty told him he would spend time with me alone. "Perfecting the illusion," he said. "I plan to use Billy in my show again, as he is the consummate performer. You do understand."

How could Dan object? I was to do the shirt pull at the next night's performance, which made me special. I looked to Dan, who I knew would want me to do well in the show. He nodded. We had one more drink before I was whisked to Monty's room.

He was different this time. Instead of a command to strip, he poured whiskey, and as I sipped, he began to undress me. "Better ways than a shirt pull," he said as my coat hit the floor. As he unbuttoned my shirt, he set aside my glass, brought his lips to mine, and I knew my first kiss ever, as Dan and I never stopped for that. He then finished taking off my clothes.

When he reached down for my dick, he had to tug but once to bring on a come that sent me spurting onto his leg. I began to apologize for soiling his pants, but he wouldn't have it. "Nonsense, sweet Billy," he said before he kneeled to lick away a drop on my cockhead. As he did so his fingers found my bottom crack and he pushed into me, which caused me to gasp.

"Such a pristine passage," he offered. "How I want to dirty it."

He then stood and threw off his clothes, revealing the cock I coveted. I expected him to put me on the bed, but instead he pulled me to him, his cock up between us like some log, and he kissed me again, open mouth this time, that snake of a tongue in pursuit of mine. I did my best to do what I thought he wanted and when he finally pulled back and said "delicious," I guessed I had done right.

Suddenly he declared we must fuck and pushed me onto the bed. When I got onto all fours, he threw me over onto my back and pulled my legs up onto his shoulders. He then drove his prick into me. I could only grab mine and hold on.

Dan had not done me this way. Never had I seen the face of the man fucking me, and I found it thrilling, as Monty was a handsome devil and his dark eyes fairly blazed as he went at me.

"You drive me mad," he declared as he gave it to me. "You are mine, Billy Barrow. I claim your every inch. I shall fuck you to hell and resurrect you to heaven by way of my prick. You are my angel, sweet Billy." He carried on like this all the while he drove that cock into me, working his manly magic. As he pumped in and out, I told him I was his to keep forever. He then became urgent and his expression drew into a grimace as he grunted out his come. When he had issued his last, he pulled out, let down my legs, and rasped, "Never enough."

I thought him done, but he rolled me onto my stomach and raised my bottom, which I took to mean more of his dick. Instead he commanded me to hold still, and I felt his breath on my buttocks and then his tongue. "No," I cried.

"Shush, Billy. Men do this. Now lie still. You'll like it, I guarantee."

He ran his tongue up between my buttocks as he held them apart, poking my center with his tongue, which got my hand to my dick because he was right, I liked it, awful as it was. He made slurping sounds, like I was good beer or sweet pudding, and then he did the unthinkable. He put his tongue in. This was too much and I attempted to pull away but his hands were iron on my hips, holding fast as that snake of tongue began to fuck me. And here I must confess I came into the bedding, crying out as it was good and bad all at once.

He fed back there for some time, then finally pulled out his tongue but did not put in his dick to fuck me proper, if such a thing can be found proper. He got off the bed to pour drinks, which we downed quickly. He then pissed the pot and washed at the basin before taking his dick in hand. He stood pulling it, which was some sight, important man like him doing what all of us drovers did every chance. "Look at it, Billy, for you will have it again and again. You are my magic now, sweet boy." The prick was stiffening with his attentions and he squirmed his hips as he brought himself along. I could not help but take up my own rod, as the sight before me was most arousing. At last, Monty settled into a chair, dick still in hand. "Come sit on me, Billy," he said.

"Sit?" I asked, having no idea what he meant.

"Astride. Climb over me and take my cock up you as you sit down. Come on. Men do it all the time. There are hundreds of ways to fuck, Billy, and I mean to try them all. Now get on."

I felt clumsy climbing over him, but once my legs were astride, I saw the appeal. His knob poked my hole and I had only to ease down to have it up me. Once in, I sat fixed on him and had to smile at such a position as it was most exciting, especially us being front to front.

"Back in the saddle," he said. "Astride your stallion, horse cock up you. Now ride me."

He lifted me to show how and I then took over, bouncing on the prick, which pretty much drove me crazy. My dick was hard as a gun barrel but I let it flop about, too worked up to even grab hold. After a bit of this, Monty said, "Easy now, I don't want to come too quickly," so I slowed until I just rocked on him. He fairly beamed with pleasure and my heart all but leaped from my chest at the sight of his satisfaction from none but a lowly cow puncher. His hands began to roam over my chest, settling onto my tits, and I was most surprised when he leaned in to lick one. He attended it a good while, sucking and nipping, which grew it to a hard little nub. His free hand rubbed and pinched the other one, and I saw the wizard knew everything about a man.

Finally he eased back and told me to resume my ride. "Make me come, sweet Billy. Make your steed spurt his stuff. Let the horse cock fill you." I began to bounce on him, at which his eyelids fluttered and he grabbed me at the waist, cried out, and bucked. The expression he wore was one I will never forget, this fine man caught up in the most base thing a man can do. Driving up into me, he emptied himself, then sank back into the chair and declared, "I am spent, dear boy. You have every drop."

I climbed off and he staggered to the bed, threw back the covers, and got in. "You may join me, Billy. Stay the night so I may have you on the morrow."

I got in and he put an arm around me to pull me close. His last words were, "You are mine, Billy Barrow."

I thought of Dan for a second, but he didn't seem to matter so much anymore.

❖

The day did not greet me so much as the wizard did, mouth on my stiff dick. But he didn't stay down there as expected. He threw back the covers and stuck his butt up like some dog in a field. "Fuck me, Billy boy," he growled. As I lay stunned at the sight, he reached back and pulled apart his cheeks. "I need your cock, Billy. Stick it in and give me a fuck. Make me yours as I have made you mine."

I sat up and just looked, for I could not believe he wanted this. Not a magic man who could make men believe in wonder. Not a man who had fucked me in a chair the night before. Yet there he was, in a position I often took, and I think it was knowledge of how good that felt that sparked me most, butt sticking up like that, begging to have it. I got a hand on my rod and worked it to get some wet, which I slicked down the shaft. I then got in behind Monty and did it, stuck it in, which caused him to cry out, grab himself, and start pulling. I then commenced the ride of a lifetime and watched myself pump in and out of him as he wanted. And even as I saw myself doing it, I thought on how it was, that I had my dick in this great man, this wizard. No trickery now, just me in his bottom. Fucking made us equals.

Doing a wizard was like nothing ever, him with all his powers and me with just my dick. I thought on his trickery as I went at him, pumping with a fury, thought how there was no illusion now. I was making him mine as he had made me his. And he kept on asking for it. "Fuck me, Billy, fuck me."

I was proud that I lasted longer than usual, but my juice finally hit the boil and rose up to a powerful spew. I called out I was doing it and Monty called back, "Give it to me, Billy, make me yours." He then groaned and I knew he shot his stuff same time as me.

Soon as I was done, I pulled out and fell over. Last thing I heard before I fell asleep was Monty saying, "Dearest Billy."

❖

The room was hot when I next woke. And I was alone. I had
no idea of the time, but bright as it was, I knew the sun was high. I
sat up and wondered on Monty. Maybe he went to get breakfast or
to see to theater business. But then I got to looking around and saw
his coat was gone, as well as his valise. All his things. The dresser
top was bare of his brushes. I got up to open drawers and found all
empty, as was the wardrobe. Only evidence he left me was in the
piss pot.

It made no sense, so I dressed and went downstairs, but he was
not there so I went to my room to see Dan, but he too was absent.
Having no idea what to do, I went out front, thinking maybe to go
over to the theater, but there sat Dan, kicked back like he had no
care, which I suppose he didn't.

"He is gone, Billy."

"Who?"

He chuckled. "Your magic man. He and the others caught the
Abilene stage an hour ago."

I looked up Front Street as if the stage might still be in sight,
but saw only how foolish this was so I took a chair next to Dan.
My thoughts raced around to where I could not catch a one. Finally
I managed a few words. "He told me I would be part of his show
tonight."

"Theater ad said just two performances."

"Didn't notice."

I hoped Dan would say no more as a hurt was crawling up
through me like some other kind of snake, this one poisonous. It
had the wizard's voice and kept saying "Billy boy" and "dear sweet
Billy," saying I belonged to him and him to me. All of it serpent's
lies. Or maybe trickery. That was it. He did me same as he did the
crowd at the Lady Gay. "He tricked me," I told Dan.

"All men will trick you."

"Not you."

"I stand corrected," said my friend. "All but one."

Part of me wanted to cry, the boy part I suppose, but another
part looked back at the night, the fucking, the licking, doing things
in a chair. I had gone new places with Monty even though he had left

me. Tears rose, the boy part hurting, and Dan must have seen, as he said we should go get a meal.

"Sounds good," I managed, looking at him like I forget to do sometimes and seeing what I've always liked, his dark hair and handsome face. "After that can we go back to our room?" I asked.

"You think I'll be enough after a wizard?"

"I learned some things last night."

"Tricks?"

"I'll leave you to decide."

THE ASSISTANT
MEL BOSSA

Mark snaps his head back and away from Eddie's rough hands. "Hey! Watch it, man. You're gettin' this shit in my eyes."

"I can't see a fuckin' thing." Eddie slaps Laddie's shoulder. "Hold the flash up higher," he orders her.

Laddie whines, "But my arm hurts."

Sitting with his back pressed against the cement blocks, Keegan watches the odd scene. Eddie, who sports a six-inch Mohawk, is dyeing Mark's hair in the dark. Keegan hangs back with the dogs, still unable to stand. He has pulled a flimsy blanket over his legs, but the shivers keep coming. It's August, the city is hot as an oven, but all day, he has had these chills.

Eddie shakes the small bottle hard again, and his bulging forearm shines white under the flashlight's glare. He is using dollar-store conditioner, mixed in with some blue methylene. "Why are we dyeing your hair in the middle of the night again?"

"So it'll dry around my ears during the night," Mark says a little too boldly. "Don't you know anything about coloring fucking hair?"

"What d'you say to me, fag?"

"Never mind."

Mark has told Keegan that Eddie spent a month in jail last year, and since then, everybody is a *fag*. Tonight, Keegan hopes to stay off Eddie's radar for one more day. The plan is still to catch a ride out East, where he will meet his great-uncle Jack. The great-uncle doesn't know he is coming. But he will give him a job with his crew when he sees how able Keegan is. Yes.

Two weeks ago, a day after his arrival in Montreal, Keegan dropped his duffel bag in this very spot here and came across Eddie and his friends. Now Eddie has taken a liking to him and says he has big plans for him.

Laddie's flashlight dims a few times and finally dies. The street lamp across from their improvised camp site is busted, and today's smog still hangs a thick veil over the moon. In the darkness, Keegan hears Eddie slap the hospital latex gloves off his knotted hands. "We're done," Eddie says. He is probably twenty-five—older than all of them. He has a head like a pack of bricks and small wooden eyes. He came from New Brunswick last April. That's all Keegan knows.

No one likes to talk about where they came from. Only where they are going. West most of the time.

But West is where Keegan is from. So here he is, moving in the opposite direction. It has always been so for him.

Eddie tosses the bottle into the street and stoops down by Keegan. "How you feelin', Bee Boy?"

Bee Boy is his street name now. Because of his blond roots coming through his dyed black hair.

"All right, I guess."

"Yeah, well, you're still burnin' up." Eddie touches a calloused palm to Keegan's head. His touch does not feel good, but it is a touch nonetheless. Nothing about Eddie ever feels good. Eddie slides down next to him and lights a cigarette. "You'll be okay in a few days."

Laddie and Mark lie side by side in a sleeping bag, sharing a bottle of beer, talking quietly.

There is no noise. Just the sound of a car rolling past the park every few minutes. Inside those cars, people are on their way to somewhere, driving by this park, seeing only darkness and bushes. Seeing nothing but an empty space waiting to be filled with condos.

Tonight, the fever is like this street—it is all over him. Inch by inch, it will swallow him, until he becomes nothing but a stain on the pavement.

"Still thinking about catching that bus to Halifax?" Eddie asks, petting one of the dogs.

Keegan answers Eddie's question with a slow nod and makes himself comfortable against the block. He lost his pillow today. And his favorite book.

"How you gonna get the money?" Eddie is like a shark, waiting for him to tire out. "Any new ideas?"

The fever makes Keegan stupid and weak. Two things he cannot be tonight. "Dunno," he says. Hearing his own voice in the night makes him want to cry. He is lonely for someone to hold on to. Mark has Laddie, and Eddie has a different girl every other night. Keegan has not been touched since he left home. The fever is making him horny—his body is burning up, aching for some kind of release. He wants a strong hand inside his pants. He remembers Jonas, his boyfriend from back home, and hates him even more tonight. That prick. That double-talking bastard. "I guess maybe I'll have to call my great-uncle or something," Keegan says, trying to stay cool. His dick has been throbbing inside his jeans all evening. There is nothing on these streets but want and need all the time.

"The same great-uncle you said would call your stepdad and turn you in?"

Keegan's stepdad would love nothing more than to have him back home again. Home in that house with nowhere to go. But he will never go back. Not even in his coffin.

"You know how much an ass like yours is worth around here?" Eddie is a man in no hurry. A man holding another man's head underwater, watching the last air bubbles escape to the surface.

Of course, it has always been about *that*. Keegan has known it from the time he turned twelve. "God, did you see those baby blues," his mother's friends would say. "That boy sure is going places."

But those places always turn into dark corners.

"I'm no hustler."

Eddie crushes his cigarette against the pavement. "You might not be a hustler, but you *are* a faggot." His hand weighs on Keegan's thigh—heavy as lead. "You thought I hadn't noticed, right? You think I'm stupid or something?"

Keegan shivers with fever and apprehension, but tonight, he would let Eddie tear him up if it meant coming hard.

Eddie is only a hater. "I got five hundred dollars' worth of loitering and vandalism tickets hanging over my fuckin' head. You think I'm gonna go back to the slammer? Didn't I take care of you in the last two weeks?"

Mark and Laddie are asleep. Wrapped around each other, they are safe in their union. Safe in their denial.

"The state that you're in right now…Well, I just don't know what's gonna happen to you, Bee Boy."

The night took a breath hours ago, but just won't exhale. If only he could get well. If only he could make eighty-nine dollars tomorrow. Eighty-nine dollars. That is all that stands between him and the great blue sea. His great-uncle manages a docking crew. All day, his men pile things into containers. Keegan is going to pile those things too, and then one day, he will pile himself right into one of those boxes and float away from this continent.

"Within a week, you and me would be set up. Nice room. Clean sheets. No hassle."

"I'm no hustler." Keegan lays his head back, trying to keep his teeth from clattering. Maybe he will let Eddie put his rough, hating hands on him.

But Eddie only pats his knee. "Right, that's what you guys all say." Brusquely, he snatches the blanket off Keegan's body and walks away. "It's *my* fuckin' blanket," he says before spreading it out over a patch of cracked pavement where some grass pokes through. "You want a blanket, you earn it." He calls his dogs over.

And of course, they obey Eddie.

❖

Silently, Keegan sits up.

The urge to take a piss is nagging him. Everyone is asleep. It must be four a.m. The sky is touched with blue. With great effort,

Keegan rises. The world runs circles around his head, and he leans his hand against the cement block, gulping for air. He is thirsty. He looks around for some water, careful not to wake anyone. He finds half a bottle of Evian and drinks it greedily.

An electrical storm is inside his mind. He can almost hear it rolling over his brain. The fever still has a strong grip on him, and the hunger too.

Love is a four-letter word, and that is all it is.

Fuck is also a four-letter word, and a much more profitable one at that.

Keegan takes a few unsteady steps and then a few more. He listens—someone is whispering out there. A girl. He really needs to piss. He walks off in the opposite direction of the voices, looking for a spot. This park is huge and notorious for its night crowd. You never really see anybody. You just know they are there, killing time and themselves in the process.

A hundred feet from where Eddie has set them up for the night, Keegan finds a cluster of trees and unzips his jeans. His piss streams out of him.

Eighty-nine dollars. Eighty-nine dollars, and God let this fever go away, and I'll be all right.

He finishes and zips up.

"Do you have a light, please?"

Keegan jumps. "No," he says, walking off, leaving the man in the long black coat and fedora hat behind him.

But the man is standing in front of him again. "I found one… Never mind." He lights his cigarette and the flame illuminates his eyes for a moment. They are beautiful laughing brown eyes.

But there is no lighter in his hand. No match.

The man sweeps his hat off. His hair is shoulder length, thick and dark as his coat. "Hi," he says in a quiet voice.

Keegan tries to make out the details of his face, but he only sees the eyes, clean of malice, yet mischievous, staring back at him. "Hi," he hears himself say.

The man steps forward. "You're not feeling well." He turns up his palms.

Wait, where is his cigarette?

Keegan takes a step back. "I'm okay." He wants to leave. "I'm okay," he says again, not moving.

"What's your name?"

"Keegan."

"I'm Hyphen." The man's hat rolls over his forearm, up his shoulder, and gently settles on his head again. "Nice to meet you here."

"How'd you do that?" The fever is making him see things.

"Just a little trick."

The sky pales across the horizon, and Keegan watches the light move over the man—Hyphen—until it is on his face...inside his almond eyes.

And he sees Hyphen is as young as he is.

Hyphen looks up at the sky and back at him. "Well, good morning," he says with a smile. He holds his hand out to him.

Keegan looks down at it. Hyphen's hand is clean, with fingernails smooth as glass. "I gotta go," Keegan mutters, turning away from Hyphen's touch.

But three steps away, Hyphen stands across from him again.

"Now, okay, how the fuck did you do that?"

"I used your peripheral vision against you." Hyphen moves closer to him. "It's just an illusion." He rubs his index and thumb together. And there is a white card there. "I'm a street performer." He offers the card.

Keegan walks off.

"Wait." Without a touch, Hyphen stops him. It is his eyes that keep Keegan from walking away. Large and expressive. "Can I talk to you? Can I help you—"

"Leave me alone, okay?" Keegan breaks free from Hyphen's stare.

"All right," Hyphen says softly. "I'll keep an eye out for you."

"I don't need you to—" But when he turns around, Hyphen is gone.

Keegan stumbles back to Eddie and the gang. All are asleep,

save for the dogs who watch him settle up against the cement block again. Soon, they too are peering at the world through half-shut lids.

Keegan is slipping into an uneasy sleep, but something scratches his chest under his T-shirt. He peeks into it—there is a piece of paper there, half-stuck to his breast. He looks up to the top of the blocks. What? Who? There is no one there. Heart in mouth, he pulls out the card from his shirt. Reading the words, Keegan stops breathing for a few seconds, his mouth opening slightly.

Take the two pills in your back pocket. You'll feel better. Don't worry, it's only Advil.

❖

The sun burns him into the pavement.

Keegan opens his eyes, and for a minute, he is unsure of where he is and what time it is in his life. Is he late for work again?

"That is so fuckin' creepy!" Laddie is yelling and yelping with laughter.

Keegan sits up, and a dog licks his hand. "Hello," he greets the animal, struggling to tear himself out of sleep and into wakefulness.

"Do it again," Mark says.

Hyphen is sitting atop a block, his legs hanging over the edge, his hat on his lap. Laddie and Mark sit as his feet, looking up with childlike expressions on their faces. Eddie is not here.

"Hold your hand out to me."

"What are you gonna do?" Laddie asks. Today, she has tied up her dreadlocks in a great big matted ponytail. "Tell me first."

Hyphen laughs at her suspicion, and then, slowly his eyes meet Keegan's. "Good morning again." He jumps off the block and walks to him.

Keegan stands—he is feeling much better, steady on his legs.

Hyphen stops close to him and they are eye to eye. Hyphen's skin is brown from the sun, and his eyes are speckled with amber. When he smiles, his whole face blooms. "You feel good?"

"Yeah, I do." He does. He really does feel good. He scratches his head and laughs quietly. "Who are you?"

"You guys know each other?" Mark asks, frowning at them.

Hyphen does not look at Mark, no. He stares deep into Keegan's eyes, soothing him and turning him on all at once. "You hungry, Keegan?"

He is so hungry, he could eat one of Eddie's dogs.

"Come on." Hyphen nudges his head to the street. "Yes?"

When they cross the street, Keegan feels the weight of Mark's and Laddie's stares burn hotter than the sun on his back. But the fever is gone, leaving so much space inside him. He must be filled. He must be sated. He looks over at Hyphen. "Where are we going?"

Hyphen takes his hand. There is softness and warmth there in Hyphen's hand. There is possession and pride. Promises wait to be fulfilled in Hyphen's grip. Keegan can't imagine ever letting go of that hand. It guides him without pulling. He feels Hyphen's forearm brush against his, and his dick swells.

Hyphen leans in and his mouth touches Keegan's ear. "I've been wanting to hold your hand like this since the first time I saw you step off the bus."

"Yeah?"

Hyphen nods, smiling. "Yes."

❖

The waitress gathers up their empty plates. "You boys all done?"

Keegan is high off the food. "Yes, thank you." He looks up at the woman and blushes a little. What does she think of him? Of them? He has not had a meal sitting indoors in weeks. He is not an animal. He is not his dirty clothes.

"You don't want any dessert?" Hyphen looks into his face. The sun comes through the dirty windowpane, dancing in his brown eyes. "No?"

Keegan shakes his head. He wants to reach out and touch Hyphen's smooth hand again, but fiddles with his napkin instead.

The waitress drops the bill on the table and Hyphen produces a credit card out of his hefty, overpacked wallet. "Thank you," he says to the waitress, offering her the card. She looks at him. She looks at the card.

Keegan is not breathing.

The waitress leaves with the card.

"Where d'you get that card?"

Hyphen waves the question off. He is spreading his paper napkin across the table. "Gimme your fork," he says. Keegan watches Hyphen place the fork gently in the middle of the napkin. Hyphen's hands move like a breeze over the fork. He folds the napkin over the fork two times, covering it completely. "You're watching?"

Keegan leans in a bit. "Yeah," he whispers, staring at Hyphen's hands, aching to feel them on his skin once more. The food and sleep have made him strong, and everything on him is hard. "Show me."

Hyphen does not move for a moment, and desire, like a sandstorm, moves across his face, clouding his stare. "I wanna kiss you right now," he says under his breath.

Keegan makes a sound like he is hurt. His dick hardens, rubbing up against his jeans.

The waitress comes back with the receipt and Hyphen signs it without a blink. "Let's go," he says, getting up.

"Where?"

Hyphen pulls Keegan off his chair and their chests touch. "Somewhere we can be alone." He turns and leans over the table, looking down at the folded napkin. In a swift gesture, he yanks the napkin open.

There is a knife where the fork used to be.

❖

The man at the hotel's reception desk returns. "I'm afraid this card's been canceled," he says. His eyes are mean black slits in his face. "Would you come with me for a second? My manager would like to—"

"Are you a good runner?" Hyphen says this into Keegan's ear, already tensing his upper body toward the hotel lobby exit.

"Go," Keegan cries, stabbing for the main doors.

They run for four blocks, never looking over their shoulders or at each other. Hyphen's boots slap the concrete and his breath is ragged, but he keeps up with Keegan, until finally he grabs his arm and pulls him into an alley. "Holy shit," he gasps, bending over.

Keegan peers around the corner of the alley, at the street. "We're okay, I think." He is barely out of breath. Perhaps he still has his health after all. "You're a thief. Some kind of klepto, right?" He looks back at Hyphen, who is catching his breath. "Is *that* your street magic?"

Hyphen's eyes search Keegan's face. "No, just trying to survive, that's all." He steps closer to him, but does not touch him. "I'm going on the road and I'm gonna be huge, Keegan. I'm gonna be bigger than Copperfield. Bigger than Blaine, or Angel." He glides his index along Keegan's mouth, pushing the tip of it between his lips. "But I'm missing something." He leans in, his mouth skimming Keegan's. "More like someone."

"What do you want?" Keegan's voice gets caught in his throat.

"I want you to be my assistant. No one else. It has to be you." Hyphen leads him to the wall behind them, until Keegan's back is to it and they are safe out of view—hidden by a large blue recycling bin. "I've been waiting a long time for you. A long and lonely time. I need your eyes. They make the magic so much better. So much more real. It has to be you looking at me…do you understand?" Hyphen puts his hands on Keegan's face, holding it between his fingers.

In his mind, Keegan can hear the crowd. He can see himself, dressed in a black-on-black suit, his white-blond hair slicked to the side, his blue eyes painted with dark kohl. He is locked in a glass box, the cool water climbing over his calves, his thighs. The crowd watches with bated breath. The water reaches his neckline and they gasp. Hyphen circles the glass prison, his face a mask of incredulousness—what has he done to his beautiful assistant now?

"Say yes," Hyphen whispers, his hands moving down to Keegan's shoulders, then down again to caress his chest, under his shirt. "I'll take you everywhere. We'll see everything." He kisses Keegan's mouth, and Keegan opens his lips, hungry for Hyphen's tongue. They fumble for each other, a little clumsily, and Keegan pulls Hyphen by his hair, pressing the length of his body to his. He can hear people walking by the alley, talking.

What would happen if they were to see him like this?

Hyphen slides his hand over Keegan's tense stomach, his swift fingers reaching his belt, unfastening it.

Every thing Keegan has worried about all of his young life—it is all gone. All of those years were nothing but a long, well-executed illusion. Reality is magical to him at this moment, real and alive in his hands.

Hyphen slips Keegan's pants down. Keegan's cock is full, springing out of his jeans. They could be discovered. Someone could see. And this notion, like the air on the tip of his cock, excites him greatly. Hyphen kneels and looks up at him, running his tongue over Keegan's shaft, but leaving the head of his dick always untouched. Keegan holds back from groaning, aware of the crowded street just a few steps away. He turns his head, peering over the bin at his side. Hyphen's tongue is agile, licking Keegan's balls, moving up and down his dick slowly and hungrily.

"Oh, oh fuck," Keegan whines as if in pain, but still, Hyphen's tongue does not reach the head of his dick. He can't help watching people walk by them. What if they could see him like this, thighs spread wide, his cock engorged and Hyphen's mouth tasting it. Sweat beads hang on Keegan's lips—it is hot and there is no air. He grips Hyphen's hair harder now, his balls churning with a climax he knows will bend his knees and make him cry out. Hyphen's hand is inside his own pants, and he is stroking himself hard and fast. Keegan watches his eyes glaze—Hyphen is coming. He loves the sounds he makes. He feels his pleasure—they are bound by it now, both of them greedy for the other to say his name. Hyphen's hand stops moving for a moment and he stiffens, looking up at Keegan. Hyphen's seed pumps out into his hand, and he grabs Keegan's clenched buttocks, driving Keegan's dick into his mouth, until the head of it reaches down into his throat. Keegan arches his back, his eyes on the people walking by, his cock spurting so—he feels he may black out.

Hyphen stands, his softening dick glistening with come, and pulls a red tissue out of his sleeve. He cleans himself and Keegan, smiling shyly. "You enjoyed that," he says, his cheeks coloring slightly.

Keegan leans his forehead to Hyphen's, breathing in the scent of him. "You really saw me getting off the bus that day?"

"Yes, and I've been following you."

"Why?"

"I told you. You're the one. It has to be you."

Their pants are still around their ankles. They are in an alley. Keegan has not a nickel to his name. He knows nothing of this boy.

"What? What is it?" Hyphen asks, worried.

No, he knows nothing of this boy.

But for once in his lonely life, he is in love.

❖

The night is creeping up on them.

Today, Keegan has seen what Hyphen can do. He is a brilliant performer—charming and witty. Three times, Hyphen drew a crowd of fifty or more people, and in this jaded city, this is impressive. When Hyphen's hands glide and fly over the simple objects he carries or demands from the crowd, Keegan wants to be those quarters, cards, and ribbons. He could disappear inside Hyphen's sleeve and come out changed.

This afternoon, they stood face-to-face, the sun burning red and falling off the earth, and Hyphen said no boat, no containers, no great-uncle could take Keegan to the places he was meant to go.

Now they walk up Saint-Laurent Street, sharing a slice of pizza. Once in a while, Keegan looks over at Hyphen, and his heart jolts. He is here and he is real.

As they pass Prince Arthur Street, Keegan spots Eddie and his dogs. Eddie is panhandling tonight. Clad in his black jeans, white T-shirt, and red suspenders, Eddie squats by a store entrance, holding up a sign that reads *Need funds for drug research.*

Hyphen stops, hanging back a little. He must have read Keegan's expression. "I don't like him," Hyphen says, tossing his head in Eddie's direction.

"He saw us." Keegan waves at Eddie, his stomach knotting. "I don't like him either, but I don't want any trouble from him. Let's just act like nothing's up, and by the time he knows it, I'll be gone."

"With me?"

Keegan nods quickly. "He's watching. Come on, let's go see him before he thinks I'm blowing him off."

They stroll up to Eddie. They exchange a few words. Eddie is watching Hyphen through his pale wooden eyes, smiling thinly. He wants to know if what Mark and Laddie say is true. Can Hyphen really make things disappear? Word on the street is, Hyphen is a wanted man. Fraud. Identity theft. Keegan listens, unaffected. What does he care if Hyphen steals a dollar from every law-abiding citizen in this rotten city? He cares nothing about that.

"So, you guys will be there, right?' Eddie is counting the change in his box.

Keegan has lost track of their conversation. "Where?"

"At the blocks. We're gonna have a little celebration."

"And what are we celebrating, Eddie?"

Eddie's eyes narrow and he laughs through his nose. "Life. Whatever." His thick fingers dive in and out of the dog's black fur. "Bee Boy, you gotta be there. Your friend too. If you don't come, I'll take it real personal, seein' you're gonna be leavin' us and all."

So Eddie knows everything. He has eyes on every corner. There is no way around this night.

Walking away, Keegan stops Hyphen. "I don't think we should go to the blocks tonight."

Hyphen grabs Keegan's hand and squeezes it. "Don't worry. We'll be out of here tomorrow, but we gotta play it cool with him."

But Keegan worries anyway.

❖

It is dark, but Laddie has hung a few colored glow sticks around the Frost fence. Keegan and Hyphen sit a little away from the group, side by side, their hands locked together.

"Relax now," Hyphen says quietly. "Look at him, he's drunk. We'll be out of here soon."

Eddie is drunk all right. He is talking at the top of his voice, swinging his bottle of rum, ranting about his latest brawl. He hasn't bothered Keegan tonight. He has barely looked at his face. This makes Keegan sick with nerves. He notices how Mark and Laddie keep looking back at the street. They are jumpy.

"We should go now." Keegan moves to get up.

But Eddie announces he is leaving. He has a girlfriend on Guy Street, waiting up for him. Immediately, Mark and Laddie spring to their feet, glancing back at the street again. Now Keegan's whole body is telling him to go. "Hyphen, come on."

Eddie gathers his dogs, but Mark and Laddie are already across the street, calling him. "Hurry! They're driving up," Mark shouts back.

Keegan's spine stiffens. "Oh, shit," he says, seeing the police cruiser pull up, sirens off.

"Get out of here." Hyphen shoves him. "Go!"

Keegan stands there. "No."

"Get out of here, Keegan!" Hyphen shoves him much harder. And Keegan tumbles back, his eyes questioning Hyphen, but he knows. He knows. There is not time, and there is nothing he can do. He sprints through the bushes, scratching his arms and neck, bolting for the end of the park.

He hears male voices calling out for him to stop, but it is dark and they will not shoot. He runs faster—through and out the park, jumping over the sidewalk, hitting the street, vanishing into it.

❖

"Tell me where he is," Keegan yells. His vocal cords are raw from lack of sleep. He is pushing his forearm against Mark's throat, enjoying the red veins bulging in Mark's eyes. "Where's Eddie, you fucking asshole."

All night, he has planned this. Looking for Mark and Laddie. Eddie too. All night, Keegan walked up and down the streets, his hands deep in his pockets, his eyes scanning faces.

Mark makes a noise and it doesn't sound good. There is no use in killing him this morning. Keegan pulls back, but still grips his collar hard. "You set us up."

Mark chokes and spits. "I…I…look…you know how Eddie is." He finally catches his breath, but his voice is broken. "Eddie wanted him gone…I don't know…he has this fascination for you—"

"Fuck you." Keegan stares Mark down, holding back the tears. "Fuck you and fuck Eddie. And fuck Laddie too." He shakes his head, stepping back. "Tell Eddie he'll never see me again, and if he does, I'll make sure I'm the last thing he ever sees."

"Right," Mark snickers. "Right." He laughs softly, his eyes dumb and blank. "Sure, I'll tell Eddie that."

Keegan looks at the street. Hyphen is out of reach.

"Look, Bee Boy, Hyphen's not gettin' out on bail this time. He's in there for good. They're gonna pin every fuckin' thing they can on him. He ain't comin' outta there for a spell—"

"Fuck you," Keegan whispers, turning away. "He's coming for me."

❖

But three weeks have passed.

Keegan sits in the bus station, his ticket in his hand. Halifax is a terrible name for a town. It sounds like a disease. His great-uncle says he will like it there—plenty of fresh air and iodine for the nerves. Uncle Jack will not turn him in.

Keegan looks down at his hands. They are clean. He runs his fingers through his short hair—he is a blond again. The lady at the mission gave him a pair of good pants and a blue shirt. The shirt is stiff around the collar and smells like old books.

What can he do?

Hyphen is awaiting trial on seven different charges. Word on the street is, he is facing four to five years.

Five years is a quarter of Keegan's life.

It is too long.

Keegan blinks, his throat clamping up, but he will not cry anymore. The great big ugly bus rolls up.

Eddie has gotten a girl pregnant. She is sixteen. Her father has promised a large sum of money to anyone who will drop Eddie off on his porch.

Eddie has left town.

Keegan stands, and for a moment, he feels watched. It has been like this for three days. He looks around, sensing eyes on him.

But there is no one watching him, except for the bus driver.

Keegan lugs his duffel bag full of books and drawings. When he gets to Halifax, he will work and save, and find a lawyer. He will come back for Hyphen.

He shoves his bag in the under-compartment and climbs aboard the bus. He is the first one in, and he sits in the back, watching people board. He looks at their faces. Their clothes. He is bored with them already.

At last, the bus driver announces their departure as if there was anything to announce but twenty-two hours of misery. Keegan settles himself into his seat and closes his eyes.

He dreams he is standing in a glass box, looking out at the world through cool water.

❖

"Did you see that?"

"Wait, wait, do that again."

"Melissa, leave your book. You gotta see this."

"Watch his hand."

A woman screams and then there is laughter.

"That's impossible," a girl says.

Keegan opens his eyes and peers out into the narrow space

between the seats. People have clustered around a seat at the front of the bus.

"Show her the other one," a man demands. "The one you did before."

Keegan's heart thunders, sending shock waves through him. Already his body awakens, his dick filling at the thought of Hyphen's hands and the imprint they have left all over his skin.

"Judy, look at this," a man says.

There is a silence.

"Ladies and gentlemen, in order to do this next trick, I need an assistant."

Keegan is frozen, his view of Hyphen blocked by a man's broad back.

A young and pretty girl bends over a little in the aisle. "I'd love to be your assistant."

"Hmm," Hyphens says. "I don't know. Any other volunteers?"

Keegan stands, his knees shaking under him. But he is strong. "I'd like to give it a try."

All eyes dart his way.

Hyphen gets out of his seat and turns around. He tips his hat. "Why sir, I think that would work." He smiles devilishly.

Keegan makes his way to the front of the bus, his hands clammy, his breath leaving him. "How did you—"

But Hyphen winks at him. "It's going to be a long ride. Let's save that story for later." And ignoring the gasps and shocked looks around them, he pulls Keegan close and tenderly kisses his mouth.

A man grunts his disapproval, and soon people are returning to their seats, most of them embarrassed, and some clearly disgusted.

Hyphen pulls back and laughs. "I think we just lost our audience."

"No shit."

"Come." Hyphen motions to the back row. They settle into the seats and Hyphen drops a pair of cuffs, a magnetic card, and a photo ID of what looks like a city worker on Keegan's lap. "I'll tell you how I did it if you take the assistant's oath," he says into Keegan's ear.

"The oath?"

"Swear you'll stand by me, never pull me out of anything—even if that very thing is Death herself—and never, ever, tell anyone what magic really is."

Keegan nods.

"Now, tell me about those boats and how those containers work."

"Are we taking our act to Europe?" Keegan smiles, nudging Hyphen's shoulder. "Is that the plan?"

Hyphen only laughs.

"Okay, but can I ask you something? As your faithful assistant, of course. What is magic anyway?"

Hyphen slides his hand up Keegan's thigh, reaching the bulge in Keegan's jeans. "This," he whispers. "This is the magic, baby."

And Keegan feels it.

He believes in it.

Old-Fashioned Expectations
Joseph Baneth Allen

My latest assignment for the *Skeptical Inquirer* was a relatively simple one.

All I had to do was figure out how Christofi Zirmis performed his "Man from Atlantis" illusion and condense it into a two-thousand-word article for the next issue. Simple in concept, except my subject was extremely difficult to pigeonhole. Without a doubt, Zirmis was one of the premier illusionists of the twenty-first century, and perhaps one of the most baffling.

Growing up in Hollywood as the only child of immigrants, an early interest in performing stage magic had led him to spend many after-school hours at the much-vaunted Magic Castle. A series of wildly successful performances there when Zirmis had turned eighteen launched his career as a stage magician. His reputation for performing breathtaking illusions rapidly grew.

He was barely two years into his career when President Jacob Cumberland had invited him to perform during a televised performance at the White House. I was covering his performance for the paper's Gallery section. Zirmis had me when he flashed a warm smile to the general audience as he walked into the State Dining Room. He was an extremely handsome young man, hard to ignore.

I was expecting to get a few paragraphs out about how a young magician awed the cynical politicians, pundits, and a few members of the Hollywood elite at a presidential fund-raising affair. Polite applause had greeted Zirmis as he strode to the center of the room.

Boyishly thin, he was dressed in a simple black Classic Peak Lapel Ralph Lauren tuxedo. The only hint of nonconformity was the purple and green plaid cummerbund that peeked out from his buttoned tux jacket.

His hands moved upward with a flourish.

"Mr. President, Mrs. Cumberland, and honored guests," Zirmis began. "It is a great honor and privilege to be asked to perform here tonight. So I've come up with a very special illusion in honor of President Cumberland that merges our great nation's past with its present."

Zirmis might have been just a skinny twenty-year-old twink in a tux, but he certainly knew how to tease, capture, and pique an audience's interest.

"Uno, dos, tres," he said. His hands danced in time to the singsong rhythm. Out of nowhere, three life-sized dollar bills with legs and Air Jordans on their feet appeared to the right of him. There were a few oohs and ahhs scattered around the audience.

"Cuatro, cinco, seis..." After another wave of his hands, an equal number of raptors right out of a *Jurassic Park* movie appeared on his left. All of a sudden, the dollar bills jumped up in alarm and took off running. With their jaws wide open, the raptors followed right behind them.

Riotous laughter rippled among the few Republicans in the State Dining Room who had been invited to the evening's festivities. Earlier in the day President Cumberland had signed a bill increasing the top tax rate to thirty-seven percent for those who earned over a hundred thousand dollars annually.

Cameras from Fox News, CNN, NBC, ABC, and a few dozen other networks captured Zirmis's illusion and broadcast it live. Obviously, nobody on the White House staff had bothered to determine if Zirmis was a Republican. I found out later that he was, and still is, a Libertarian.

Zirmis's illusion of Jurassic raptors chasing and gobbling up tax dollars was talked about by political pundits right up to Election Day a year later—when President Cumberland, a Democrat, lost in a landslide.

That election night had also cemented Zirmis's reputation as the illusionist who brought down an unpopular presidency. At that time, I had so wanted to bring him down for ruining what should have been an easy re-election for Cumberland. I still did.

Now, ten years later, Zirmis could have had a lifetime contract at any of the top hotels here in Las Vegas. Yet he eschewed any bookings longer than two weeks and only performed in Sin City at the Flamingo Hotel. He also rarely gave interviews anymore. His last interview—pictures, mainly—appeared five years ago in *People.*

He is a rarity among Greek men—a tall natural redhead with emerald green eyes that sparkled with good humor and teasing bedroom promises. He had definitely filled out nicely since our paths crossed in the White House.

With his dark olive complexion, Zirmis gave the impression of a freshly struck match whenever he stepped onto the stage. The strategically placed blond highlights in his coiffed ringlets added gravitas to the illusion of being the living embodiment of flame. He wore a traditional black tuxedo with casual confidence.

I had studied every aspect of Zirmis's performance before he stepped out onto the stage at the O'Sheas Theatre this evening. It was my fourth time doing so this week. Zirmis is what's known in the showbiz vernacular as a "song and dance man." His show combines musical comedy with dance, romantic intrigue and, of course, magic.

Onstage he was now engaged in a playful tango to Biagis's *Soledad, la de barracas* with an attractive leggy brunette whose red dress nicely accentuated her shapely curves. She was the fourth partner to appear in his arms since this part of the act had begun.

"What is your name, my dear?" Zirmis asked with a butter-melting smile.

"Peter," gruffly replied the burly and balding dark-haired man now in his arms. Peter wore the same dress and was indeed shapely, if you took his beer belly into account.

Laughter filled the theater as the tango came to an abrupt halt. Zirmis brought a hand to his lips in mock horror as Peter curtsied and exited from the stage. Granted, lame. But still funny as hell, even after seeing it multiple times.

"Atlantis, Atlantis, we want to see the Man from Atlantis!" a rowdy bunch of theater goers three rows behind me chanted. Within a minute, the whole theater reverberated with the demand for a vision of a mythical man from a fictional lost city. I knew it was coming next. The switching tango dance partners bit was the second-to-last illusion of his usual nightly performance.

Zirmis didn't encourage the reincarnation cult that had sprung up from the seeming reality of his Atlantis illusion, but he didn't discourage it either. I had been tasked with figuring out how he brought a mythical city and its inhabitants to life onstage, and then debunking it.

Zirmis help up his hands for silence. After about two minutes more of chanting and applause, my fellow audience members complied with his request by settling back into their seats.

"Now, be honest," he coyly said. "How many of you just came just to see me strip?" All the women and about a third of the men in the theater gave him a bawdy standing ovation, and I joined in. Nothing in my freelancing contract had stipulated that I couldn't ogle Zirmis as I delved into his stage act secrets.

"Very well, ladies and gentlemen, prepare yourselves for a glimpse of a civilization and a people lost to the depths of time," Zirmis said. The theater now went dark except for one golden spotlight centered squarely on him. "Prepare yourself to meet my ancestor—the Man from Atlantis!"

Stepping out of his ebony Florsheim lace-up dress shoes, he threw his arms back with a flourish. The black tuxedo he wore parted into separate pieces that vanished into the dark stage behind him.

Only white swimming trunks remained on his smooth, muscularly lithe body. Shadows fleeing the spotlight nicely outlined his pecs and the other firm lines of his body. The golden trident embroidered exactly right on the front of his swimming trunks accentuated the swell of his ample cock underneath. The audience went wild with applause and catcalls.

"Hey, hey, now," Zirmis joked. He pointed at his face with a

V-sign from the fingers on his left hand. "My eyes are here, not down there." He laughed, pointing downward with his right forefinger. More laughter erupted out of the audience, along with a few camera phone flashes.

More than once I found myself wishing I could have smuggled opera glasses or a pair of small binoculars into the theater, but the roving ushers would have ejected me. Zirmis had strict rules on what you could and couldn't bring to his performances.

If my judging of his curved bulge with my unaided eyes was correct, Zirmis had left only the question of whether he was cut or uncut to the audiences' imagination. Several more minutes passed until the giddy laughter and applause died down sufficiently enough for Zirmis to continue.

"Join me now, as we call forth the Waves of Time," he said, taking a step backward. The spotlight focused on his smiling face, upraised arms, and upper torso.

A casual observer never would have noticed the-oh-so slight tensing of his deltoid muscles as he began rising slowly in the air. Scattered applause and ooh-ahhs filled the auditorium, but his ascension was no mystery to me. He had obviously stepped into a small harness being raised by invisible wires into the air. By the way his feet dangled, I doubted he stood on a platform.

"Ladies and gentlemen, by my rights of inheritance as Poseidon's Heir, I call forth the Waves of Time," he called out. "The Waves of Time will erode the barrier of centuries and return me to as I was in Atlantis."

Zirmis had created a rather nifty backstory for his Waves of Time on his website and program literature. By immersing himself in water filled with tachyons—a scientific implausibility to put it kindly since the faster-than-light, time-traveling photons don't exist—Zirmis's DNA reverted back to its ancestral state.

By my rough estimate, Zirmis hovered about thirty feet off the stage. We heard ocean waves crashing as he began falling backward. The audience gave a collective gasp as Zirmis swan-dived backward into the darkness. Light suddenly washed the stage, revealing a counterclockwise rotating wall of turquoise water that filled its entire width and breadth. A bulge began forming in the middle of the water cocoon, which edged closer to the audience.

"Oh my God, I've just got wet!" several men and women in the first row exclaimed. Laughter and whooping erupted everywhere.

My earlier attempts in the week to get a peek into how Zirmis and his crew set up the props for his "Man from Atlantis" illusion weren't successful. Backstage security at the Flamingo's theater was tighter than anything found at a Justin Bieber concert. Zirmis kept all the tricks in his magician's hat tightly under wraps through the auspices of the Atlantean Guard, his own private security force.

Not a lot was known about the men who made up the Atlantean Guard. They were a smorgasbord of full-spectrum hunky men who carried themselves with a bearing that suggested prior military service. All wore white jumpsuits with a gold trident embroidered over the heart. Rumor was that the men were unpaid volunteers personally hand-picked by Zirmis. If so, he certainly had a great appreciation for masculine beauty of every nationality.

Whether or not Zirmis paid them with cold cash or warmth provided on bended knees was irrelevant to me. What was relevant was that they were fiercely loyal to the stage magician. I had observed this firsthand when I happened to chance upon Simon Owen trying to bribe one of them the day I had arrived at the Flamingo.

Simon was a features writer for the American entertainment beat of the *Daily Mail*—a British newspaper a few pegs above their usual trashy tabloids. He was also a drunken overnight mistake I made a few years back. Beer goggles were definitely needed by anyone who was toying with the notion of actually sleeping with him. Upon seeing him, I ducked behind a nearby slot machine that had just been vacated and fed it quarters while I kept an eye on him.

I watched as Simon tried to bribe the Atlantean Guard member blocking a side theater entrance with a few pound notes. The muscular blond shook his head, rejecting the offered cash. There was way too much distance and noise around me to hear what Simon offered the young man next, but he must have gotten one doozy of a response. He turned beet red. A few seconds later, suits from the

Flamingo's own security force restrained Simon and escorted him off the premises.

Simon's experience with Team Zirmis was just the latest in the long line of journalists who tried, albeit unsuccessfully, to penetrate the magician's inner world. I still wanted to give my least favorite mistake a swift kick up his broad backside. As a result of his shenanigans, the Atlantean Guard was probably now on even a higher alert for any intrusions by journalists.

Getting into Zirmis's shows at the Flamingo was relatively simple thanks to Reginald Simpson, a senior editor at the *Skeptical Inquirer*. Published by the Committee for Skeptical Inquiry, the international magazine regularly went after magicians who claimed their tricks and illusions were attributed to special occult powers.

Simpson had Zirmis in his crosshairs ever since the magician's Man from Atlantis illusion developed a cult following who honestly believed some sort of time travel was involved. Zirmis never claimed this, but his refusal to talk about how he created his Atlantean illusion irked many, especially since he had given up all the tricks of the trade behind his Jurassic Raptors and Tax Dollars illusion.

All Simpson had needed was to get tickets to a Zirmis show for several nights in a row in advance, then give the assignment to some writer who was unknown to the magician. Simpson was a fan of the hard science writing I did for the print syndicated Cox News Service, so I was a logical choice. I was also a Zirmis fan, but I didn't tell Simpson that when I accepted the assignment.

Now I was again trying to puzzle out the Wave of Time. How people in the front row were getting wet was simple to figure out. Someone had synchronized a small, yet highly portable sprinkler system that could easily be hauled on and off stage. The bulging wave looked like a solid wave of impenetrable water. How it was generated was a bit of a puzzler, but I assumed holographic lasers projected it against a particulate background to give it the illusion of depth and motion.

Now the wave stopped spinning and began flattening out. Zirmis was in the center of the illusion. Or, I should say, a spectacular emerald-tailed merman who looked exactly like the Greek magician was in the direct center in the water above the stage. He wore a silver crown adorned on its four corners with gold tridents. He carried a gold trident in his left hand.

"I am Betylus, philosopher king," boomed out a voice, deeper than Zirmis's own normal dulcet speaking tone. He spread his arms. "Welcome, visitors, to the time-lost city of Atlantis." A pod of twelve mermen with a rainbow variety of muscular bodies and tails swam behind him against the imposing ivory towers capped with golden spires. The sight caused a moment of stunned silence before wild applause and cheers erupted from the audience, accompanied by another unanimous standing ovation.

Betylus smiled and bowed in appreciation before he and his burly mermen were reclaimed by the impenetrable turquoise waters of the Waves of Time. The stage went dark again, only to have a single gold spotlight break the black symmetry into uneven pieces.

Smiling, Zirmis stepped into the spotlight with a damp towel wrapped around his waist, and the wild applause resumed. His forehead was crowned with damp ringlets. He bowed before the spotlight was extinguished.

All I could do was clap and hoot in unison with my fellow audience members. Sure, he was probably a fraud, but I couldn't help being intrigued. As far as how he did the illusion, I was clueless. And beginning not to care. He fascinated me and intimidated me at the same time. He could have his pick of the Atlantean Guards, so I knew I'd never get a chance with him. Still, the fantasy made me hard enough to have to wait until the audience filed out of the auditorium before I could stand up without getting arrested.

Ambling out of the theater, I decided to head straight to my room and go to bed after typing up my observations of Zirmis's performance tonight. Maybe I'd be able to sneak backstage tomorrow.

❖

In my recurring nightmare, Grandpa smiled at my eight-year-old self sitting in the chair beside his bed.

We were in his room at the Memory Care Unit at the Heartland Long-Term Care Facility out on Normandy Boulevard in Jacksonville, Florida. Mom and Dad had brought me there for our usual Sunday afternoon visit. I had been left alone with him as they went off and consulted with the head nurse on Grandpa's condition. He had not recognized us, and he seemed even more withdrawn than usual.

Grandpa and I used to be inseparable. He had been an architect by trade, but magic had been one of his hobbies. He had come to live with us until Alzheimer's disease began picking away at his memory like I did with scabs on my arms and legs. I still felt like it was my fault that he was in a tiny room at Heartland instead of back home.

Everything was fine until two months ago. It was spring break from Mandarin Elementary School and I was enjoying my freedom from homework. Mom asked me to watch over Grandpa while she drove to Publix to pick up a few things.

Grandpa had been sitting on the couch with me. Today, at least for now, he knew who I was. We were watching the animated *G.I. Joe* episode where Lady Jane and the Baroness were having a cat fight inside of Cobra Commander's top secret headquarters.

A trickle of music from the ice cream truck passing outside the house caused Grandpa to look away from television.

"Hey, buddy, let's go get an ice cream cone," Grandpa said. "My treat."

"Okay," I replied. I didn't think Mom would freak out if we got ice cream. But by the time we got outside, the ice cream truck was just passing out of sight.

"Let's go follow it," he told me, heading straight for the garage where his 1995 green Chevy Impala had been parked several months ago. Mom started it on a regular basis to keep the battery alive. She had left the garage open since she was only running a short errand.

"Maybe we should wait until Mom gets back," I suggested. Still, I got in the passenger's side when he beckoned me to.

"Nonsense, buddy. She'll just say we can't go. Now buckle up."

Reluctantly I did as Grandpa asked. Mom was going to pitch another one of her royal conniptions for sure when she found out what we had done. I just knew it. Everything was going fine until we caught up with the ice cream truck. It was waiting to make a turn at the intersection. Instead of braking to a stop, Grandpa hit the gas pedal.

"Hit the brakes Grandpa! Hit the brakes!" I cried out, but it was too late. The Impala collided with the rear end of the truck. My body lurched forward, restrained by the seat belt and cushioned by an air bag.

"Grandpa, are you all right?" I asked. He didn't respond. "Grandpa?"

The air bag blocked my view of him. Reaching out, I felt for his hand. It was felt limp and wet. Startled, I pulled my hand back. It was covered with his blood. I started to scream and was still screaming by the time the paramedics arrived.

❖

Mom didn't pitch a conniption. Neither did Dad. Both were relieved that nobody had been seriously hurt. Grandpa just had a scalp wound that bled a lot.

"It's nobody's fault about what happened, Saul," Dad told me. We were waiting patiently in the waiting room at St. Vincent's Hospital, Mom still hugging me. Her eyes were blotchy from crying.

"I never should have left Dad alone," she whispered from time to time.

Grandpa had to stay in the hospital for a few days for observation. By then, Mom and Dad had told me that he needed more care than he could be given at home. So despite all my pleading and promising to watch Grandpa better, he was admitted to Heartland. We visited with him every day we could.

He hadn't remembered who I was since he got there.

"Hello, buddy," he said, smiling.

"Grandpa, you remember me!" I cried. Despite knowing that he'd probably forget me again in a few seconds, I was bursting with happiness. I had him back for this moment.

"Of course I do," Grandpa replied, smiling. "Now, I don't have much time left, buddy, and I need to give you something. Hold out your hand."

I leaned forward with my hand out and waited.

Grandpa took his white gold wedding ring off and placed it in my open hand.

"Now close your hand."

I did as he asked and waited. His ring felt cold against my fingers.

"Saul, your grandma and I've been talking," he said. I grew scared. Grandma Sarah had been dead for four years now. He couldn't have been talking with her, unless...

"We want you to have my wedding band. You're going to have need of it one day," he told me. "It's the only way you'll be able to prove your heart's true intentions."

He waved both of his hands over my closed one.

"Abracadabra!"

I no longer felt his ring. Puzzled, I opened my hand. His ring was gone.

Grandpa smiled and leaned back against his pillow.

"We'll meet again, buddy. I promise you that. Sarah, I'm ready now."

He closed his eyes and drew one final breath.

"No!" I screamed. I heard nurses running toward the room as the heart monitor flatlined. "No! Wait, Grandpa! Please don't die! Please..."

I woke up drenched in sweat.

Taking a deep breath to calm myself, I threw off the cover and stumbled out of bed. Thankful that no policemen were breaking down the door to my hotel room to see who was murdering me, I took a quick shower and got dressed, placing my pass key in my pants.

"Thank goodness the Flamingo has soundproof rooms," I muttered to myself as the room door closed behind me. Making my way down the hall, I turned right and headed to the elevator alcove, recalling my past attempts to call forth Grandpa's ring with girls and then guys when I realized it was cock I liked. All ended with failure. With any luck, there'd be an empty car that would provide me with a quick escape from the hotel.

Normally I would go out for a run whenever my childhood horror replayed itself in a Technicolor dreamscape, but jogging was out of the question here in the neon landscape of Vegas at one o'clock in the morning. I didn't want to keep getting stopped by policemen and pimps.

Thankfully, there was only one other person waiting for the elevator. He was a tall man dressed in regular jeans and an oversized simple white sweatshirt. Only his hands and face betrayed his dark olive complexion. A bandana hid his hair, and he wore a pair of sunglasses with dark lenses. His whole body tensed as he saw me approach. He stole a quick glance at me, and then smiled in relief.

"Thought you were some tabloid reporter who's been dogging me," he said.

The familiarity of his voice tugged at the outskirts of my memory. Then it struck me who he was. What on earth was Zirmis doing on the floor where my room was? Celebrities staying at the Flamingo were usually sequestered in one of the penthouse suites on the top floor. Or perhaps he was just getting back from a late-night fuck session with one of his Atlantean Guard members.

The vision that conjured made me feel hot and flushed but emboldened me. I no longer saw a potential fraud, just an incredibly handsome man with potential. Sure, he could have anyone he wanted, but we were alone. And maybe I had a few tricks of my own up my sleeve.

Resisting the urge to reach out and remove those ridiculous sunglasses from his face, I decided to hazard calling him out.

"Aren't you Christofi Zirmis?" I half expected him to bolt down the hallway.

A boyishly shy smile played across his thin lips. "The one and only."

My look of utter disbelief over his admission must have been a doozy.

"If you need proof, I could always disappear in a puff of smoke," he teased. "Do you prefer blue or pink haze? By the way, it's not fair that you know my name and I don't know yours."

"I'm Saul." We shook hands as I gave him a nervous smile. "Rather you didn't go anywhere. I mean, I'm just surprised to see you here on this floor. Blue. I like blue."

Oh boy, nothing like being way too obvious. My heart was jackhammering from being this up close and personal with him.

"Best way to distract nosy press hounds," Zirmis said. "It's a bit of stagecraft every magician and performer learns early in their careers."

"Very ingenious and subtle use of misdirection," I said. "While the press jackanapes are camping out on the top floor, you can get a night's rest in your room on another floor."

"Oh, I'm not looking for a complete night's rest."

Playful banter? I was liking this more and more.

"I would have thought a member of your Atlantean Guard could have provided you with any needed distraction."

"Nothing little about them," Zirmis laughed almost hysterically. He quickly sobered up. "I prefer being with a regular guy. Someone who knows how to cuddle and pillow talk till dawn and who doesn't fall asleep after having one orgasm."

I was a regular guy. A regular guy who swallowed hard as the down light announced the arrival of the elevator and the doors slid open with a melodic ding.

"Oh look, it's full up," Zirmis said. He smiled at the single occupant inside. "We may catch the next one…going down."

The guy smirked knowingly as the doors swallowed him up.

"You're joking, right?" I quipped nervously. Damn. Screw journalistic ethics. How I wanted him in my bed. "I'll turn around and you'll disappear in a puff of blue smoke."

Zirmis pulled off his dark glasses and revealed those emerald green eyes that only held sincere honesty in their depths. He pulled up the sleeve on his right arm and offered me his hand.

"See, it's not a fake arm that will detach when you grab hold of it."

I grasped it, and he squeezed my hand with equal measure.

"My room," I told him.

Once inside, I pulled Zirmis into my arms. As our mutual kissing became more passionate, my hands slid underneath his shirt and inside his pants, exploring the firmness of his body. He moaned as my fingers began teasing his ample nipples.

Most of our clothes were scattered on the floor by the time we had moved atop the bed. I paused only long enough to remove his briefs and mine, tossing them onto the floor.

My lips and tongue explored every inch of his body. Zirmis moaned as my tongue teased the tip of his cockhead. I eased as much of his ten-inch, gloriously uncut cock down my throat as I could without gagging. His neatly trimmed red bush brushed up against my lips. He enjoyed having his cock sucked while I gently tweaked his nipples.

His hole tensed when I first penetrated it with a finger. It was tight. So it had been a while since Zirmis had a cock inside him. By the time I had loosened it up with three fingers, Zirmis was begging me to fuck him. I paused only long enough to slide a condom on. Then I placed his legs over my shoulders and gladly obliged him.

He was nuzzling against my chest by the time I fell asleep.

Nearly an hour later, I awoke to the movement of Zirmis sliding out from under my arms. I tried my best to keep my emotions in check. Turnabout was only fair in the universal scheme of things, I supposed. Why shouldn't he use the same method I had employed when I escaped from Simon's bed months ago? I sighed. I think I had fallen in love with him. Sadly, the feeling apparently wasn't mutual.

"I'll be right back, Saul," he promised. His lips brushed against mine. "You're not getting rid of me that easily. I just want to borrow your computer to send a quick e-mail to my majordomo and let him know who I'm with and where. Otherwise he'll unleash the guard to track me down."

My relief at knowing he was only leaving temporarily was suddenly blotted out when I realized my article on him was still up on my computer. But by that time, it was too late. He had read it.

"What the fuck!" Zirmis turned back to me. Anger now raged in those emerald eyes of his. "You're writing an article debunking me? You fucking little press whore!"

He raised a clenched hand as if to strike me. Then his eyes grew wide in astonishment. "I'm a stupid bitch. Now I recognize you. You were there when I one-upped President Cumberland and made a fool out of him." He raised his palms outward. "I'm out of here."

"Wait, no, please, Christofi, wait, please hear me out," I cried, getting out of the bed. He roughly brushed me aside as he was gathering up his clothes.

"There is absolutely nothing you could possibly say that could prevent me from leaving," he said.

Grandfather's last words about his wedding ring now came flooding back to me.

"It's the only way you'll be able to prove the true intentions of your heart," he had told me. Somehow Grandfather had known I would need help in keeping the man I wanted to find out if I loved enough to spend the rest of my life with.

Crying, I got down on bended knee. *Please, please help me, Grandfather*, I silently prayed. Zirmis was just about dressed now.

"Christofi, wait!" I cried before he headed out the door. He glared angrily at me.

"Nothing up my sleeve." Trembling, I closed my left palm.

"Abracadabra!"

I felt the coolness of Grandfather's wedding band in my hand. Zirmis was astonished when I opened my palm.

"Care enough to support a poor, struggling writer who's going to e-mail in his resignation to the editor?" I asked, hoping against hope.

Grandfather's ring went flying as Zirmis bowled into me.

"Only if you teach me that trick," he said. Any reply I wanted to make was silenced with his lips firmly on mine.

MAGIC TAKES A HOLIDAY
RALPH SELIGMAN

Silence spread among the audience as the stagehands hoisted the man-sized cage, now covered in velvet. The only sound in the theater was the squeak of the pulley lifting the cage pull by pull, until its bottom was ten feet above the stage. The lights dimmed and a single spotlight highlighted the red velvet as the cage began to swing, slowly at first, then acquiring a circular motion. One could hear the tension of the rope on the pulley above the cage.

The cage now resembled a pendulum, moving side to side. Someone in the audience coughed nervously. The viewers were clearly uneasy with the motion of the cage and the fact that nothing else seemed to happen. From backstage, someone suddenly yelled, "The rope won't hold!" as the cage slipped down a few inches at a time. Another voice screamed, but before anyone could take action, the cage plummeted to the stage, its four sides collapsing outwardly as the velvet cover billowed down and flattened on the stage. Giorgio the Magnificent was not there!

The audience rose up to see what was lying on the stage. Then, realizing that once again they'd been fooled, burst into thunderous applause. There was no encore, no one to appear on the stage to take a bow.

❖

By the time the cage had lifted off the stage, I was already on my way to my dressing room. I washed my makeup away in the sink and trimmed my goatee and sideburns to an everyday length.

As the theater emptied, I was already in a taxi with a small travel bag, heading toward the airport. I was not going to need much at my destination. Even the clothes I wore would be unnecessary. I had long yearned for this trip. For once, I had no performance schedule to adhere to or rehearse for. For once, I was doing something that I was both hesitant yet excited to do, contrary to my instincts and professional experience.

A successful magician, or more aptly, an illusionist, is adept in the art of control—of not only the props, one's moves and what should be seen or not, but also control of the audience. They, themselves, must feel they have control while being led in the direction the magician wants them to go. In the professional parlance, it is referred to as the art of misdirection, but I consider it the complete opposite. I direct the audience exactly where I want their attention to be.

This time, I was going to relinquish control and leave my fate in the hands of someone else. The mere thought of this caused a stir in my groin, a good indicator that I was about to embark on a welcome adventure the likes of which I had never seen before.

I arrived at the airport with my small bag and a sealed envelope in my hand. Written in a commanding script on the outside of the envelope were the terminal number, the airline name, and the time I was to report at the counter. Until the boarding pass was handed to me, I did not even know my destination. The counter attendant, a handsome man in his mid-twenties, directed me to the airline club lounge, a perk included with my first-class ticket. The man maintained eye contact with me long enough for us both to recognize we were kindred spirits. I would not have minded a short romp with him in one of the mini-rooms inside the club room, but my instructions were clear. No sex for at least one week before the trip. Not having a current companion, it was not difficult; I needed to focus on my last week of performances anyway. Had the circumstances been different, however, that young airline employee would have fit the bill nicely.

I boarded the plane at the assigned time. A comfortable window seat and a glass of my favorite wine helped me feel quite welcome.

My host-to-be must have had a connection with the airline, and must have exercised great care studying the questionnaire I had filled out and sent to them a few weeks ago. I had no knowledge who this man might be, only that the club through which I had "booked" my adventure had guaranteed his expertise and reliability.

The flight was uneventful. I was not very hungry for the dinner that was offered to me. I did not bring reading material with me and the airline magazine offered articles about places I had little interest in visiting. The crossword puzzle was partially, and poorly, completed. I put the magazine back in the pocket in front of me, leaned back, and tried to relax. The pilot startled me awake when he announced our descent and the cabin crew started collecting plastic glasses, aluminum cans, and the poorly folded remains of newspapers. I was almost there.

Leaving the airplane was a cinch, being right in the front of the plane. I only had my carry-on bag with me, so I didn't need to wait for luggage. As I left the security area, I looked for my ride. A dozen chauffeurs stood around with paper signs, folded in half with names handwritten with a black marker. I finally spotted one with a sign with my name. The man was tall and broad-shouldered, sporting a salt-and-pepper goatee. The bill of his cap shielded the bright airport light from his eyes, casting a shadow over them. His uniform was elegant and crisply pressed. I approached him and said: "I'm Gregory Goldlink."

We exchanged pleasantries about the flight and the weather as we walked to the parking lot. "The Master is pleased to know of your timely arrival," the driver said in a deep voice. Once we arrived at the luxury SUV, he opened the back door on the passenger side and said: "We have a forty-five-minute drive to the house, sir. Make yourself at home. There is a package and instructions for you in there," he continued as he walked around the car to the driver's side.

I entered the SUV, sat down, and closed the door. The smooth, black leather seats told me my adventure would be luxurious. No one could peek inside due to the heavily tinted windows—in fact, I could not see what was going on outside either. The engine started and I leaned back in my seat. Across from me were a mini-bar and a leather-covered box. I poured myself a glass of scotch and leaned back. I realized then that the leather-covered box was the "package" the driver had mentioned earlier.

I drew the box toward me and opened it, finding a letter containing handwritten instructions:

> *In this box you will find the only items you will be wearing at the residence. While on your way to the residence, please remove all your clothes, jewelry and other accessories you may have on your person. Be assured that your garments and property will be returned to you at the end of the engagement. Failing to follow these instructions to the letter may result in undesirable consequences.*

This much I had anticipated when I signed up for this adventure. I took off my shoes, my jeans and shirt, followed by my underwear and socks. The temperature in the SUV was pleasant, so I did not feel uncomfortable. My watch and my neck chain went into my travel bag. However, there was one personal item I would not part with. It was a custom-made titanium chain, about three inches long, less than a quarter of an inch wide. An Italian craftsman made it to my specifications.

Each link fit neatly into grooves in the adjacent links, making it very thin. Also each link had two small barbs at each end. When the links are twisted, the barbs lock in, turning the chain into a solid, but light, bar. This bar can be used to pick all sorts of locks, just like wire picks other magicians like Houdini had used before me. Houdini's wife would pass the pick to him as she kissed him before getting tied up and locked and after he was checked for such contraband. I was sure then that I was going to be checked from top to bottom, so I had few choices of where to hide my chain. One choice was between my toes, another, my mouth, but I finally settled to wrap it around the ridge below the tip of my cock, and then covered it with my foreskin. The feeling of the small chain on my cock was reassuring, as it gave me some sense of control.

I reached into the black box and withdrew a leather harness. The smell of the leather was intense and intoxicating, blending in with the strong leather smell of the SUV's upholstery. Not having kept good track of time, I rushed to put on the harness, followed by a leather jock strap. I snapped one of the leather-covered elastic back straps and inhaled through my teeth as the strap bit into my buttocks. It felt right. The codpiece was snug but comfortable. Obviously the list of measurements I had to submit prior to this trip were used to custom-make the leather pieces. I finally buckled the leather gauntlets on my wrists and fetters on my ankles. A black silk robe completed the outfit. I put on the robe, tied the belt and sat back for the remainder of the car ride.

We arrived forty-five minutes after we had left the airport. By that time I had helped myself to another shot of scotch, so I was comfortably relaxed.

The SUV slowed down and turned into what I thought was a long driveway or side street. I heard a garage door open, then close as we stopped. The driver came to the door on the side where I sat and handed me a leather mask. I put it on, surrendering my final sense of independence.

The driver held my arm firmly as I stepped out of the SUV. The garage floor was cold. He led me a few paces forward and said: "Two steps up." We walked several feet forward on tiled floor and then he coaxed me to turn sharply to our right, as if we turned around a wall. A door opened in front of us. The driver, steering me like a car, announced, "Ten steps, down. Banister to your left." I stepped down and mentally counted the ten steps, feeling the smooth, cold floor at the bottom. We continued walking to the far end of what seemed like a basement.

I sensed the presence of someone there. A pair of hands grabbed my wrists and attached the D-Rings to hooks attached to chains. Then my ankles got attached the same way. Leather straps crossed my back from wrist to ankle. The sound of the chains rattling prepared me to be hoisted off the ground by my arms and legs. There would be neither a false bottom nor a trapdoor for me to make an exit now.

I was being lifted, spread-eagled, to what I assumed would be waist height for someone standing by me. Once I was in place, I felt a slight rocking back-and-forth motion. I heard someone walking around me, assessing me, gauging me. This had the right effect and my cock was getting hard in the confines of the jock strap. I could feel the pressure of the chain at the head of my cock, both reassuring and frightening at the same time. *Did I make a mistake keeping it on me? Will I be discovered? Will I be punished?* That thought made my hardening cock jump. I felt my face reddening.

A hand pulled the metal ring in the middle of my chest, putting me off balance, startling me. The hand released the ring and moved over my chest hair, first slowly, then in increasing circles. The hand was large, slightly calloused, firm and strong, tugging at different parts of my pelt, causing goose bumps all over, making almost every hair on my body stand up on end and hum.

The circles widened and the fingers brushed my nipples, first the left, then the right until they were hard. My tormentor took note of this and started focusing on my nipples. He stood behind me, his leather-encased groin brushing the top of my head. The musk of the leather and his crotch were strong. I craned my head back to take in more of the odor and lick that package.

"No! Not yet," a deep, masculine voice commanded me. He resumed pinching my nipples, pulling them up, then releasing them, alternating from one to the other. As the intensity of the nipple play increased, I arched my back each time, inhaling through clenched teeth. The coolness of the inhaled air contrasted with the heat of the excitement that caused me to sweat.

The man then began working his way down my chest, tormenting me with the smell of his crotch in my face. He rubbed his hands over my chest, grabbing tufts of hair, pulling them up and releasing, making me gasp in the delicious pain.

He was already past my belly button and was reaching toward the jock strap. I suddenly realized that I still had the chain lodged beneath my prepuce. Even though my cock was hard, the hood of skin still held against most of my cockhead, but any manipulation down there would cause the chain to be revealed. It was my turn to exclaim, "No! Not yet!"

"Who gave you permission to talk, slave?" asked the man gruffly.

"Sorry, sir," I responded.

"Very well, slave," he continued, "we'll save that for later. I'll be back." He left me wanting more; high and dripping wet, I heard him go up the stairs. He called for the driver and told him to go into town to get some supplies. He closed the door and I heard the latch click. I knew my being left alone was a deliberate move to increase my sense of isolation and subjugation.

A few minutes later, I heard the muffled footsteps heading to the garage. Then I heard the engine start and the sound of the SUV pulling out. The garage door closed and for once, I was all by myself.

I had prepared for this moment. When I attached the gauntlet on my right hand, I had flexed my muscles so that it would have some wiggle room when relaxed. With some effort, I was able to slip my hand out of the gauntlet. I pulled the mask off my eyes but left it on my head. My body suddenly tilted down on that side, since I no longer was held up by the chain there. I pulled with my left hand and regained my balance. Then I bent my right knee. Reaching with my free hand, I released the chain off the fetter on that side. Carefully I reached to my left ankle and did the same. Supporting myself with my legs, I was able to free my left hand.

I finally was able to check out the space where I was confined. As I had guessed, I was being kept in a basement. The floor was finished concrete. Aside from the sling I had been attached to, I saw other instruments of pleasurable torture. A horse, like the kind one would see in a high-school gym, was there, and next to it I saw a wooden structure shaped like a large X, which I recognized as a St. Andrews cross with leather cuffs attached to the ends of each section of the cross. A rack of whips and cat-o'-nine-tails was on the wall. In one corner, I found a small bathroom with a shower, and next to it, an army cot with a pillow and woolen blanket. The shower was inviting, but it would expose my insubordination. Some other things I did not even recognize were spread all around the room, including a large red toolbox, the kind you might see at an auto mechanic's shop.

With some trepidation, I climbed to the top of the stairs and studied the doorknob. It was a simple indoor lock. I dug into the jock strap, pulled back my foreskin, and removed my chain. I felt the phantom sensation of the chain around the corona of my penis. My cock twitched at the thought. I twisted the chain in two segments, creating a C-shaped tool that I placed between the face and the strike plates, hooking the improvised tool around the latch assembly. I grabbed an end in each hand and pulled. The latch disengaged. I pulled the knob, but it just moved a bit. There was a hasp with a padlock on the other side.

I looked at the hinges. There were only two. I grabbed the pin of the top hinge and, with some effort, was able to pull it out. The bottom pin came out more easily. I pulled the door toward me, leaving it attached only to the hasp and padlock.

To my left was the door to the garage. Ahead of me was a well-appointed kitchen, with track lighting and chrome. It was very manly and modern, large enough to prepare food for a big group. Beyond the kitchen was a large dining room with a glass table for up to twelve place settings. The living room was furnished with comfortable furniture and a black grand piano. On the wall above the piano, next to a window, was a black shadowbox with a silver magic wand inside. I got closer to it and saw a plaque that read: *To Neptuno in Gratitude for Contributions to the Craft.*

Neptuno? Neptuno was my Master? He was a well-known magician whose specialty was underwater tricks. One of his trademark openers was pulling out a live lobster from a top hat. His name was Preston Cipriano, and his stage name used to be Presto Poseidon, until the movie *The Poseidon Adventure* forced him to change his name to Neptuno in the early 70s.

I wondered if it was simply a coincidence we shared the same fetish, but it could not be. He must have gleaned my identity from my profile, so I was curious as to why he was drawn to me. Did he want to use my sexual interests to extract some trick information, or was this simply fate? Did he like my quirks and interests? I had to let this adventure play itself out. Even though my aim was surrendering myself to him, at least I had a slight edge.

I explored the mansion a little more. It was quite interesting and well taken care of. Obviously he's done well for himself, but I did not find much in terms of props or magic information. I figured he must have a separate workshop, perhaps elsewhere on the property. I headed upstairs and, through a window at the landing, I was able to see the main gate and driveway leading to the house.

I suddenly saw the gate opening. I rushed back down to the basement, closed the door, and replaced the pins in the hinges, putting myself back on the sling. Thinking my cock would soon be otherwise engaged, I placed my chain lock-pick inside my mouth, between my gums and my cheek. On it I tasted my own dick sweat. I smiled, thinking, *I taste good!*

I heard the garage door open as I finished reattaching my right hand to the sling. All I needed now was to slow down my breathing and stop the sling from swinging. Both were skills I'd practiced many times for my performances.

I heard the kitchen door open and the noise of paper bags being carried in.

Neptuno didn't come back to the basement right away, but at length he unlocked the padlock and the door opened with squeaking hinges. I panicked, thinking that the door did not make any noise the first time I was brought down to the basement, but I remembered the door was already open when I took the steps down.

Blindfolded again, I could only hear what was going on around the basement. Something heavy was being moved toward the center of the room. Then someone came to me and unhooked me from the sling, feet first, then arms, and guided me to the center of the room. I recognized the mixture of body and leather smell, and knew it was my Master. I felt my way around and touched the suede top of the horse. My Master positioned me over it, facing down, securing my arms and legs to its legs. My feet barely touched the ground, and all I could do was grab the legs of the horse to brace myself for what was to come.

My Master reached around my chest and continued the tit play he had started earlier. He kept twisting my nipples back and forth, as if he was trying to find a shortwave station on an old-fashioned radio.

He let go of my tits and turned his attention to my ass. He kneaded my cheeks deeply, softening the muscles, making me feel relaxed. Without a word, he quickly dispensed full-palm slaps, alternating from cheek to cheek. I winced at the stinging pain and cried out loud.

"Quiet!" he commanded. I tried to keep my mouth shut. I felt my ass cheeks glowing red from the slaps, when I sensed a soft caressing from one cheek to the other. A light breeze cooled my buttocks, but it was not meant to last. The cat-o'-nine-tails' light brushing of my ass gradually turned to rhythmic whips on top of the already sensitive skin. I yelped a few more times, again being admonished to be silent.

The whipping was followed by more kneading of my red-hot cheeks, and then he crouched down behind me, his knees popping audibly. With both hands on my ass cheeks he spread them apart, exposing my eager pucker. He licked gently around my hole, starting with wide circles and gradually getting closer to the center. His tongue met my hole and worked itself in, deeper and deeper each time. I relaxed both my body and my ass, bending my knees slightly, allowing him to enter further with that delicious tongue. With his free hand, he snapped the elastic band of the jock strap, tormenting and delighting me.

The trance state I reached while he was rimming me, ended suddenly when he rose from the crouched position. He unsnapped his leather codpiece and worked his dick to a hard erection, his balls slapping against his upper thighs. Meanwhile, his other hand worked his fingers into my asshole, first one, then another, until three fingers were being pushed in and pulled out in a steady rhythm.

His fingers were soon replaced by a thick cock. Even though he had primed my ass, first with the tongue, followed by the fingers, entering proved to be difficult, so he let a bit of drool drop from his mouth directly on the tip of his cock and the penetration was resumed. With his spit mixing in with the pre-come oozing from his slit, he slowly began to enter me. Little by little his dick worked its way into my ass.

Years ago, when I was just coming out and still a virgin, I asked my friend Ted, who was more experienced than I, how one enjoys anal sex. I knew I wanted it, but I did not know what to expect. I also wanted to know how big a dick one could accommodate up one's ass. I had experimented sticking a finger up my hole, but one finger was not a hard cock.

Ted explained it to me this way: "Think of the largest turd you've ever squeezed out your butt. Most penises are not as wide or long as that. Also think of the pleasure you had as that turd came out of your rear end. Now multiply that pleasure by hundreds of strokes, in and out of your hole." He paused as I thought about it, and the more I did, the wider the smile on my face became. Ted nodded, realizing that I knew I was ready to get fucked.

Neptuno kept a steady beat as he plunged his hard cock into my ass. At times he slowed down the rhythm. I involuntarily raised my butt off the horse, trying to make the cock enter me deeper than he intended. He did not go for that. Control over the fucking was his. Instead of driving his dick deeper in me, my ass cheeks got more slaps and whippings, while the head of his cock teased my pulsating hole.

My cock strained inside the leather jock strap. I could feel my pre-come being squeezed between my lower belly and the jock strap, both trapped on top of the leather-covered horse. Each time Neptuno plunged his cock into my ass, my nuts pushed against the base of my cock, making it pulse to the same beat. My hard cock rubbed against the leather jock strap, and I had to hold back my moaning as I felt I was nearing orgasm.

Neptuno was not about to come in my ass. He pulled out,

leaving me wanting more. I took a deep breath and relaxed on top of the horse. My head hung down and I could feel the blood rushing down to it.

My Master walked around and pulled my hair, forcing me to lift my head. His groin was close to my face, forcing me to smell his essence as well as my own. I opened my mouth carefully so as not to drop the chain I was hiding in it, sticking out my tongue to taste the cock that, just moments ago, was plunging into my ass. He took a step back, away from me, to make me reach further for the prize.

To my surprise, he turned around and backed his hairy ass into my face. Without further prompting, I licked the firm ass mounds he presented to me. He must have bent forward, or was leaning on something to keep his balance as I worked my tongue over those fuzzy cheeks. One of his hands reached around and opened up the ass crack and my tongue found the sweaty, salty bottom of the crack. Even with my limited range of motion, I worked my tongue up and down the crack, allowing myself a little bit of control at the same time I exercised my self-control.

I wanted to eat that asshole but I took my time, knowing that was exactly what he wanted me to do. I was both smelling his essence and driving myself crazy with desire to please him. Slowly and steadily I worked my tongue through the crack, once in a while nibbling at the hairy ass, understanding through his moans that that was exactly what he expected from me. I took a final run of the crack and found his asshole. It was relaxed and ready to be worked on. I took on the task with great pleasure. My tongue explored his hole for quite a while until he stepped away from me.

I was able to lower and rest my head again. I heard my Master puttering around the room. Soon enough he released me from the horse and moved me to the St. Andrews cross. One by one my limbs were attached to its four arms with my back against the cross.

Some other noise from the room told me he had opened the toolbox. He played with my tits until they were hard and erect, then he attached a tit clamp with rubber tips to my left nipple, putting some pain and pressure on it. Neptuno let the chain attached to the clamp hang free, and I felt the downward pull on my chest. He then grabbed the other end and worked it through the inside of my jock strap behind my ball sack. The other clamp, going back up, was attached to my right nipple. The chain was taut enough that any time I moved, or was made to move, both my nipples and my groin enjoyed some tension. The pain was remarkably delicious until Neptuno started plucking the chain like a harp. I arched my back with each painful tug, the chain pulling on both sides, drawing my nuts up. My cock jumped.

My Master retrieved the cat-o'-nine-tails again. He did not whip me, even though I was ready for more punishment. Instead he threaded the handle behind the chain on my chest, its weight pulling on my nipples and my groin.

I had not noticed earlier that the St. Andrews cross was attached to a mechanism. I heard the grinding of a handle being turned behind me, then suddenly the top of the cross lurched forward. I moved gradually downward while the base of the cross stayed fixed to the ground. I could not tell at what angle I was when the cross stopped moving. I only knew that the weight of the whip pulled on my tits and nut sack.

Neptuno came around and rubbed his crotch on my face. I opened my mouth to allow him to do as he pleased with me. My tongue moved out to taste him. He allowed me to lick his nuts, then his cock. I tasted my own ass on his cock. I leaned forward as far as my tethers allowed me and took the head of his cock in my mouth. I ran my tongue over the engorged bulb, tasting the sticky pre-come gathering at the slit. Concentrating on the rim of the head, I ran my tongue around the sides of the bell-shaped cockhead. I tasted the edges, going around from the underside, where the two ends meet below the slit, then around in one direction and back in the opposite one. I could tell my Master was enjoying this. I felt him pull forward as he arched his back to allow me more access to his dick.

He stopped me briefly to unsnap my codpiece and free my cock from the confines of the leather jock strap. My cock and balls dropped naturally and the cooler air of the room made me realize how sweaty and pre-come-covered my dick had been. Rather than dampening my excitement, the coolness stimulated me, and my cock rose to a full erection, aided by the pull of the chain from my nipples to my ball sack. In turn, the weight of my fully engorged cock pulled further on the chain, and so the tension on my tits increased.

I felt Neptuno's rigid cock brush my lips again and I opened my mouth wide. As soon as his dick entered my mouth and rested on my tongue, I embraced it with my lips and let him slide in and out, but not fully remove it from my mouth. I slid my tongue over the veiny cock as it pistoned inside me. I felt the tip reach my throat and I angled my head up a bit to accommodate it. It slid freely past my uvula, and I moved my head to the rhythm of his thrusts, doubling the friction on that meaty shaft.

My Master picked up speed in his lunges inside my mouth. I felt his right hand reach behind my head to give him leverage. His left hand was pushing down on the handle of the whip, making the chain pull down on my nipples and up on my cock. As his rhythm increased, my own cock reached its top hardness. His panting matched my own breath.

Just as his come started to surge out of his cock and into my mouth and throat, my cock also reached its climax and, without any direct contact other than the chain, I came, spurting more than I had ever had before. His loud moans blended together with my muffled whimpers. Gradually his thrusts slowed, but he kept his cock inside me, allowing me to taste the last drops of come and to run my tongue all over the softening meat.

He finally pulled his dick out of my mouth, his breath slowing down. I craned my neck toward where I assumed his face might be and said, "Thank you, Neptuno!"

"Be silen…what did you call me?" he yelled.

I gulped, still tasting him in my mouth. "Neptuno, Master, sir," I replied.

He silently unhooked me from the St. Andrews cross, holding me so I would not drop to the ground as he steadied me on my feet. I felt his eyes intently focused on me as he pondered what to do with me. He slowly lowered me and had me kneel on the floor. I could feel a wet spot by my left leg. Must have been my own come.

I heard him pace the floor back and forth. I knew what he must have been feeling. For someone like either one of us, where full control of our environment and all its parameters is crucial, having something go amiss can be distressing. All we can do is try to regain our sense of balance and go on with the performance. He and I entered this tableau with specific aims and expectations. My thoughtless need to gain some control had now disturbed his role in this sex-play. The small chain buried by my gums exposed my shame.

"I'm sorr—" I tried to say.

"Hush, slave!" he answered gruffly, still trying to regain composure. I lowered my head demurely. He left the room, closing the door behind him. I stayed as I was, kneeling on the concrete floor, feeling the come drying on my leg. I do not remember for how long I remained in that position. My legs were getting numb and I shivered from the coldness of the floor when the door at the top of the stairs opened again.

I heard Neptuno's footsteps coming down the stairs again, approaching me. He removed the clips from my nipples and the chain from under my scrotum. Then I felt a warm blanket being wrapped over my shoulders. Neptuno grabbed my arm and helped me rise from the floor. I was unsteady on my feet, so he reached around my back with his arm and walked me toward the steps.

We walked up the stairs one by one. I counted them in my head to make sure I did not miss any. The way he led me made me realize we were headed to the kitchen. He sat me at the kitchen table.

"There is a mug of hot coffee in front of you," he said. "Do you take cream or sweetener?" I shook my head. I reached blindly for the mug, grabbing it by the handle. My hand shook as I lifted it up. I steadied it with my other hand and brought it to my lips. It was hot and delicious, and I had not realized how thirsty I was. After a few small sips, I held it in my hands, letting the warmth seep into me. I turned my head toward where I thought Neptuno was sitting and nodded gratefully.

"I release you from your bondage now, Gregory," he said. "Close your eyes. I will now remove your eye mask. The kitchen light is bright." I closed my eyes as instructed. I opened my eyes gradually and looked in front of me. At first I saw a pair of broad shoulders, framed in a leather harness like mine, a hairy chest, matted by sweat. Then I looked up. A smiling, benevolent face with a well-trimmed salt-and-pepper goatee greeted me. The chauffeur!

"Yes," he said, as he noticed the incredulous look on my face. "It was me all along."

"What about the different voices?" I questioned. He went ahead and explained that besides being a magician, he also had been a ventriloquist. We talked for what seemed hours, having coffee and sandwiches he had prepared for us. He asked me how I managed to discover his identity and I answered truthfully, showing him my little chain. He laughed heartily once he realized that we had both been tricked by the other.

I spent that night in his bed with him, making love and sharing each other fully. The following day he drove me to the airport, with me sitting in the passenger seat of the SUV next to him. He kept my leather gear in his basement dungeon, asking me to promise to come back.

I did.

Magic Lantern
William Holden

Wednesday, October 17, 1742

"Go fetch the constable." A cloud of smoke encircled us.

"What do I tell him?" Avery reached for my hand. His fingers trembled against mine. "We cannot admit to having our hands involved in such things. People will see us as witches, using such magic in the way we did. We could be executed!" His voice rose with fear.

"Tell him only what you must and no more." I turned to him. "Do not worry yourself so. I shall take care of things here before your return." I laid a gentle kiss upon his lips, smiled, and then walked into my master's bedchamber. The front door closed, leaving me alone to think of how we would conceal the truth.

Tuesday, October 2, 1742

"Mr. Apperwhite, where have you been? It's been a fortnight since I've heard word from you. There has been business that needed tending to that I have not been trained for."

"Mr. Ayers, you are nothing more than my apprentice, an extra hand that I must say I did not ask for. Therefore, I do not feel it necessary to report to you where my travels take me, or for that matter the purpose of my travels. You will be good to remember that, young man."

"I merely was expressing my concern..."

"You need not worry yourself. I have traveled a great distance to obtain these items." He placed a large bag upon the table. "The contents of this bag will assure my future. With the new knowledge I have obtained, I shall become the most respected man in the Church of England—and the most feared among the citizens of London."

"May I inquire as to what you have acquired that can bring about such a state?"

"You may do so, but you will not receive a response from me." He glanced at the door as if waiting for someone. "You may be my apprentice, Mr. Ayers, but this is one project of mine you shall have no part of. Is that understood?"

"I beg to differ, sir. I am here to serve you and to learn from you. If you do not allow me that—"

"Do not lecture me on my obligation to you!" He slapped my face. If it hadn't stung my skin to such a degree, I would have laughed at his feminine manners. "I will not be insulted by my servant. If I had not promised your father an apprenticeship for you, I would have you out on the street for such behavior." He tossed the bag over his shoulder. "I shall be in my workshop. Do not interrupt me."

"Yes, sir." I watched Mr. Apperwhite's hips sway as he left. I wanted nothing more than to shove my erect prick between his ripe, unused buttocks. I disliked everything about Mr. Apperwhite, but something about him gave rise to such devilish thoughts that I worried I might act upon them out of frustration or, worse, true desire. My prick rose as I thought of his body, stripped and exposed. I unlaced the front flap of my breeches and coddled my prick, needing to give myself a moment's pleasure before he beckoned me for a gin. A fire built in my belly as I imagined the scent and taste of Mr. Apperwhite's body.

I pulled my stiffened prick out of my breeches, rubbing its clear, sticky excitement over the thick trunk. I closed my eyes imagining his mouth upon me, bringing me to the height of pleasure. Perspiration gathered in the pits of my arms as the need to release my secret lust reached a feverish pitch. A knock came to the door. My prick responded with a quiver as it receded in my grip. I laced up my breeches and wiped the excitement off my hand. The knock came a second time as I reached the door.

"Is Mr. Paine Apperwhite at home?" a man several inches above my height inquired. His outfit, while properly fitted, did not speak of a high social standing. He was a bit rough around the edge, something my personal taste in men could appreciate.

"May I inquire as to what it is you wish to see him about?" My eyes skimmed over his tight fitting outfit.

"My name is Avery Winfield. Mr. Apperwhite hired my father to print these broadsheets. I was instructed to bring them here the moment they had dried." His eyes sauntered down my body. I felt my prick rise with his attention.

"Please, come in." I stood back so Mr. Winfield could enter. Before I could close the door, Mr. Apperwhite bounded up from the depths of his cellar.

"Are these the broadsheets?" He snatched the package from Mr. Winfield's arm. "Your father never disappoints." He opened the wrapping. "These are perfect." Without so much as another word, Mr. Apperwhite returned to his workshop.

"Do you know what is printed on the broadsheets?" I questioned, curious to know what Mr. Apperwhite was up to, but more importantly allowing me additional time with this handsome beau.

"I am sorry to say that I do not." He walked over to the bureau. "This is dreadfully rude of me, but may I help myself to a gin?"

"You may as long as you pour one for me."

"If you wish to know what the broadsheet says, why do you not just ask?" He handed a cup to me.

"If only it were that simple. Mr. Apperwhite has forbidden me access to his workshop or any knowledge of this new project, which he says will make him the most feared man in all of London."

"That is quite a statement. I suppose I could ask my father…"

"I must leave this house at once!" Mr. Apperwhite appeared almost out of nowhere carrying the large sack on his back. "There is too much at stake to leave my project in my own home for prying eyes to see. Mr. Ayers, look over the house and take care of any business that arises. I will not leave word as to where you can reach me."

"You mustn't be serious?" I looked at Mr. Winfield, who was staring at me in a curious way.

"There is nothing left in the house that your eyes cannot see." He opened the door and left the house without further comment.

"Here is your chance, Mr. Ayers." Mr. Winfield smiled.

"My chance for what?"

"To find out what Mr. Apperwhite is up to." He took the empty cup from my hand. "Let us follow him and see where it leads us. It shall be wicked fun." He bowed mockingly as he held my waistcoat for me. "I do hope that you will allow yourself to call me by my given name: Avery. I do hate formalities."

"I would like that, Avery. You may call me Heath." Our immediate closeness brought with it the heady scent of his body. My prick spat against my linens from the release I never granted it.

"Shall we?" Avery opened the door for me. I exited with him at my side. "I noticed when he left that he went toward the Thames. There he is," Avery whispered in my ear.

"Do you think he is going to St. Paul's?" I questioned as we turned on Fleet Street.

"He is acting with great regard to privacy. I would not think the cathedral would be the most suitable place." He rested my elbow in the palm of his hand. "There he goes." He pointed into the moonlit street. "He's heading in the direction of Covent Garden. What business could he possibly have there at this time of night?" We quickened our step to keep pace with him.

"You blokes need'n a fuck?" A woman three times our age came upon us without warning. "I would guess that the two you have fine tools. I might consider doing both at one time." She laughed as she threw her arms about us. "Which one is gonna get under my cover and which one gets their tonker up my arse?"

"It is not in either of our interest to fuck your diseased muff." Avery pushed her off us. "Whatever you believe your talents to be, they would not pleasure us in the least." Avery put his arm about my shoulder, quickening our pace.

"Fuck'n naffs." She spat as she lashed out with her foot, striking Avery in his buttocks. "I can get finer men than you to fuck." She continued to curse us even as we disappeared down another street.

"We've lost him." I stopped, looking about. "Fucking whore."

"Let us continue our walk. It's a beautiful night; perhaps we might be able to locate him."

"If you don't mind, I need to make water before we continue. I shall only be a moment." I walked further into the alley as I unlaced my breeches. The crisp night air caressed my prick, causing it to stiffen in my hand. I shut my eyes and took a deep breath, enjoying the feel of the hot stream spouting out of me. As I squeezed the final drop out, a new sensation arose from that region. I opened my eyes to witness Avery's hand cupping my affairs.

He shook his head as if to silence me before I had uttered a word. He gripped my prick. It swelled from his attention. He smiled as he laid a kiss upon my lips. He coddled and stroked my eagerness, causing such dizziness that I almost lost my footing.

"Oh, you devilish man." I gasped between breaths. "I have not been touched to this degree in years. Keeping this pace you will surely hasten my impending release."

"I shall not let you spill your seed on this sodden ground. Please, shove that hefty prick up my ass before any more time passes." He released my prick, turned around, and dropped his breeches. He grabbed his knees, thrusting his hips in my vicinity. "I beg of you to fuck me and do so with abandonment."

"You have the most perfect ass in which to play." I fingered him as I knelt behind him. I spat and then licked his ripe ass. The heavy masculine odor of his body made me drunk with desire. His body quivered against my face as I drew small circles over the tight puckered skin. I nibbled upon his ass, letting the dark brown hair that lay across it draw damp lines against my face. "I shall carry your scent with me for days." I groaned as I stood up. I stroked my prick before plunging it deep inside him.

"Mother of mercy, the sting of your prick is grand." His voice echoed down the narrow street. "Yes, my beloved, fuck me, fuck me. Oh, you are such a beast."

I felt his body shift as my thrusts of insertion reached a feverish pace. I clutched his narrow hips to steady his footing as the fire grew in my belly. His buttocks tightened about my throbbing prick, squeezing and priming me till I could no longer refuse my body's demands. I leaned into his body as the first of my release escaped me.

"Oh, yes, Heath. That it is. Fill me with your hot seed." He reached between us and fondled my tender satchel, sending pleasures of delight through my body of the likes I had never known. The second and third release exploded into him, wetting our connection. I filled him to such an extent that the final release immediately sprayed forth from his ass.

I pulled my softening prick from him. He turned to kiss me. I ignored his advance and fell to my knees, where his stout cock met my mouth. I sucked him with my lips and tongue until his prick spasmed, shooting thick ropes of his pearls into my mouth. I swallowed as another rush of his heat replaced the first. I continued to suck him as his firmness receded. His prick fell from between my lips.

"You, my handsome new friend, are quite the devil yourself." Avery smiled before he kissed me. His tongue slipped into my mouth and licked the remnants of his own spilt seed. He broke our embrace. "I would desire nothing more than to take you home and do to you what you have just done to me, but we are still in search of Mr. Apperwhite, are we not?"

"Yes, but I would not know where to begin to look for him." I laced up my breeches, enjoying the lingering moisture on my prick. We made final adjustments to our outfits and then took up the search where we had left it. The night was alive with whores and drunkards, arguing, pissing, and fucking. Fires built to keep the less fortunate warm against the chilling night rose up on nearly every corner of the city. "We have been out here for hours." I stopped, turning toward Avery. "We are no closer to finding Mr. Apperwhite than when we started."

"Perhaps it was a foolish gesture after all." Avery pulled me into a shadowy corner of the street. He peered around the corner and then kissed me several times with quick, light lips. "I would very much like to spend the night with you, if I am not being too bold."

"You are not." I smiled and kissed his cheek. His rough whiskers pricked my skin. "You shall come home with me. My bed is quite adequate for two." We stepped back onto Russell Street with a new purpose, one that had nothing to do with Mr. Apperwhite.

Tuesday, October 16, 1742

"Good evening, my love." Avery winced as his voice echoed through Mr. Apperwhite's house. "My apologies for speaking out so intimately." He gave me a quick kiss.

"No need for that, Mr. Apperwhite is not at home." I poured two gins.

"Where is he this evening?"

"The same place he's been for the past fortnight, though the location still is unknown to me." I lit my pipe. "People are starting to talk his name in the streets, some expressing fear while others pride. Whatever he is doing cannot be good."

"It is not. A former acquaintance told me that Mr. Apperwhite has been touched by the Lord, giving him the gift of foresight. Several of my former intimates have been to his shop, Phantasmagoria, and now will not speak to me unless it is to condemn me for my unnatural desires. If I can be permitted to speak my own thoughts, I believe it is not the Lord that has touched him, that he is in fact using magic to perform his deeds."

"Did your acquaintance know of his location?"

"He would only confirm that his shop is indeed in Covent Garden." He finished his gin as he lit his pipe.

"Then we must go out at once." I opened the door. "This time we must find him before he destroys us all." The streets were quiet this time of night, though we knew Covent Garden would be alive with the scavengers of the city.

"Heath, one moment." Avery broke the silence that had fallen around us. "Over there." He pointed down Bow Street to a large group of individuals drinking by a fire.

"What about them?"

"Perhaps they know of Mr. Apperwhite's whereabouts. If he is as dangerous as we believe he is, then they must know of him, or perhaps can tell us if they have seen him." We walked toward the group, keeping a friendly distance between the two of us. "Excuse us, gentlemen, oh, and pardon me, m' lady. We were wondering if you might be able to assist us."

"Gentlemen?" One of the men grumbled as he looked about the group. "I do not believe there has been a gentleman in our presence for some time." He chortled. The others followed. "Covent Garden is not a wise place to find oneself lost in, especially at night. You don't know who you might run into—"

"Pardon me, sir. We are not lost," Avery interrupted, a move I was not quite comfortable in him doing with these drunk and obviously rough men. "In fact, I live not too far from this very place. We are just looking for an acquaintance of ours. Most people in this city know of his name: Mr. Paine Apperwhite. We hope that perhaps you know of him or his whereabouts."

"I do not like to get involved in other people's business. Though I doubt business at this time of night is what you were conducting." The old man looked toward the others. "Do any of you know of this Mr. Apperwhite?" They all murmured that they did not. "You boys do not belong out here at this time of night. Go home to your warm, well-appointed homes before you find yourself floating in the Thames." He spat. It dripped down his chin. He wiped it with the back of his hand.

"You fecker." The woman spat before turning toward us. "You boys pay him no mind. The man you are looking for came through here less than an hour ago. He was talking gibberish that the Lord speaks to him and that we all had to pay for our sins. He headed down Bow Street."

"Thank you, m' lady. You have been most kind." I bowed to her. Avery followed my lead.

"Mind your own business, you old cunt," the man grumbled as we took our leave.

We walked along the deserted streets with no sign of activity within any of the shops that we passed. The moon, like a resentful lover, played peek-a-boo behind the clouds, covering us with intermittent darkness. I was close to giving up on this near-impossible search when I noticed the flickering of light coming from a shop window. I pulled on Avery's arm, directing him to follow. We crept up to the window and peered inside. Translucent cloth hung from the ceiling, cutting the room into three dissimilar spaces. Through the shroud of curtains, we could see Mr. Apperwhite sitting in the rear of the shop with a small painters brush clutched in his hand.

"What is causing the light from the candle to be so vibrant?" I spoke what my mind questioned.

"I cannot say for sure. It is almost as if his worktable is sheeted in glass, but that would be most impractical, and not to…he's getting up." Avery's whispered tone rose in excitement. "Come, this way." He grabbed my arm, pulling me into a narrow space between the two buildings just as Mr. Apperwhite opened the door.

I heard his footsteps approach our direction. He stopped just a few feet from where we hid to light his pipe. "My magic show will soon be the end to all sin in this city," he muttered to himself as he continued down the street.

Avery peered around the corner before stepping back out onto the street. He pulled me with him. "I fear Mr. Apperwhite is sick in the head. First he talks of God and of the Church, and now he has turned to dark magic. Perhaps we should not get involved."

"That is precisely why we must." I walked toward the shop, pulling out a heavy brass key.

"What are you doing?"

"We are letting ourselves into his shop to see what dangers he is up to." I turned the key. The lock disengaged. I opened the door. "Are you not coming inside with me?"

"I shall stay outside and notify you if he returns." He lit his pipe and anxiously looked down both sides of the street.

"I will not be long." I closed the door and turned my attention to Mr. Apperwhite's shop. The candles still flickering in the back of the room convinced me of Mr. Apperwhite's intention of returning. The reflected light of the candles drew me toward a small area in the back of the room. Hidden behind the drapery was an odd metal box that looked to be some sort of lantern. Lying next to the box were twenty or thirty rectangular pieces of glass. I stared in disbelief at the exquisite, yet terrifying scenes painted on the surface of each piece. Naked men portrayed in sodomitical acts with blood pooling at their feet. Other images depicted a faint yet discernible face with an expression of contempt blended into the clouds. Beneath the stare of the clouds lay naked men struck down by fire from the sky. My concentration was broken as Avery came running into the shop.

"Heath, he is coming back!" Avery stopped and stood beside me as his eyes caught the painted images. "What in the Lord's name…" The front door opened, startling us both. "We must go," Avery whispered to me. Over here." He took my hand and led me behind the drapery to an open area that contained a small table and two chairs sitting opposite each other. Avery pointed to the corner, pulling me behind several wooden shipping crates. Mr. Apperwhite escorted a young man into the room.

"Please take a seat, Mr. Archer." Mr. Apperwhite motioned to the chair that sat with its back toward the box and painted glass. "As I mentioned to you earlier, I have been touched by our Lord and have been asked to speak on his behalf, to free you and others like you from your sins." Mr. Apperwhite took a seat across from the stranger.

"If it were not for the five pounds you paid me, I would not be here. I am not a sinner." Mr. Archer looked about the room with uncertainty.

"Lying is looked upon to be the beginning of a sinful life. Those who partake cannot be trusted. They must look upon their vile ways, even by force. The images I saw when I looked upon you in the street tell a different story, one of growing lust of the worst kind, one that is never named but must be tonight in order to free you from the sodomitical intentions that lay in your heart. You have ungodly desires for other men. You betray the Lord that has given you this life. That is why I have brought you here this evening: to show you the visions that the Lord has blessed me with, visions of your future if you continue these unnatural ways."

"I have never—"

"Silence!" Mr. Apperwhite's tone echoed his irritation. "I can see the deceit in your eyes, Mr. Archer. It is time to renounce your sins against the Church of England. Purify yourself in front of me, and the Lord." Mr. Apperwhite extinguished the candles as he stood. Avery and I looked at each other in fear and curiosity as Mr. Apperwhite slipped behind the drapery. A light flickered behind the drapes, and then the room, which housed Mr. Archer, glowed with the reflected light. "This is what the Lord sees when he looks upon you, Mr. Archer." An image suddenly appeared against the drapery that lined the back of the wall. I could see the fear rise in Mr. Archer's face as he looked upon two men fucking.

I let out a small gasp as I watched the image of the two men begin to move, as if they were fucking right before our eyes. Mr. Archer began to whimper as the blood in the image began to drip, pooling about the men's feet. A third image appeared over the others. Fire fell from the sky, striking the two men down. That was all Mr. Archer could take.

"Please, no. Yes, yes I have the lust inside me. Please, Lord, forgive my sinful desires." He fell to the floor and wept. "Surely there are worse sinners than I, as I have yet to act upon these desires. Please, have mercy upon my tainted soul. Give me the strength to stand tall once more." His body trembled as the light from the lantern dimmed.

"You have witnessed firsthand the blessing that the Lord has given me." Mr. Apperwhite knelt down beside Mr. Archer. "Come with me. Let me take you out into the night and show you the world through the eyes of a new man." Mr. Apperwhite steadied Mr. Archer as he rose to his feet. "The Lord has forgiven you, my friend. It is time for you to repay his kindness and locate more men to save." Mr. Apperwhite looked behind them. A stiff rise in his breeches told a different tale, a tale of hate, and betrayal against us all.

"Yes, thank you. I will bring thousands to your door and help you spread the word of truth." Mr. Archer wiped his tears as they fell to a troubled smile across his lips.

"We must find a way to put an end to this." I stood from behind the crates once the two men were gone. "I cannot let these innocent men fall for such trickery."

"How are we to stop him?"

"Mr. Apperwhite may be seen as an upstanding citizen of this city, but I am sure that he has the same desires within him that he is condemning. He is striking out against us out of fear of his own lustful desires." I walked over to the drapery that hung on the back wall. With a few forceful pulls, it fell to the floor. "Fold this up. We're taking it and all of his magic with us."

"What will we do with such things?" Avery shook the lightweight fabric and folded it onto itself. "We know nothing about performing such magic."

"Perhaps not, but I have a few tricks of my own." I gathered several of the pieces of glass with images he had not used upon the poor man. Others I smashed against the table. "Mr. Apperwhite will be in a rage when he returns. We must be ready for him." I grabbed the magic lantern as Avery opened the door. We ran through the streets as quickly as the rutted ground would allow. Our clothes were wet with perspiration by the time we entered Mr. Apperwhite's home.

"I will get his gin ready." I spoke through heavy breaths as I set the magical items on the table.

"What are you placing in his spirits?" Avery questioned as he came upon me.

"Opium," I answered as if nothing was amiss.

"How did you obtain…?"

"A God-fearing man I have never been, nor will ever be." I smiled at him. "I use to introduce a little of this to men I wished to have. Even the most righteous man would give up his ass to me once his mind became clouded. Opium is one of the reasons my family forced my apprenticeship upon Mr. Apperwhite. They are paying him great sums of money to bring me into the Lord's graces."

"I see it is not working."

"It is not." I winked at him. "Now, let us take the items we have gathered into his bedchamber."

"I am starting to believe that you have a plan; one that I would be most interested in hearing."

"I will tell all, but as we work. We have little time to get this right."

By the time we had finished, Avery was quite versed in my plan. We adjourned to the parlor to wait on Mr. Apperwhite's arrival. Our time was limited for immediately upon taking our first sip of gin Mr. Apperwhite stumbled through the door, full of liquor and fury. He had either lost or misplaced his wig. His shaved head glistened with perspiration. He slammed the door as he stared about aimlessly. His eyes caught our gaze. Our quiet demeanor must have been too much for him to take, for he soon took his rage upon us.

"You fucking naffs. I am out being robbed while the two of you are living well off my money. You, Mr. Winfield, you are not even in my employ, and yet here you sit with Heath in my home!"

"Mr. Apperwhite!" My voice rose as if the news of the thieving was a shock. "You were robbed? They did not hurt you, did they?" I ran up to him, pulling his waistcoat off his shoulders.

"Do not touch me!" Spittle flew from his lips. "Pour me a gin before I throw you both out of my home."

"Of course." I followed his orders and poured a large glass of gin. "What did they take?" I asked as I handed him his drink. "Did you contact the constable?"

"They ruined me is what they did." He took a long drink from the glass. "Months of study and wealth were destroyed. If I find out who has done such heinous acts against me, I swear on the good Lord's name…" He paused to finish off the gin. "No…no, I could not…did not contact the constable. This is a personal matter, one that I must take care of without involving anyone." He looked at me with half-shut eyes. "Do not stare at me with that expression. Get me another drink." He threw his arm out, pushing me toward the cabinet that held his precious liquor. I refilled the glass and handed it to him, anxiously awaiting the effects to become evident.

"Mr. Apperwhite, you are not looking well." I looked over at Avery. He approached us. "Perhaps you are falling ill to something. Shall I send Avery to the apothecary?"

"And what, waste more of my precious money?" The glass slipped from his hands, shattering against the floor. "I do seem to be a bit light in the head. Perhaps it is the events of the night that are causing such dizziness."

"Mr. Apperwhite, let us help you to your bed, where you can lie down. I am sure by morning you will feel better." I took hold of his arm. "Avery, would you be so kind as to help me?" We guided Mr. Apperwhite to his bed.

"What do you think you are doing?" Mr. Apperwhite inquired.

"I am removing your shoes to make you more comfortable," Avery responded as he placed the shoes on the floor.

"Theodore?" Mr. Apperwhite questioned. "Oh, how I miss your friendship."

"Who is Theodore?" I whispered to Avery. He shook his head in response. "Mr. Apperwhite? It is I, Heath Ayers."

"Oh, Theodore, you wretched scoundrel. Are you wishing to lay your hands on me?"

"We shall be in the parlor if you need us," I replied without acknowledging his question." I took Avery's hand, leading him out of the room.

"He does not know who we are."

"That is my hope, for I do not want him to remember us come morning. He must believe without any doubt that what he will be suffering this evening is the Lord's doing, not ours."

"The tricks that you have devised to play against his mind are quite telling about you."

"They are no worse than the trickery and magic he was performing in his shop. We are creating visions against one man, while he was attacking hundreds with his evil ways."

"Please, do not feel I was striking out against you with my words. On the contrary, I am becoming quite fond of you. I only hope that once this is done, our intimate friendship may continue." His faced flushed with a romantic hue.

"I believe there is a greater purpose at hand. I want nothing more than to have you by my side…"

"Oh Lord, why have you befuddled me so?" Mr. Apperwhite shouted from his room.

"It is time we begin our own Phantasmagoria." I delivered a kiss to Avery's lips before slipping into the darkened room and hiding behind his armoire. I opened the back of the lantern and lit the oil lamp. The light in the room shifted as the flame cast shadows against the walls. The effects of this magical lantern excited and troubled me at the same moment.

"Lord? Is that you?" What more do you wish of me?" Mr. Apperwhite spoke out as he watched the shadows dancing about him. He reached out in all directions as if trying to touch them.

With a forceful whisper, Avery pushed his voice into the room. "Paine Apperwhite, you have done a great injustice to me. You must suffer for your sins."

"No, please, Lord. Everything I have accomplished, I did in your name."

I slipped the first of several pieces of glass through the front of the lantern. The soft cotton of the drapery behind Mr. Apperwhite's bed took hold of the image. A face appeared out of the magical clouds. Mr. Apperwhite noticed it immediately. He knelt upon his bed. His hands stretched out in front of him. I slipped the second image into the lantern. The image of a naked man came into view, his prick erect with need as he looked upon another man in the distance.

"Why are you forcing me to witness another man's body?" Mr. Apperwhite fell back against his bed. "Is it not a sin, to look upon one man's prick? Why, Lord, are you tempting me with these images?"

"You must give in to your secret desires, Paine Apperwhite." Avery moved to the edge of the bed to bring his voice closer. "No longer fear what you believe to be a sin. I shall show forgiveness toward you."

"No, I cannot do as you request, my Lord. Please do not ask this of me."

I slipped the third image into the lantern, bringing the two men together in an embrace. I shifted the three pieces of glass, giving the illusion of movement. Mr. Apperwhite's hands trembled as he tried to unbutton his blouse. I slipped the third glass out of the lantern, replacing it with a fourth—the men in the act of sodomy.

"God have mercy on my soul!" Mr. Apperwhite panted as he tore into his blouse. He sat up in bed, tossed his tattered fabric to the floor before unlacing the front flap of his breeches. He pulled out his prick, which was thick with need. He petted and coddled it as he stared at the trickery we had created.

"Is it time?" Avery came to me.

"Yes, he is ready." We moved to the foot of the bed. We embraced each other. We kissed in what most would call unnatural ways. Mr. Apperwhite looked upon us. He leaned back against the bed. He pulled his breeches from his legs, kicking and panting like a ferocious dog. The heat of his body in the stagnant air of his room surrounded us. I quickly pulled the images of the two men from the lantern. Mr. Apperwhite, noticing the shifting light, looked behind him, then again toward us.

"The Lord hath delivered unto me the men from my vision!" He unlaced his undergarment, exposing a mat of tight, curly black hair covering his chest. His hand once more returned to his erect prick. He fondled himself as we stood before him.

Avery kissed me as I let my undergarment fall to the floor. He cupped my ample affairs with both hands as his tongue slid down my neck. He nibbled, then bit my tits, sending a ball of fire through me. I gasped his head to support my weakening knees as he moved his tongue down my body, licking the perspiration off my near hairless body.

"Yes, yes. Take his prick within your mouth. Suckle it like a newborn baby would a mother's tit!" Mr. Apperwhite begged through heavy breaths. "Oh, you heavenly devilish men, let me witness that which I cannot experience."

I nearly lost my footing when Avery took obedience from Mr. Apperwhite, taking the entire length of my prick into his mouth. I gasped as he squeezed his throat, milking additional quantities of my clear nectar from the folds of skin that covered my prick. I took it upon myself to use his mouth as if it were his arse. I fucked his face, stopping briefly with each forward thrust to hold his face against the damp, musky hairs of my sex.

"You rascals are delivering such fits of pleasure. If only the Lord would allow me to touch your nakedness, to lay greedy kisses upon your lips, and to taste your seed as it spills from your full spouts."

Avery looked up at me with a mouth full of my glistening prick. He smiled as best he could. I knew what was running through his mind: that we needed to fulfill Mr. Apperwhite's prayers and let him have the two of us. Avery looked up at me. I nodded my silent approval as my prick fell from his mouth, leaving a thick rope of my early release dangling from his chin.

I walked over to the side of the bed. Mr. Apperwhite appeared shocked by my closeness, or perhaps it was the fact that he could interact with us. My eyes stole glances of his nakedness. Thick white ropes of his pleasure lay drying amid the hair of his body. He had spilt his seed without a murmur. Without a word of my intention, I drew circles about his erect tits. His body quivered from my caress. Avery came up beside me. He ran his fingers up the inside of Mr. Apperwhite's leg. I witnessed Avery fondling his own heavy satchel as he did the same to Mr. Apperwhite's much smaller affairs.

"My Lord, you devilish men can touch me!" He gasped. "Thank you, Lord, for bestowing these pleasures upon me." He reached out and touched my prick. It moved from his advance. He pulled his hand away as if scared my prick had a mind of its own. His hand came away damp with my excitement. He slipped his fingers into his mouth and tasted of me. "The nectar is sweet upon my tongue. Do not waste more time with your temptations. Do it now. Favor me with the thrust of your insertion." He tossed his arms over his head and raised his legs, offering me his glory.

I pulled his hips toward the edge of the bed. He squealed with delight from my handling of him. I stroked my prick to its fullest length before piercing Mr. Apperwhite's ass. His screams of painful pleasure echoed through the room as I sank my prick into the deepest levels of his body. I gave no warning to my thrust, nor did I delight in tenderness.

His ass gripped my prick, causing such a fire in my belly that I thought I might release. I pulled my prick out, rubbing my excitement over his tight, hairy entrance. He wiggled against me. He begged for me to fuck him. I obeyed. I thrust myself inside him without pause. His moist, hot hole caressed my throbbing member as it penetrated him.

"Yes, that is it. Fuck me like a whore!" Mr. Apperwhite yelled as tears fell from his eyes. "Oh you bring such devilish urges to me, I do—" His words ended as Avery shoved his prick into Mr. Apperwhite's mouth, using it as if it were a willing ass.

I looked upon my most cherished friend as he straddled Mr. Apperwhite's face. My own thrusts grew in force as the fires burned for him. I leaned against Mr. Apperwhite's body until I had him doubled over upon himself. I inhaled the acrid scent of Avery's ass. I slipped my tongue between his perspiring buttocks. The taste of him invaded my mouth, causing such rapture that until today I had never known. I nibbled on the puckered skin of his ass as my tongue made quick little darts inside him. His flavor and scent caused my own delirium. I knew my release would be upon me soon, for no man could withstand such delights as I and not give in to the ultimate of natural urges.

My satchel tightened against the pounding of Mr. Apperwhite's ass as I reached the final barrier before pleasure. I groaned with such force against Avery's ass that his buttocks shook against my face.

"Yes, my devoted love," Avery bellowed when I shoved my tongue into him as the first release of my seed shot through my throbbing prick filling Mr. Apperwhite with my need.

Mr. Apperwhite's muffled yells of excitement vibrated against the two of us, sending great waves of pleasure through our connected bodies. I fucked Mr. Apperwhite harder as another release drew near. As my spunk gushed forth for a second and third time, my wails of pleasure against Avery's ass brought forth his own release.

"Mother of mercy," Avery screamed as I felt the rush of his excitement expel from his body. Mr. Apperwhite's gurgling moans escaped his parted lips as he drank of Avery's hot flow. I pulled my tongue from Avery's ass and straightened my body. I withdrew from Mr. Apperwhite's ass as a final burst of seed shot from my prick. Even as I ended, Avery would not give in. He continued to fuck Mr. Apperwhite's mouth. Thick rivers of his pearls ran from the edges of Mr. Apperwhite's lips.

Mr. Apperwhite gasped for air as the prick slipped from his ragged mouth. His body, covered in a thick cover of perspiration, shook and trembled. I walked to where Avery stood. I kissed him, letting him taste the remnants of his own ass that still lingered upon my tongue. Mr. Apperwhite lay in a state of calm; he was still breathing, but there was no sign of his waking. I took Avery by his hand and led him out of the room, closing the door behind us.

Wednesday, October 17, 1742

I awoke to the light of the morning upon my face and Avery's body curled about mine. I lay listening to his slumber as his warm breath beat against my neck. I did not want to disturb my handsome friend, but knew we should check on Mr. Apperwhite.

"Good morning, my love." I rolled over and kissed his lips. He stirred and then opened his eyes. A smile rose across his face.

"Good morning to you." He returned my kiss as his hand slid down my body. He wrapped my prick in his hands and coddled me until I was stiff with need.

"We must wait for that." I held his hand as my prick spat its morning tears. "We should dress and see if Mr. Apperwhite has risen from his troubled sleep." I tossed the sheet off our nakedness, letting my eyes witness the joy of Avery's body damp with the night's perspiration, stiff with his own desire, and covered with the softest hair I had ever touched. With reluctance I pulled myself from his embrace. "You may wait here if you wish." I pulled the gown over my head. Its soft silk fibers fell about my body. "If I find Mr. Apperwhite still asleep, I shall come back and let you bring me off." I leaned over the bed and kissed him.

The air of the house felt different as I walked through the parlor toward Mr. Apperwhite's bedchamber. I rapped upon his door and waited for a response, and when none came I took it upon myself to open it. My eyes alit upon a sight I had not expected.

"Avery," I called out. "Come quick." I could hear his bare feet against the floor as he approached.

"My Lord." Avery came to a sudden stop next to me. "What has he done?"

"It appears Mr. Apperwhite was more troubled than we knew." I stared at his naked, lifeless body as it hung from one of the beams near the ceiling. He swung gently over an overturned chair beneath his feet.

I pulled my pipe from my gown and placed it between my lips.

THE MAGICIAN'S ASSISTANT
LOGAN ZACHARY

A ndrew, most magicians' assistants are female. You can apply, but…" the perky female voice said on the phone.

"What time is the audition tomorrow?" Andrew looked at himself in the bedroom's full-length mirror and turned from side to side to see how his tight leather pants hugged his legs and ass. They fit him like a second skin, sleek against his tan torso. His arousal grew along the left side of his fly, showing his religion. His big, thick religion.

"Your interview will be the last one of the day at four thirty. Don't be late," she warned.

"Is there anything I need to bring or prepare?" He smiled a white, even grin in the mirror.

"Do your best tricks? I don't know what else."

"I thought I was assisting the magic tricks."

"You are the distraction for his sleight of hand. Eye candy and misdirection."

He ran his hand down his bare chest with its fine pattern of hair over each muscled pec, down his sculpted abs, and through the thickening fur. He looked into his amber eyes and winked at himself. His sun-bleached hair flowed in waves of unruly cowlicks.

"I'll work on that."

"Good luck, and we'll see you tomorrow." She ended the call.

Andrew walked to his closet and pulled out a black dress shirt with ornate stitching and smiled. He was ready and knew what he had to do. He knew what tricks he would bring to his audition, and this pirate shirt might help. His eyes glowed with excitement in the bedroom light. Hopefully, his new career would take off tomorrow.

❖

The next day at four, Andrew stood offstage as the last girl tried to catch the gold rings Aleksander Armstrong threw to her. One bounced and rolled offstage. Another rolled around and around on the floor, making the metal hum as it finally came to rest. The girl looked to be sixteen years old, dressed in a pink leotard with a pink skirt that stuck straight out in all directions.

A few people sat scattered around in the audience of the theater and avoided eye contact with each other for fear of laughing. Aleksander held the last two rings and clicked them together. He released one, and as it fell, they hooked together. His free hand rubbed his forehead. Fatigue and frustration made his eyes hurt; dark circles made them appear to sink into his face.

Sweat beaded on the girl's forehead as her face burned with embarrassment.

"Next," Aleksander called.

The girl fled the stage and brushed past Andrew, almost knocking him over.

Andrew walked to the center of the stage and stepped into the spotlight. "I'm Andrew Dayne, and I'm here to be your new assistant." He struck a pose and waited. The black shirt was open across his hairy chest, and the lace that ran from eyelet to eyelet hung loose. His black leather pants highlighted all of his attributes. High-top black boots covered his feet, making him look like a modern-day pirate.

Aleksander stared at him, his eyes drinking in every detail. A faint smile curled the corner of his mouth. He had never worked with a male onstage before, but this man sizzled. His eyes burned bright and a halo seemed to circle around his body. He'd have to learn how he made the spotlight do that with black clothing. It was amazing.

"Have you performed magic before?" Aleksander's eyes narrowed.

"I have studied magic for years in many guises."

"If you have studied so extensively, why don't you want to be the magician?" Aleksander walked around him on the edge of the spotlight's circle. He inspected every inch of the man.

A dazzling smile crossed his lips and showed perfect white teeth. "I haven't found the perfect partner yet, and I don't need to be the center of attention. My skills speak for themselves."

"Do you expect equal billing? Like Penn and Teller?" Aleksander paused behind him, checked out his perfect butt, and continued around.

"This is your show, and I'd be your assistant. If you wanted my name in lights next to yours, who am I to argue? But I am willing to earn what's right, not demand it."

"You sound pretty sure of your skills." Aleksander stood in front of him, nose to nose, and looked him in the eyes.

Andrew met his gaze and held him there. The air between them tingled, charged like before an electric storm. The energy flowed over the men and grew as the hair on their bodies stood on end.

Aleksander broke the silence. "What tricks are you able to perform?"

"I can do anything you want." Andrew felt a stirring in his pants. As he breathed, he felt his arousal swell and push down his pant leg. He tried to maintain eye contact as not to call attention to his groin. He longed to see his effect on Aleksander.

Sensing Andrew's excitement, Aleksander inhaled deeply and felt his own body start to respond. A musky male mix of exotic spices and midnight filled the space. "Let's see what you can do." He walked to the edge of the stage and picked up the lost ring, along with the one someone had placed on the end. He spun suddenly and threw one to Andrew.

Andrew caught it without a blink. Another ring flew at his head, and it was suddenly in his other hand. The next one flew low to the stage, and his foot flipped it up and he caught it between the two, linking all three together. The last two rings whizzed through the air. Andrew raised the chain of three, and the two clinked onto each end.

Aleksander came over to the spotlight, and Andrew handed the rings to him. "Impressive. The rings locked for you." He looked at the chain and pulled on them. All five gold rings remained linked. "What else can you do?"

"What would you like?" Andrew whispered in a low and sexy tone.

"Surprise me," Aleksander cooed back.

Andrew stuck his hand in his tight pants pocket and pulled it out. As he opened his fist, a burst of light flashed out of it and a ball of fire rolled and flamed in his palm. It spun faster and faster as it rose and hovered about his hand. His amber eyes glowed with an unearthly light, and his blond highlights blazed like the sun. Even the hair on his chest glowed with solar rays.

Aleksander reached into his pocket and did the same trick.

Andrew tossed his ball to Aleksander, who did the same. The flaming orbs spun faster and faster, the light intensified and burst into a shower of sparks that rained down over each man's hand, not a single hair singed from the falling display.

Those in the audience clapped. Andrew looked out into the audience. He had forgotten they were even there. He smiled and gave a slight bow. Aleksander stepped in front of him, blocking him from view.

"What else can you do?"

Andrew drew his hand up along Aleksander's leg, barely touching his aroused bump. "I can pull a rabbit out of"—his finger traced along his shaft—"a hat. Card tricks, catch bullets with my teeth." He smiled a big toothy grin.

"Hey, Aleksander, is this going to be much longer? It's been a long day, and I think we've seen enough to make our decision," called Matt Singer, his manager. "And, Andrew, I think we'd like to see more of you."

"Would you like to see a lot more of me?" Andrew teased Aleksander.

Aleksander spun around and fought the flush that he could feel rising up his neck. "You guys can head home. I do agree with you, Matt. I think Andrew has been the best assistant of the day."

Andrew reached forward and caressed his ass.

Aleksander tensed his butt cheeks, and his voice rose. "I would like to see more of Andrew onstage," he turned and lowered his voice, "and off." He reached back and grabbed Andrew's hand before it did any more damage. "Could you stay just a little bit longer? I have one more trick I'd like to try."

Andrew's eyes widened. "I would love to stay." He continued to hold Aleksander's hand.

The scattering of people left the theater. As the door slammed shut, the men onstage headed to the right wing.

A huge square shape was draped with a blue satin curtain. "Have you seen the water chamber of death?" Aleksander asked as he pulled the sheet off the glass tank filled with water. "I usually go in and my assistant has a curtain that covers the tank as we switch places."

Andrew looked at the top of the tank and felt along the cool, damp glass with his hand. "Is there a trapdoor?"

Aleksander smiled and winked at him. "Do you trust me, and better yet, do you believe in magic? Real magic?"

Andrew's amber eyes glowed. "I do, do you?"

Aleksander cocked his head to the side. "Do you...are you...?"

"What?" Andrew challenged him with his stare.

Aleksander pulled off his shirt over his head and tossed it to the floor. "Let's try this one now." His skin was smooth and pale, and his body looked sculpted. He unbuckled his belt and unzipped his fly, revealing black square-cut shorts underneath. He kicked off his shoes and stepped out of his pants. A healthy bulge filled the pouch in his shorts.

Andrew licked his lips as he scanned his new boss's body from head to swelling head. "I'm not sure..." His voice trailed off.

"You have the job, you know that already. This will be fun, our first training session." Aleksander bent over to remove his socks. His tight butt stretched the shiny cotton material and hugged his assets.

Andrew almost reached forward to caress the beautiful sight.

Aleksander turned and looked at him. "Well, are you going to strip down too? We don't want your clothes to get wet, do you?" He raised his eyebrows in question, but the suggestion took on another meaning.

Blood rushed into Andrew's loins, stretching the leather tighter. "Maybe we should start by pulling a rabbit out of a hat."

Aleksander laughed. "You're my assistant. You said you know magic." He stepped to face Andrew, feeling his hot breath on his face. He unlaced the rest of Andrew's shirt and exposed his hairy chest. "I can feel it in your heart."

Andrew's flesh burned where Aleksander touched him. His heart rate increased, blood thundering in his temples. Pain from the pressure in his pants made him step forward to relieve some of the tightness.

Aleksander slipped the pirate shirt down Andrew's arms and watched it float to the ground. It folded itself on the way down and landed in a neat pile. His blue eyes glowed to green as he seemed to take control of Andrew.

Andrew's boots kicked off easily and settled next to his shirt. "I'm not sure."

Aleksander's hand touched his bare chest. "It'll be fine. This is one of the highlights of my act. Seeing your hot body, wet and floating inside, will get the audience on their feet. It'll get me..."

"Get you what?"

He smiled but didn't answer. Touching the side of Andrew's face, he climbed the ladder to the back of the water tank and opened the lid. "I wish I had warmed the water. You should take off your pants."

"That will be a problem. I'll leave them on."

"Suit yourself." Aleksander opened the lid and pushed it back. He sat on the edge of the opening and dangled his feet inside. "Brrr. Once I'm inside, you need to close the lid and then step on top of it.

I'll knock on the glass three times and you pull the curtain up over your head. Take a deep breath and hold it."

"What do you want me to do? How does this trick work?"

"Just do as I tell you, and I'll do all the work."

"But don't I need to do something?"

"Just close the lid, stand on top, and pull up the curtain and count to three." With that, he jumped into the tank. He sank to the bottom and then floated. As his feet touched, he opened his eyes and smiled at Andrew. He pointed to the top of the tank and then to his wrist. *Hurry*.

Andrew watched as a bubble came out of his mouth and rose to the surface. He thought of removing his leather pants, but there wasn't time. He scurried up the ladder, his long toes clutching the steps as he climbed. At the top, he pulled the glass lid back and sealed the tank. He leapt on top of the platform and centered himself. He looked around and found handholds on the curtain rod. He pulled it up to his waist and looked down between his legs.

Aleksander floated beneath him. He reached through the water and tapped on one of the sides.

One.

Andrew lifted the curtain over his head as high as he could, sweat running down his side from his hairy armpit.

Two.

He inhaled deeply as tap number two sounded beneath him. He smelled his own scent of sweat, damp leather, and excitement. Closing his eyes, he clamped his lips together.

Three.

Suddenly, Andrew was the one inside the tank, soaking wet and floating in the cold water. He almost inhaled a mouth and noseful of water, but instead, he counted.

One.

Two.

Three.

And then Andrew found himself standing back on top of the tank, dripping. Exhaling the air in his lungs, he dropped the curtain and watched it fall. He looked down at his wet, bare feet and saw

Aleksander pushing up from the bottom of the tank and grabbing at his throat.

Andrew hurried off the top of the tank. His bare feet slipped, and he almost fell. His toes curled around the rung as his fingers worked the latch, but the metal didn't release.

Aleksander pounded on the glass as huge bubbles of air escaped out of his mouth.

The latch wouldn't open.

Andrew slid down the ladder and stood looking up into the water chamber of death. Aleksander struggled to breathe. He looked around and saw a huge pipe wrench, picked it up and lifted it over his head, ready to smash the glass.

Aleksander waved his hands. *No.*

Then Andrew understood: if he broke the glass, all the water would rush out, and as it expelled onto the stage, Aleksander would be cut to shreds. He dropped the wrench and leapt to the small ledge alongside the tank. He placed his hands on the glass and motioned for the magician to do the same.

Aleksander sank to the bottom of the tank and struggled to hold what breath he had left. He placed his hands on the glass inside in the same place as Andrew's outside.

One.

Two.

Three.

Skin touched skin, and Andrew pulled Aleksander out of the water tank. A wall of water followed him, but as he emerged from the tank, he gasped for air and spat out a mouthful of water. He stumbled and collapsed into Andrew's arms.

With the water and the extra weight, Andrew's feet slipped, and he fell to the floor, pulling Aleksander on top of him. Pelvis to pelvis, the men rubbed against each other as they rolled on the ground. Their fingers were intertwined as they finally came to a stop.

"What did you do?" Aleksander spattered into Andrew's face.

"What did you do? I could have drowned."

"You could have drowned? I was the one in the tank. What did you do?" Aleksander released Andrew's hands, but kept his hips pressed down, holding his captive to the floor. He ground into Andrew and his cock, still semi-erect, grew. He felt Andrew's arousal swell against his. "I was outside of the tank and as I started to rescue you, I found myself back inside."

"You didn't tell me the trick."

"But you did a trick of your own, didn't you?" He thrust his pelvis and ground it in a circle, hard-on to hard-on, warming their quickly chilling bodies.

Andrew shivered.

"We should get those wet pants off you and warm you up. There's a shower over here too." The magician pumped against him one more time and pushed up to kneeling. He stood and held out his hand. "I'll show you where we can warm up." Aleksander led him through the maze backstage and to a narrow staircase that descended to the dressing rooms.

Aleksander pushed open the door bearing his name and picked up two thick towels as he headed to the shower. He pulled off his wet shorts and tossed them in a plastic bucket. He turned to Andrew and held out a hand. "Do you need some help? Wet leather is hard to get off." His erection bounced as he bent. "With that raging inside, it may be difficult."

Andrew unbuttoned his pants and worked the zipper, but he wasn't able to get them down.

"I told you." Aleksander pulled on the wet leather and revealed a rounded hip. Andrew's thick pubic bush came into view, as did the base of his thick cock. He pulled on the other leg and revealed more penis. With the pressure removed, his dick swelled even more. One more tug and his pants peeled down his legs. Andrew's cock flipped up and slapped him in the mouth.

The wet tip shot out a pearl of pre-come that landed on his lower lip. Aleksander licked the salty-sweet and swallowed. He stuck out his tongue and licked the mushroom end of Andrew's dick. More clear liquid poured out and flowed over his tongue as he swallowed him inch by inch.

Andrew looked down and touched the side of Aleksander's face.

Aleksander noticed the goose bumps over his body and slowly let the massive dick slip out. He held the pants until Andrew stepped out of them, then he picked them up and slung them over a chair back. "This way."

The shower stall was huge, and steam flowed as soon as the water was turned on. Andrew stepped into the spray, feeling the heat warm him. Aleksander watched as the water cascaded down Andrew's body. His golden brown skin glistened in the water and his hair was plastered to his skull.

Andrew tossed his hair and shook his head, sending water around in all directions. Time seemed to slow, making the gentle rainfall hang in the air as Aleksander stepped into the hot spray. A bar of soap appeared in his hand, and he lathered Andrew's back. He worked lower and lower, foam running down between his muscular butt cheeks.

Andrew pushed back as Aleksander's fingers explored his crack. His erection strained, waiting and wanting to get washed next. Aleksander spooned Andrew, running his hands up his torso, through the hair, and over the pecs. Andrew's nipples rose as his palms rolled over them.

As Aleksander felt Andrew's aroused points, he pinched them, teasing them into sensory overload. His cock slipped between Andrew's legs and rubbed against his low-hanging balls. The men rocked their hips back and forth, more lather and foam flowing between their bodies. Large blobs splattered on the floor and swirled around the drain. The hot spray and steam warmed both men, but the friction between their bodies added more steam and heat all on its own. The soap disappeared, and Andrew reached forward and turned the water off.

"Towel?" Aleksander wrapped a fluffy one around Andrew's shoulders and started drying himself.

They dried off, but Aleksander's raging hard-on stuck out proudly despite his work to hide it. "Can you do magic?"

Andrew stopped rubbing his hair and looked deep into his eyes. "Isn't that why I'm here?"

"No. Real magic, not sleight of hand or dime-store tricks."

"Smoke and mirrors and black wires?" Andrew's erection still stood. He walked into the dressing room and lay down on the floor. His penis flopped on his belly. "Get over here."

The magician walked over and straddled him. He dropped his towel and looked down at the naked man. "What did you want to show me?"

Andrew closed his eyes and extended his arms out to the side. When he opened them, they glowed. "Up."

Aleksander laughed, watching his own cock rise. "Like that's magic?" But then he realized his whole body was rising off the floor. "Andrew, what are you..." Energy flowed around the room and swirled around the two naked men. The hair on their bodies rose as if static electricity crackled over them. Aleksander bent his knees in an attempt to lower his center of gravity, but he still hung in the air.

As Andrew looked up, he saw a perfect ass—smooth and nicely shaped. A thin line of black hair ran along its crease and darkened at the tender opening. He took a deep breath, motioned with his arms, and began to rise, water dripping from his wet back. He grabbed his erection and stroked his shaft several times. Pre-come oozed out of the tip, and he smeared it over the massive head. His body rose higher until it was between Aleksander's legs.

Aleksander's butt shifted as Andrew's wet hard-on slipped along his crack and teased his hole. He bounced gently up and down on his cock and felt its slippery tip. Aleksander pushed backward, driving himself onto the invading member. He brought his arms out to the sides and extended his fingers. Sparks and tingles shot out of the tips, and he moved more freely, now under his own control, not Andrew's.

With the extra weight suddenly lifted from his aura, Andrew's body bored into Aleksander's with more force. The tip of Andrew's cock entered and spread Aleksander's tight opening. More man-made lube poured out of him and slicked up the spot. Andrew reached up, grabbed the floating pelvis, and guided it down onto him.

Aleksander threw his head back as another thick inch entered him. "Use your wand on me, deeper, harder."

That was all Andrew needed. He thrust again, and his fat tip popped into the tight hole. Once past the muscle, the rest of his shaft entered easily. His thick bush tickled Aleksander's tight ass floating above him. His balls slapped the muscled cheeks. He pulled his hips down and almost came out, only to drive back into Aleksander, all the way to the hilt, again and again, faster and harder.

The force of his thrusts pushed Aleksander forward, but instead of going up, he arced forward as if on an axle. His head spun down as Andrew's pelvis pushed up. Andrew fell backward, and his body tensed as his head neared the floor, but only his hair brushed the ground. As he spun upward, Andrew extended his spine, making both men rise another foot into the air.

Aleksander matched the force of his rotation even as he pushed his butt back onto Andrew. He only slowed the spinning of their circle, making it an even and steady loop. Their bodies moved as if on the Zipper ride at the state fair, spinning head over heels as Andrew plowed into Aleksander. Their magic blended together, working in tandem as they spun in a sex circle.

Andrew drilled into him deeper and harder, and Aleksander rode him as they flew through the air. Who needed smoke and mirrors? They had each other, and their magic flowed. The room glowed a warm gold, with sparks of red and explosions of orange. Purple and pink pulsed in time with their hearts, faster and faster.

Andrew reached between Aleksander's legs and found his magic stick and started his own spell. The power in the room swelled, pulsating in time with the magicians' thrusts and heartbeats, growing and quickly filling the space. Energy flowed around them like an electric storm, streaks of lightning zipping from the two men who were now one.

"Faster, harder, faster, harder," both men chanted as their pleasure grew and grew.

One charged particle ran across Andrew's ass as he thrust into Aleksander, adding more stimulation to both men's exposed nerve endings. Pre-come flowed out of Aleksander's cock and over Andrew's hand. As his hand became coated, energy from the room made the lubricant glow brighter and brighter with each stroke. Andrew brought his hand to his lips and licked the salty-sweet fluid, and at the taste of charged ambrosia, his balls let loose, exploding out of his wand into Aleksander.

Aleksander's body acted like a lightning rod, conducting all the power and energy, making it flow through him and out of his dick. The energy bolt shot out with the creamy load as it splattered across Andrew's chest. A blob entered his open mouth and surged through Andrew's body and out of his fleshy wand, only to be recycled in the loop of magic.

Faster and faster the pleasure entered one man only to exit and enter the other. Both men spun in one direction as the energy flowed into the other.

Andrew yelled as all of his body's nerve endings screamed.

Aleksander came again and again. The room glowed brighter and brighter, blinding the magicians. He gasped and shot the rest of his load, one huge deposit, and the room exploded with light.

The theater shook and trembled, then fell into total blackness.

❖

One by one the lights came on, glowing dimly yellow, casting faint shadows and turning into enough light to reveal the room. Two naked bodies lay huddled together on the floor, neither one moving. As the last light came on, the men gasped and exhaled a huge breath.

"What was that?" Andrew asked in a whisper.

"How the hell should I know?"

"You're the magician."

"And you're not a man of magic? Where did you learn your tricks?"

"I've always been able to do them."

Aleksander waved his hand around his totally trashed dressing room. "You've always been able to do this?"

Andrew laughed. "Not this, but, you know, magic. All I need to do is think, and it happens."

Aleksander wasn't able to move. His body was drained.

Andrew rolled onto his back and scanned the room. "Look

what we did." Clothes were tossed around the place, hangers were embedded in the walls, and papers slowly floated to the floor in a slow circle; bottles were shattered, makeup streaked the mirror. All the furniture was pushed into the corners, as if tossed by a tornado. "Where are my clothes?"

"Who's going to clean up this mess?"

Andrew flicked his finger and said, "Clean."

All the items in the dressing room swirled around and around and returned to their proper place. The furniture, which looked as if it was tossed about like a child's dollhouse, slid back into position. Even Andrew's leather pants reappeared on the back of the chair.

"Thank you," Aleksander said as he pushed up to a sitting position. "Wow, what a ride."

"You haven't seen anything yet." Andrew's amber eyes glowed.

"You mean there's more?" An evil look came into Aleksander's eye. "Or did you mean you *wanted* more?" He snapped his fingers as he fell back onto the floor and rolled onto his side to watch.

Handcuffs appeared on Andrew's wrists and held him securely to the wardrobe.

"Let's see you get out of this one, Houdini." Aleksander crawled over and kissed Andrew.

"Watch me." And the lights flickered, energy rose, and...

AFTERWORD

Tricks of the Trade is the third anthology of erotica I've edited for Bold Strokes Books, and I've enjoyed each and every one thoroughly. Putting these together is a labor of love, and reading the stories written around these admittedly odd themes I've come up with is a real joy and amazement to me.

So, the first round of thanks goes out to the authors who have contributed their wild imaginations and hard work to make my vision a reality. They are truly the backbone of these books, and any accolades are due to them first.

Credit also goes out to Radclyffe and her amazing team at Bold Strokes Books, including editor extraordinaire Stacia Seaman and Sheri, who has designed some of the most interesting covers I've ever seen.

And, as usual, nods and tips of the top hat go to William Holden and Dale Chase for their continued support (or is that enabling?) of my madness. On the home front, Ryk Bowers also deserves my thanks, as this is the fifth book of mine he's lived through without murdering me in my sleep. Yet.

But as this is being put together in late May of 2012, I've just returned from the annual Saints and Sinners Literary Festival in New Orleans, a reminder to thank Paul Willis, Amie Evans, and Greg Herren (as well as the evil Mark Drake) for making that conference a reality every year. If it were not for the lessons I've learned there and the contacts I've made, I would have absolutely no writing career at all. Please bless (or blame) them.

As always, however, we all need to thank you readers out there. You have many choices to pass the time away. Thanks for choosing us, and we hope you'll return again and again.

CONTRIBUTORS

JEFF MANN's books include three collections of poetry, *Bones Washed with Wine*, *On the Tongue*, and *Ash: Poems from Norse Mythology*; two books of personal essays, *Edge: Travels of an Appalachian Leather Bear* and *Binding the God: Ursine Essays from the Mountain South*; two novellas, *Devoured*, included in *Masters of Midnight: Erotic Tales of the Vampire*, and *Camp Allegheny*, included in *History's Passion: Stories of Sex Before Stonewall*; two novels, *Fog: A Novel of Desire and Reprisal* and *Purgatory: A Novel of the Civil War*; a collection of poetry and memoir, *Loving Mountains, Loving Men*; and a volume of short fiction, *A History of Barbed Wire*, winner of a Lambda Literary Award. He teaches creative writing at Virginia Tech in Blacksburg, Virginia.

LEWIS DESIMONE (lewisdesimone.com) is the author of the novels *Chemistry* and *The Heart's History* (both from Lethe Press). His work has also appeared in *Chelsea Station*, *Christopher Street*, *James White Review*, *Harrington Gay Men's Fiction Quarterly*, and the anthologies *Dirty Diner*, *Second Person Queer: Who You Are (So Far)*, *The Mammoth Book of Threesomes and Moresomes*, *Charmed Lives: Gay Spirit in Storytelling*, *Best Gay Love Stories: Summer Flings*, *I Like It Like That: True Tales of Gay Male Desire*, and *My Diva: 65 Gay Men on the Women Who Inspire Them*. His contribution to the latter was highlighted on *Salon* and reprinted in *Ganymede* and *Best Gay Stories 2010*. He blogs regularly at SexAndTheSissy.wordpress.com and can be reached through his website. He lives in San Francisco, where he is working on his next novel.

ROB ROSEN (therobrosen.com), author of the novels *Sparkle: The Queerest Book You'll Ever Love*, *Divas Las Vegas*, *Hot Lava*, *Southern Fried*, and *Queerwolf*, has had short stories featured in more than 150 anthologies.

JAY NEAL finds it easier—and more satisfying—to construct the imaginary events entangling the life of an unusually sophisticated, nineteenth-century, red-headed Cockney con artist with Victorian law courts than to concoct an interesting yet honest short autobiography detailing his life as a suburban denizen. Neal's enjoyed spinning fictional tales now for fifteen years, traveling to far-flung times and places and getting to know people who don't actually exist, but always returning home to his partner of twenty years, with whom he leads a grand life of domestic tranquility in the suburbs of Washington, DC, where they fulfilled a long-held dream by being married in 2010.

XAVIER AXELSON is a writer and columnist living in Los Angeles. His columns include interviews with counterculture celebrities, artisans, singers, writers, performance artists, politicians, and activists. While his writing has been called "raw, dirty, and absolutely beautiful," Xavier hopes to push boundaries of what is expected in the horror and erotic genres.

TODD GREGORY is the author of three novels (*Every Frat Boy Wants It*, *Games Frat Boys Play*, and *Need*) and has edited numerous anthologies, including *Blood Sacraments*, *Rough Trade*, *Wings*, and *Raising Hell*. His own collection of short erotic fiction, *Promises in Every Star*, will be released by Bold Strokes Book in late 2012.

'NATHAN BURGOINE (http://redroom.com/member/nathan-burgoine) lives in Ottawa with his husband Daniel. His previous erotic fiction appears in *Tented*, *Blood Sacraments*, *Wings*, *Erotica Exotica*, *Afternoon Pleasures*, *Riding the Rails*, *Dirty Diner*, *Melt In Your Mouth*, and *Sweat*. His non-erotic fiction appears in *Fool for Love*, *I Do Two*, *Saints + Sinners 2011: New Fiction from the Festival*, *Men of the Mean Streets*, *You Can't Shoot the Cancer Squad* (the second *Machine of Death* anthology), and *Boys of Summer*. His nonfiction appears in *I Like It Like That* and *5x5 Literary Magazine*. He has never made a coin dance.

DALE CHASE (dalechasestrokes.com) has written male erotica for fifteen years with over 150 stories in magazines and anthologies including translation into Italian and German. She has two story collections in print: the IPPY silver medal winning *The Company He Keeps: Victorian Gentlemen's Erotica* from Bold Strokes Books and *If The Spirit Moves You: Ghostly Gay Erotica* from Lethe Press. Her first novel, *Wyatt: Doc Holliday's Account of an Intimate Friendship*, was recently published by Bold Strokes Books. Chase is currently at work on an erotic novel about John Wesley Hardin. She lives near San Francisco.

MEL BOSSA is the author of *Split*, a Lambda Literary Award finalist. Her third novel, *Franky Gets Real*, was nominated for a Foreword Book award. She lives in Montreal with her partner, a visual artist, and their three children.

JOSEPH BANETH ALLEN grew up in Camp Lejeune, North Carolina. An avid reader and writer, his short stories have appeared in *Blood Sacraments*, *Wings*, and *Riding The Rails*. His nonfiction has been published in *OMNI*, *Popular Science*, *Final Frontier*, *Astronomy*, *Florida Living*, *Dog Fancy*, *Pet Life*, *eBay* magazine, and many others. He has also received the Disney Showmanship Award for his work on promoting *The Nightmare Before Christmas* and other animated movies. He now lives with his family amongst an ever-growing collection of Big Little Books, Gold Key Comics, and G.I. Joes in Jacksonville, Florida, where he continues to write fiction and nonfiction.

RALPH SELIGMAN is a bilingual interpreter and translator. He recently translated the landmark book *Loving Someone Gay* by Donald Clark, PhD, into Spanish. He has a story in Jerry Wheeler's *Tented:*

Gay Erotic Tales From Under the Big Top. Ralph lives in Kansas City, Missouri, with his husband, author Wayne Courtois, and their two cats. He dedicates this story to Wayne and in memory of Ted Williams, a fatal victim of clergy bullying.

WILLIAM HOLDEN's (williamholdenwrites.com) writing career spans more than a decade, with over forty published short stories in erotica, romance, fantasy, and horror. He is co-founder and co-editor of *Out in Print: Queer Book Reviews* at www.outinprint.net. His first collection, *A Twist of Grimm*, is a Lambda Literary Finalist. His most recent works include *Words to Die By* and his historical novel, *Secret Societies*, both by Bold Strokes Books.

LOGAN ZACHARY is a mystery author living in Minneapolis, Minnesota, where he works as an occupational therapist and is an avid reader and book collector. He enjoys movies, concerts, plays, and all the other cultural events that the Twin Cities have to offer. His stories can be found in *Hard Hats, Taken By Force, Boys Caught in the Act, Ride Me Cowboy, Best Gay Erotica 2009, Ultimate Gay Erotica 2009, Surfer Boys, SexTime, Queer Dimensions, Obsessed, College Boys, Teammates, Skater Boys, Boys Getting Ahead, College Boys, Men at Noon, Monster at Midnight, Homo Thugs, Black Fire,* and *Rough Trade*. He can be reached at LoganZachary2002@yahoo.com.

ABOUT THE EDITOR

Editor of *Tented: Gay Erotic Tales from Under the Big Top* (a Lambda Literary Award finalist) as well as *Riding the Rails* and *The Dirty Diner* (both Bold Strokes Books), **JERRY L. WHEELER** lives, works, and writes in Denver, Colorado. Co-founder of *Out in Print: Queer Book Reviews*, reading for the blog takes up much of his time. What's left is misspent in fleeting encounters with men best described as trashy. Some on work release programs. Despite this predilection, he still manages time for writing, including short stories, essays, book reviews, and a novel-in-progress called *The Dead Book*. Please feel free to contact him at either www.outinprint.net or at his website, www.jerrywheeleronline.com. Furry men with tats and shady backgrounds, please step to the front of the line.

Books Available From Bold Strokes Books

Straight Boy Roommate by Kevin Troughton. Tom isn't expecting much from his first term at University, but a chance encounter with straight boy Dan catapults him into an extraordinary, wild weekend of sex and self-discovery, which turns his life upside down, and leads him into his first love affair. (978-1-60282-782-0)

Raising Hell: Demonic Gay Erotica, edited by Todd Gregory. Hot stories of gay erotica featuring demons. (978-1-60282-768-4)

Pursued by Joel Gomez-Dossi. Openly gay college student Jamie Bradford becomes romantically involved with two men at the same time, and his hell begins when one of his boyfriends becomes intent on killing him. (978-1-60282-769-1)

Timothy by Greg Herren. Timothy is a romantic suspense thriller from award-winning mystery writer Greg Herren set in the fabulous Hamptons. (978-1-60282-760-8)

In Stone by Jeremy Jordan King. A young New Yorker is rescued from a hate crime by a mysterious someone who turns out to be more of a something. (978-1-60282-761-5)

The Jesus Injection by Eric Andrews-Katz. Murderous statues, demented drag queens, political bombings, ex-gay ministries, espionage, and romance are all in a day's work for a top secret agent. But the gloves are off when Agent Buck 98 comes up against the Jesus Injection. (978-1-60282-762-2)

Combustion by Daniel W. Kelly. Bearish detective Deck Waxer comes to the city of Kremfort Cove to investigate why the hottest men in town are bursting into flames in broad daylight. (978-1-60282-763-9)

Night Shadows: Queer Horror edited by Greg Herren and J.M. Redmann. *Night Shadows* features delightfully wicked stories by some of the biggest names in queer publishing. (978-1-60282-751-6)

Wyatt: Doc Holliday's Account of an Intimate Friendship by Dale Chase. Erotica writer Dale Chase takes the remarkable friendship between Wyatt Earp, upright lawman, and Doc Holliday, Southern gentlemen turned gambler and killer, to an entirely new level: hot! (978-1-60282-755-4)

Secret Societies by William Holden. An outcast hustler, his unlikely "mother," his faithless lovers, and his religious persecutors—all in 1726. (978-1-60282-752-3)

The Jetsetters by David-Matthew Barnes. As rock band the Jetsetters skyrocket from obscurity to superstardom, Justin Holt, a lonely barista, and Diego Delgado, the band's guitarist, fight with everything they have to stay together, despite the chaos and fame. (978-1-60282-745-5)

Strange Bedfellows by Rob Byrnes. Partners in life and crime, Grant Lambert and Chase LaMarca are hired to make a politician's compromising photo disappear, but what should be an easy job quickly spins out of control. (978-1-60282-746-2)

Fontana by Joshua Martino. Fame, obsession, and vengeance collide in a novel that asks: What if America's greatest hero was gay? (978-1-60282-675-5)

The Dirty Diner: Gay Erotica on the Menu, edited by Jerry L. Wheeler. Gay erotica set in restaurants, featuring food, sex, and men—could you really ask for anything more? (978-1-60282-677-9)

Sweat: Gay Jock Erotica by Todd Gregory. Sizzling tales of smoking-hot sex with the athletic studs everyone fantasizes about. (978-1-60282-669-4)

The Marrying Kind by Ken O'Neill. Just when successful wedding planner Adam More decides to protest inequality by quitting the business and boycotting marriage entirely, his only sibling announces her engagement. (978-1-60282-670-0)

Calendar Boys by Logan Zachary. A man a month will keep you excited year-round. (978-1-60282-665-6)